THE UNEXPECTED CARD

A Mr. Boss Novel

EVEY LYON

Copyright © 2021 by EH Lyon

Written and published by: Evey Lyon

Editing & Proofreading by: My Brother's Editor

Cover concept: Tash Drake

Cover Design: Kate Farlow, Y'All. That Graphic.

over Photography: Lindee Robinson Photography

Cover Models: Adam Johns & Christina Engel

ISBN E-book: 978-1-7365752-0-8 / ISBN Paperback: 978-1-7365752-1-5

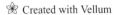 Created with Vellum

MR. BOSS SERIES

The Unexpected Card

The Broken Rule (Novella)

The Big Charmer

The Perfect Distraction

The Real Deal

ABOUT

One business trip is all it takes for the unexpected...

As co-owner of Ives & Wells, Josh is ready to nail the most important business trip of his career. But does it have to include his business partner's moody younger sister Layla escorting him to New Orleans?

As much as they hate each other, it isn't completely crazy. Technically, she's an employee and Josh is her boss. But one fight after another leads to an explosion in the bedroom... more than once.

Josh definitely wasn't planning on nailing more than a good business deal on this trip.

Unfortunately, their plan to leave the antics in the bedroom and out of the office falls apart as soon as they return home. First, because some of their mutual talents can't be forgotten. Two, because there is a business partner that may kill Josh as soon as he figures out what happened. And three, because some secrets can only be kept for so long, give or take nine months.

The Unexpected Card is a standalone novel from the Mr.

Boss series. This workplace romance is filled with banter, a swoony boss, and surprises along the way.

PROLOGUE

Josh

Six Months Ago

She has a look of disbelief on her face with her hands firmly on her hips. She is inches away from me as I sit confidently perched on the front ledge of my desk.

"I don't know what your problem is, Layla. I'm trying to compliment you on a job well done. Christ knows that I wasn't a fan of you working here." There is disdain in my voice as I keep my arms crossed.

Layla holds a hand up. "At least you admit it. If you don't want me working here, then why the hell did you agree with my brother to hire me?"

She is sassy today, probably because of what went down twenty minutes ago.

I scoff in annoyance and rub my temples with my fingers in frustration. "Layla, you're irritating as hell, but even I know you have talent. Can't we just move on from this one assignment you have helped us with?" I plead.

I didn't have any tolerance for her yesterday, most certainly not today, and I doubt I would tomorrow.

She steps closer to me. "Fine. But, Josh, remember I only helped out of respect for my brother. Dealing with you is torture on a good day."

A victorious smirk forms on my face as I raise an eyebrow. "I torture you?"

She is nailing it as it *was* rather torturous. We debated every detail of the marketing campaign.

She shakes her head in utter annoyance. "All I am saying is that it's all well and good that you compliment my work now. But you and I working together was a near disaster all because you are a complete jerk—"

I propel off my desk and step closer to her, interrupting. "Near disaster? Sounds accurate. Look, Layla, thanks for your contribution, but I think we learned that this was better as a one-time thing."

She flinches as I invade her space. Making her squirm and that action energizes me in more ways than it should.

Her finger pokes my chest and she snickers. "One time sounds like paradise. Probably your limits to impress anyhow."

A low growl escapes me from the back of my throat as I grab her wrist to take her little claw off my chest. That touch just sent a tremor between us and our eyes blaze. Still, I step closer to her. Our air supply merging.

"You really have an interest in how I impress the ladies, don't you?"

She groans in irritation. "Yeah, because that is exactly what you did twenty minutes ago."

With that blow, I grab her other wrist, which makes her body jolt, yet she doesn't pull away.

"You are impossible," I warn her.

Our gazes intensify and our breath quickens.

"Least I speak my mind," she challenges, and with that remark, it cracks between us.

Our mouths crash into one another and we dive into a deep kiss, a long kiss, our tongues quickly meeting before re-angling so we don't need to part for air. Fusing in an unexpected tango that it seems we are talented at. *Together.*

I need to silence her like this. Half of my brain reminding me she is off limits and the other half reminding me I don't care. Her luscious lips are responding to my firm imprint on her mouth and the whiff of her perfume fuels a need to keep her quiet longer. A subtle sound from the back of her throat only encouraging.

When the sound of someone coming down the hall becomes louder, I let her wrists go and we pull away. We both quickly step back. Before we even have a chance to look at each other, a project manager enters the meeting room.

"What do you want us to do?" the young man asks.

"Find someone else. Layla is just a graphic designer. It won't work with her filling in for the model. Find someone more suitable," I say. The moment the man walks out, I turn my attention to Layla.

Her fury looks explosive. "You are a moron. Really unbelievable. Let's just stick to avoiding and disliking each other. Okay?" She struts away in her black dress, too scandalous for my thoughts.

"Swell," I call out sarcastically.

1

JOSH

Throwing the tennis ball against the ceiling as I lean back in my comfortable chair behind my glass desk, I listen to the guy on the other end of the line.

"Right, just send me the overview and I will have a look. Next time, bother me when you actually have something productive to tell me," I tell my IT guy, slightly irritated, then hit the end button on the phone.

As co-owner of Ives & Wells, I expect only A-game performance, and luckily everyone in our office delivers. Landing clients and delivering top marketing rollouts are our jam, and I have no problem telling someone to step up. I would say people like me as a boss. I respect early "happy hour" Friday drinks in the office, grab an occasional donut in the break room when it is someone's birthday, and even throw on my best smile to make the women in project management get their panties wet. But the office has no illusions—if someone needs to get fired, then I am the guy to do it.

For years, I watched my father run a successful company out east and it rubbed off on me. And I want to make the old man proud. We have one of those special relationships that sons and fathers dream of.

Looking in my coffee cup on my desk, I see it is empty. Crap. I need a little caffeine. Didn't sleep well last night and as much as I wish I could say it was because of a woman working her magic in my bed... I can't.

I arrived home late due to my flight getting delayed from visiting my sister out in Colorado who decided my love life was the topic of conversation the whole weekend. My ears turned off when she reminded me I needed to settle down.

Another cup of Peruvian bean coffee from our coffee machine sounds good right about now.

But right on cue, Noah Wells—my business partner of three years—comes through the glass door to my modern office with a great view over Lake Michigan in downtown Chicago. The view alone is worth every cent of our monthly rent.

"Big news, Josh. Great news." He beams as he straightens his black-rimmed glasses. Noah's excitement looks like a guy who finally won his fantasy football draft. His short brown hair styled in pointy spikes and his green plaid shirt reminds me he is the nerdier of us two. But it is a casual day at the office, so I let his outfit go as he finds a spot on my sofa.

Hopping out of my chair, I throw the tennis ball to him as I stand and walk to the front of my desk, running a hand through my hair.

"Talk to me," I request as my hands push my suit coat to the side and find my fitted jean pockets, because—unlike Noah—I've got style.

"We got the meeting," Noah tells me, and I know what he means.

Trey Radnor, only the biggest client we could land yet. Three years ago, Noah and I broke away from our big-name marketing agency to start our own. We have done well. Really well. But Trey would take us over the edge. He owns a few hotels across the country and while the clientele is a niche, having him on board would open the door to many other names. Not to mention, he invests in so many companies himself that he alone could be enough business for us.

"This is good news," I respond as I snap my fingers and sit on the edge of my desk.

Noah throws the tennis ball around between his hands as he speaks. "You will need to take the meeting. I am still deep in the Zall account. Trey wants the meeting in New Orleans since he just opened a hotel there."

"I can do that." Not only can I do that, but I will nail this like the bulldozer I am. Plus, I could use a little New Orleans heat as the crisp autumn air has taken over Chicago.

Looking at Noah, I see there is more. "And?" I press, feeling entertained and slightly nervous.

"He wants Layla to come to the meeting. He loved her designs on the Hult account. Plus, Mindy—our in-house designer—is going on maternity leave, so Layla will hopefully pick up the slack. Not to mention, Trey comes from a family business, he likes that extra touch."

A deep sigh overtakes me, and a wave of aggravation goes through me.

Layla—Noah's little sister—who while technically is not employed by us on a permanent basis, helped us out *one time* to do freelance design work and ever since clients chase us for her to work on their accounts. Since Noah is all about ethical appearances in our office of forty, Layla reports to me when she is hired as a consultant. Looks slightly more ethical than reporting to her brother.

Maybe I should backtrack a sec and point out that she is quite talented and it's worth hiring her. Her calling me boss is just a fucking bonus that my ears and the imagination of my dick can thank the employee handbook for.

"I know you both can barely stand breathing the same air in a five-mile radius of one another. But she needs to go with you," Noah mentions again.

That woman avoids me like the plague when she can due to an incident that occurred when she did help us that *one* time, which I was hoping was her last. The incident that I like to call *Dressgate*. Since then, she makes it a point to irritate me and I return the favor in full.

Our feeling of disdain for the other runs strong. The jabs we hash out are never-ending. The buttons pushed by the other can be scorching. It's a headache.

"No. Absolutely not," I tell Noah firmly. "Plus, the designer would never come to such a meeting."

I have managed to stay clear from Layla for a solid month or two now, which has been the gift that keeps on giving. We have never had to go on a business trip together. We have always been surrounded by a buffer of people.

A good thing. A very good thing.

We are a ticking time bomb together waiting to go off, even I know that.

Noah holds a hand up. "It's what Trey wants, and the client always gets what they want," Noah justifies.

Damn, he is right. We need to nab this.

Shaking my head. "Fine. I mean, it's only what a two-day, tops, meeting?"

We could fly in on the afternoon, schmooze Trey over dinner and close the deal by next day lunch.

Find the silver lining, Josh, just anything to make this bearable.

"Exactly. I will make sure she is on the plane. I don't know why you both annoy each other so much. At least I know you know the bro code and I never have to worry about you two hooking up or some crazy shit like that. Otherwise, I would be serving your balls up on a silver platter," Noah mentions as he walks toward my door.

At least I know I will be keeping my balls undamaged because Layla rolling into bed with me is never going to happen, and no way does it cross my mind. Nope. Nuh-uh… okay, maybe once or twice.

————

GETTING ON THE PLANE, I look at row three in first class. Of course, Layla Wells is waiting in seat 3B with her arms and legs crossed, a solid glare from her green eyes, and a gray dress that fits her body to a T. A bonus of bare legs, smooth and silky. Her soft brown hair is down with natural waves and her lips are covered in some potion of red gloss to match her red nails that may just give me the image of how good they would look clawing into my skin. Her nails tapping her arms in a steady beat as if she is telling me she has been waiting.

I'm totally unaffected.

"Hey there, boss," she greets me with her eyebrow arched. Probably taking slight entertainment in the fact she gets to annoy me for the next forty-eight hours.

Rolling into seat 3A next to her, I let my hand run through my hair and drag across my freshly shaved face. Pushing up the sleeves to my white button-down shirt, I flag for the attendant. I am going to need reinforcements, ASAP.

"Layla," I greet her dryly, avoiding looking at her.

The flight attendant with blond hair and a perfect body comes to me. "Yes, Mr. Ives, what can I do for you?" she chimes.

You could do a lot. Probably involves the bathroom, your mouth, and pleasure... for me.

I give her my best smile. "Whiskey neat." Because it is twelve o'clock somewhere.

"And for you Mrs. Ives?" The attendant smiles.

Layla lets a chortle escape her and I can only shake my head at this bad start.

"This man wishes he had a wife like me. We are not married. He is my boss." Layla grins. "The same, please, but just bring me the small little bottle."

"This is going to be a long flight, isn't it," I speak aloud.

Layla nudges my arm with hers. "It could be worse; I could be your wife." She throws on a fake closed-mouth smile.

No worse would be combusting together in an activity— that I am quite exceptional at.

I make a mental note in my head to send a reminder to my dick that Layla and me disliking each other is the best policy.

Re-angling my body, I turn to her and move into her space. It causes her breath to catch and her shoulders to stiffen. But I get my kicks out of making her squirm. Hell, we probably both get off on making the other squirm.

"Listen, *sunshine*, Chicago to New Orleans is a solid two-hour flight. After which we need to nail this client. You are so quick to remind me that on paper I am your boss. Although I am positive you call me that because it turns you on like crazy. So, boss, it is. Then fine, this is how this trip is going to go. I'm your boss and you are my direct report, so you will listen, agree and this will be a smooth forty-eight hours." My voice is firm, and I recognize a hint of sweltering that only I recognize when I *may* slightly be turned-on.

Her eyes change. I cannot pinpoint to what. Annoyance? Fear? Heat? Is she aroused?

"I'm not your sunshine," she snipes. Because this woman is a little spitfire full of attitude when I am around.

But how I do enjoy having her as a sparring partner. I side roll my eyes to her. "No, you are the rain on my sunny day."

"Here you both are." The blond attendant hands us our whiskeys.

Layla opens her little bottle and downs it in one go.

"Whoa, easy there, princess," I comment, but then I remember. "Still hate take-off and landings?"

She looks at me, surprised that I remember. But then she must register that her brother is my business partner. Noah is like a Canadian bear in winter when it comes to Layla—he is protective—and she can do no wrong in his book. When their parents died in an accident when she was younger, he paid for her college and took over a sort of guardian role. They are close. Close enough that she is a topic at lunch more than I'd wish. He shares information about her that I do not particularly care to know. Such as she hates flying and has no boyfriend.

Layla has an odd look on her face, which must be from downing the gold-colored liquid and hitting her throat in one go. "Yeah, something like that," she comments.

Letting out a deep trying to relax exhale, I turn my cell to airplane mode and place it in my pocket as the plane gets ready for take-off.

Not sure where this streak of being a gentleman is coming from, but I look forward. "Just tell me again how the hell you met Radnor before." I am trying to keep her distracted. *How kind of me.*

"You were there, remember? You and Noah were having a drink with him at a bar and by chance, I was at the same bar with a friend," she recalls.

"Oh yeah, your date." That comes out as expressionless as I can.

"Wasn't my date. Clive is gay. We worked on a project together. Why am I even explaining this to you?" she wonders aloud, almost frustrated with herself.

A short laugh escapes me.

"Anyhow, Noah noticed me at the bar, and it was pure coincidence. Introduced me to Radnor and by chance, Radnor remembered my work for a few other clients. But you know all of this. You were there. Just probably had your tail between your legs since I was in a dress and we know how you get when that happens." She is feisty when she mentions that.

I roll my eyes, but I am amused.

Ignoring her quip, I ask, "And how have you ended up on a plane next to me?"

"Flash forward a few months and Noah called me to say he needed my help. Seems like Trey is giving you two a shot as long as I do the design work. But again, you know this. Just like you know that I am only doing this for Noah. Trust me, a trip with you was not part of the deal."

"Layla. Do I always bring out the best in you?" I am not at all serious.

"Do I always get your bullshit holier than thou personality that women seem to drop to their knees for?"

"Ah, so you do want to drop to your knees for me?" I give her a wry smile and I cannot tell if she is irritated or enjoyed walking into that remark.

But this conversation is working as we already made it to the runway. As soon as the engine picks up, the look of fear on her face is apparent.

Holding my arm out. "Here, grab my arm or something."

She does not even question it or look at me, she grabs my

arm and holds on for dear life. Layla is petite, which means her stronghold on my firm and well-ripped arm still feels light.

She is warm and I can feel her pulse is beating as fast as the speed of the plane. For a second, I feel for her. She may be my Achille's heel. Annoys the hell out of me. But she actually is a decent human being if you get in her good books, and we need her for this win.

As soon as we make it to the sky, she lets go. Like a switch, she voids whatever temporary armistice that was between us for a millisecond. She leans over to grab her tablet from her bag on the floor.

I cannot help smelling her macadamia scented hair as she leans over or the way her body bends forward and could so easily...

Shake it off, Josh. Whatever just flew through your head—shake it away.

Coming back to sitting she angles her body toward me to show me the tablet. "I made some of these designs as possible marketing material." She begins to swipe the screen.

And for the next two hours, we go over designs and what to expect for our dinner meeting. We keep it purely about business. Every idea I suggest, she would debate. Every suggestion she had; I would argue. Constant back and forth.

"Trust me. I play hard, then we close this tomorrow," I inform her.

She huffs. "Listen, boss, trust me when I say he is going to drag this out. Make us build a relationship with him to test us. I mean, test your agency as the best people to get the job done."

The back and forth continuing for several more minutes.

Finally agreeing to disagree.

Looking at my watch, I see we have a few minutes left in

the air. Throwing on my headphones, I enjoy the sounds of a playlist of Motown. Layla grabs my phone from my hands and looks at the screen.

"Really?! No... really?" She is surprised with my music selection.

"Pure happiness sounds, baby." I grin and I am proud of my musical taste. If you cannot get in a good mood from a little Motown, then you were possibly born as a member of Satan's family.

She laughs as she hands my phone back. "Well, this is a game-changer. Wasn't expecting this."

"I don't disappoint, Layla." There may be a cocky grin on my face.

For a moment, we look at each other and there is an odd calm between us. That moment lingers until the overhead speakers go on.

The captain announces that we will be landing shortly, and I offer my arm again. Without words, she takes it. For some reason, I felt the need to move a little closer to her that time. You know, *in case* she needed full access to my arm.

I smile to myself as I could have also sworn she was humming The Temptations, "Get Ready."

After landing, we grab our bags from the overhead and head through the airport. Someone from the hotel was waiting for us when we arrived to take us to the Sweet Dove Hotel near the French Quarter.

The hotel is a traditional creole styled colonial building that dated back to another time. Painted blue on the outside with porches and white shutters. Inside, high ceilings and beautifully refurbished. Our two rooms are next to each other and my guess is the woman of my contempt is on the other side of the wall looking at the exact same setup.

The room is filled with a four-post bed with high thread

count sheets that would probably feel fantastic for my back to lie on as a woman rides me into oblivion.

Complimentary brandy waits on a small table in the corner near a desk and chaise lounge chair. French doors to the balcony outside overlooks a green garden that looks like a tropical forest. This room is ideal for a certain type of traveler.

Looking at the guest literature on the desk next to the complimentary box of peanut brittle, I scratch the back of my head. This trip would completely be Noah's scene. He is a hopeless romantic. Me? I am a little rough on that front. I haven't had a relationship worth romantic trips in a few years.

The rose petals laying on the bed must be the hotel's way of taunting me with these facts.

These romantic references? It matters. It matters because the whole point of why Trey Radnor is looking for a new marketing agency is he wants to capitalize on the fact his hotel just won an award for the most romantic place in Louisiana.

2

JOSH

Waiting at the hotel bar, I scroll through my phone in one hand and have a club soda resting on the top of the dark wood bar in the other. A duet is playing a clarinet and piano in the corner of upbeat yet mellow jazz tunes. Couples laugh as they enjoy pre-dinner drinks, business associates have meetings discussing stocks, and women who ooze temptation waltz through the entrance sending my head into a spin.

My head quickly looks up for a double-take.

My fist clenches around my glass of club soda and I need to swallow. There is an urge to loosen my dark red tie around my neck, because it is feeling a little warm in here. I guess Layla's version of freshening up for dinner involved a little red dress to mid-thigh that passes as respectable but seems to draw eyes her way—including my own. She is fire in heels and sirens just went off in my head.

She smiles dryly as she walks—no, she sways toward me. Her hair even bounces to tempo. One thing I need to give her credit for is she is a confident soul who is comfortable in her body. Her hips swing and I am questioning what move I can do to make it a point to every man in this room that she is with me... *well sort of.*

When she reaches me, I stand—because I am a gentleman —and show her to the stool next to mine letting my hand gently touch her lower back to guide her and my eyes look around the room, shooting out some warning daggers from my eyes.

Her smell of macadamia strong. Her body flawless. Her zipper location found.

Why the zipper? Because she is a forbidden fruit. And my mind and body lock in on that fact.

Sitting back down, we look at each other. Perhaps a few more seconds than we should.

"Okay. I follow your lead during dinner," she blurts out blankly as she steals a swig of my club soda. This chick hates me but is always quick to drink from my drink glasses at every gathering we run into each other.

My head snaps back a little with skepticism. "A change of heart?"

A closed-lip smile forms on her face before she speaks. "If it means I don't need to hear you complain and moan tomorrow at breakfast, then it might be worth it. But some-thing tells me that you will be quiet anyway. Trust me, Trey doesn't want to do quick."

Rolling my eyes, I knew she would not let it go.

She raises a shoulder. "What? Some men have the skill to draw it out, make it last." She is trying to rile me, and her voice most definitely was smug.

Reminding me that our back and forth sometimes crosses the borders that make me think I may one day need to screw her against a wall from exasperation. It has never been more apparent than the last six hours.

A laugh comes out from deep in my throat. "Sometimes

you just need to go in hard," I tell her, and it makes her turn slightly pink. She even bites the corner of her lip.

Looking away then looking back at me with a confident grin. "Is that what you tell yourself as the reason you go through half the city?" she retorts.

Shaking my head. "Right, that's the image you have of me. But if that's the case then I guess that makes me experienced, which probably puts your head into a tailspin of what I could do to you."

She irks me. Her image of me is way off. Sure, I have a list of women who I could call, and they would come running to their knees *literally*. But that does not mean I sleep around on a weekly basis. No sir, I do not. No, half the time I am working seventy-hour weeks and the other half I am catching up on sleep, exercise, and keeping my over-talkative sister in line. My rather large whistle is selective and stays in check.

"Anyway. What happened to listening to your boss? Can we please re-focus?"

I need to re-focus.

"Whatever you say." She drags out as her finger plays with the rim of my club soda glass. The air between us as humid as the New Orleans heat. Her eyes I swear give me a glint.

Our tension is broken by the arrival of Trey Radnor. Layla and I give each other a look to confirm it's show time. We both stand and throw on our best faces.

"Josh, Layla, so good to see you again."

Trey is my age and inherited millions from his father. Dark hair, a little heavy on cologne, tries to pass as slick. His suit cut almost matches mine except for the color, but I am going to guess I wear it better. He shakes my hand and then takes a moment to look at Layla before kissing her face on both sides as if we suddenly have gone European style on the greetings front.

Before I know it, we are sitting at a table in the upscale restaurant of the hotel where dark wood backdrops the many candles laid around the white covered tables and more candles hang on the dark walls filled with art. If I were a man trying to romance someone from the female species, then this would be the place—I'll give Trey that.

Layla shows designs, I pitch the spiel about how great our firm would be. Drinks are flowing, good food on the table, laughter from our table fills the restaurant on several occasions. All signs are a green light for Trey to agree to sign us on.

"What do you say? Tomorrow we talk logistics of how we can make this partnership work." I grab my whiskey.

Trey holds his hands up. "Sounds good, but I don't rush into decisions."

Layla gives me a knowing look from across the table. Rolls her green eyes then turns her attention to Trey.

"A wise man." She flatters him and even pokes a finger to his arm. "Right decisions need time. Since we are the right decision, then we will be patient."

Is she flirting with the guy? Is she actually using her charm to help secure the deal?

Trey gives a soft smile. "Good, because I want to wrap this up later in the week."

A nervous laugh escapes Layla. "Later in the week?"

"You both can stay a few more days, right? We can get to know each other more; you can explore this great city and then I will make my decision," Trey explains.

"Uh, a few more days would be okay." I am doubting my own confirmation and willpower.

Looking to Layla, she looks unimpressed. Hell, a few

more days stuck with her is not my idea of a holiday either. Friction between two people tends to rub you the wrong way and put you in a bad mood.

"Great. The hotel will take care of you both."

"Excuse me for a moment," Layla comments and we all stand as she leaves the table. Probably to go to the ladies' room to let out some frustration or plan for my murder.

Sitting down again, Trey finishes his drink. "Is she single?" he asks.

Oh hell no. Tell me no. Are we stuck here a few more days because Trey thinks Layla is his next dessert? Who probably tastes like a martini—dirty martini—and lies on a bed making amazing sounds as she claws the sheets?

Need to shut this down. Noah would have a tantrum, and for some reason, I cannot grind my teeth hard enough.

Clearing my throat, I say, "You know, I think she is seeing someone."

Total lie.

A frown forms on his face. "A shame. But what happens in the big easy..." he mentions as he nudges my arm with a sly grin. My inner blood boils and I can only answer with my chin gently tilting up to show him I heard.

"Well, I will be in touch tomorrow. I am going to head out. Say goodnight to Layla for me." Trey gets up out of his seat and heads off.

Leaving me to rub my face in frustration.

Great, now I am stuck for more than forty-eight hours with Layla Wells and questioning what I can do to survive this.

3

LAYLA

My hand draws with the pen on a napkin. Fierce strokes of black ink hitting the napkin normally reserved for sitting under a strong drink. Drawing is a perpetual habit to take my mind to a happy place and right now I need a fucking Zen moment.

I returned from the ladies' room to find that I am trapped alone with Josh, but a fresh glass of brandy that I saw the barman pour was waiting for me, and I'm not going to turn down a much-needed nightcap.

This trip is turning into a disaster.

One: I only packed for two days and now we are stuck here for four days. A girl's worst nightmare. Dresses and good lingerie are two of my indulgences. I need to always have them on.

Two: I am stuck with Josh. Bane of my existence.

The man sits across from me, leaning back in his chair as he scrolls on his phone and sips on a clean scotch. My eyes take a moment to look at the view.

I mean, I am not blind. The guy is the complete package. I am not going to deny that. I give credit when credit is due.

Good looks, well dressed, and he oozes success. He has a saccharine smile that has made single women burst an ovary and married women consider leaving their husbands. Blondish-brown hair that is mussed perfectly on his head to match his hazel eyes. A sharpshooter when it comes to business deals and probably the same way in bed, which I most certainly have *not* thought about.

My phone vibrates on the table and I grab it to look at a new message. Pulling up the chat conversation, I see it is my best friend Lauren who also happens to work at the Ives & Wells office in finance.

Lauren: How is it with the boss?

She has the audacity to throw in a winking emoji.

Me: A continuous asshole who rubs me the wrong way, always has.

Lauren: Right. Why is that again?

My thumb quickly types.

Me: My brother plus Josh screams red flags.

Josh corrupted my brother. He convinced my strait-laced older brother to break away from the big agency where they worked a few years ago and start anew. It was a legal mess.

The red flags are because someone with his looks who doesn't have a girlfriend probably means he is horrible on the romance front. My brother even told me how Josh screwed up an office romance once at their last company. I don't have the patience for men who don't know how to treat a lady.

Lauren: What if he rubs you the right way?

That woman needs to stop with her winking emojis.

Me: Not happening. For many reasons. Anyhow, I literally texted you to ask to water my plant since I am away longer and now I get the third degree?

Lauren: Plant duty accepted, but for a woman who is 27 you really shouldn't become a plant or cat lady.

Me: I hate cats.

Lauren: Relax Layla, you have been working too much. Have fun tonight.

The winking emoji needs to be banned. But true, I have been overrun with design requests, which is a freelancer's dream. And maybe I should use this unexpected time in New Orleans to enjoy some downtime. It's not like I am twenty-four seven on the clock at Ives & Wells. Just need to push through a few more meals with Trey and Josh.

I put my phone back in my bag and continue to work on my little minion from Mars type creature on the napkin. Truthfully, I have been working on little cartoons for a year or two now. Just a hobby that I love to do separate from my actual design work.

My strokes are hard and rough on the napkin.

"Okay there, princess? Seems like you have some aggression you need to get out. Always were high strung." That cocky grin is plastered across Josh's face as he leans back in his seat, smug and confident.

The corner of my mouth slants up. "Just drawing your dick. Small and confused."

His tongue circles his mouth in amusement. "By all means, let me know if you need me to model for you to get a more accurate interpretation."

I am a well-poised woman who is successful at what she does and knows how to charm. I have no problem owning my strengths. I would never speak this way with a client. But Josh is not a typical client. He is my brother's business partner and sidekick at parties. I know this guy more than I would like.

Looking at the man in front of me and I am ready to play our tit for tat, I begin by changing topics.

"Well then, looks like Trey boy doesn't want to do quick

and hard," I tell Josh, satisfied that I was right. Licking my lips, I take a sip of my brandy.

Josh shoots me a hardened look. "Right, he just wants to do you."

I choke on my brandy. "Say what now, boss?"

Josh leans in closer to me by moving his chair. And I choose to ignore the tingle racing through my body. It has happened before on the odd occasion when he is present.

"Your fucking charm, *honey*. Has landed us an extra few days down here. So next time you plan on flirting with the client—think about the consequences." He breathes into my space. His tone a little cocky and I wonder what else he could say using that tone.

"Screw you," I fume.

"You wish."

I may have, but then sanity hit me in the head.

Because there is an array of options why this man is not good for me. Not to mention, I will say blue and he will say green.

Rolling my eyes, I say, "Listen, I was not flirting and whatever I did seems to have worked better than your go in fast and hard approach, which has probably disappointed the female population of the masses." I am pissed. He should show some appreciation that I persuaded the guy to keep us around.

He pinches the bridge of his nose and he seems a little on edge.

Ugh, I get a whiff of his scent and it is awakening my senses. Spring fresh and strong. It must stay on the sheets for days.

"You're welcome, by the way. I think I swerved him off you, at least for a solid twenty-four hours." Josh leans back in his chair.

My hands find my heart to fake my gratitude. "Gee, you saved me. How ever can I repay you?"

The look he flashes me tells me a thought flew through his mind. Probably something dirty or inappropriate. Probably of me on my knees and taking him in my mouth.

What the hell? Why did that come into my mind?
Brandy stat.

Oh no, brandy is gone. Time to escape.

"Anyhow. I'm off. Your aura does something to my mood." I kiss the napkin I was drawing on, leaving a firm print of my red-covered lips. My eyes don't blink, but only glare at him. I throw my napkin in his direction on the table and head off. Teasing the man always gives me a high for reasons I cannot explain.

When I reach the elevator and step in, his highness himself joins me before the doors can close. I cross my arms and look forward.

"What now, boss?" There is annoyance in my voice.

An almost evil rumble escapes him. "Oh Layla, how you love to use that boss term. You are pretty hot and bothered for someone who just had her theory proved right. Slow it was, your winning theory of how to win this deal?" he says as he punches the number three in our elevator.

"Point is?"

He moves closer to my bubble of space and places a hand on the wall behind me to lean over me.

"Do you ever lighten up?"

I give him a dirty look. "I do, actually. I was going to book a massage at the hotel spa since the guide of the hotel highlights their massages. And yes Josh, I will be very naked on that massage table." My fingers flop his tie over his shoulder as his tongue hits his inner cheek in pleasure. "I also have a session planned at the hotel gym tomorrow at seven a.m. after a solid night of Z's in the heavenly bed of my hotel room. Where I will sleep like a baby since I am what is it… right?" I tell him and place a finger on my chin as if I am contemplating.

An almost devilish laugh escapes him. "Right, and you will be reminding me for the next four days, I am sure. Just remember who your boss is, Layla."

Why did he have to throw boss around because ah, *it is* a cliché scenario that does something to me!

The man is stealing all my air and my body has a peculiar sensation that I vaguely remember as the start to being extremely turned-on. My breathing is picking up. Is he looking down my dress?

I mean, I know I made a solid choice with my dress and matching bra, but really?

The elevator doors ping open and we both begin to walk down the long hall.

"How do you get away with being such a jackass? I would hate to be your actual direct report. HR must have a field day with you," I snicker.

He loosens his tie and unloops it so it hangs around his neck. "I don't know what thoughts are in your head, but HR would only have a field day if I was sleeping with my direct report."

That thought *may* send a tingle down my body to between my legs.

"Right, and you have such a high moral standing," I scoff with sarcasm.

Josh grabs my arm, stopping me from walking, and my body zings from his touch. We are standing in the middle of the hallway looking at each other.

"Believe it or not, sweetheart, but I am not the asshole

you think I am. I have never been down the road of banging my direct report or anyone from the office."

I look at his hand on mine. What does this man do to me? Why does he rub me the wrong way, but in all the *right* places?

Jerking my arm away forcefully, we walk a few more strides to our adjacent doors.

"Ugh, my standing waxing appointment is more pleasurable than a conversation with you," I grumble and roll my eyes.

The look on his face tells me he may be wondering what I have waxed.

I wave my long finger from side to side as a devious grin forms on his face. "Tsk tsk, Josh, mind out of the gutter."

"Right. Because in your dreams I am thinking *very* dirty things about you," he responds with a sexy voice and I huff.

When did he become a mind reader?

We are going nowhere, and both look at each other in a stalemate.

I decide changing topics is the only way to go. "Give me thirty minutes and I will send you some new designs based on Trey's input."

He leans against his door with an eyebrow arched. "I thought you were heading to bed?"

"I'm too hyped up now from your douchery, so I need a distraction before I try to fall asleep."

This seems to satisfy him. "Ah, happy to hear I have affected you so much. But if you want a distraction, we know what works…" He trails off.

I look at him and I am wondering where his sentence ends, because I know where it ends for me.

My eyes meet his and for some reason, I have a feeling

our minds are looking in a mirror. Our eyes scream the same —heat and bad decisions.

Really bad decisions.

He pulls his key card out from his pocket and dangles it in the air and my feet are traitors as they step closer to him.

"You never bang your direct reports, remember?" I challenge him with widened eyes and hands on my hips.

A cunning grin spreads across his face as he stands tall and takes one step closer to me. "Never have, didn't say I never would."

We look at each other with blazing eyes, and we are on the edge of no return. The aching between my legs reminding me it's been a while and an odd sensation in my brain telling me Josh may be a release I temporarily need—ignoring all warning signs. That one careless moment flashes into my memory and the feeling of his sizzling lips.

Ah damn it, this was inevitable.

You always want what you should not have. This turn of events was always silently whispering in the back of my head and I did a damn good job ignoring it. Until now…

4

LAYLA

In a flash, our mouths crash into one another.

Holy cow, he tastes as good as I remember, and wow, firm commanding lips too.

This undeniable need takes over me. I need more of him. Our mouths devour the other as our tongues collide. It's a powerful kiss, yet feels smooth. As if our mouths have been at this for years together.

The door behind him opens and we tumble into his room. Before I have a chance to realize what is happening, his mouth is trailing down my neck and his hands are on my sides. We are a mess of starving kisses and hands roaming.

I manage to get his suit coat off and wish I had a magic wand to get us naked faster. I feel his fingers encircle my wrists and he brings them above my head against the wall. My body curves into his body and we are two magnets pressing against one another. His mouth claiming my neck. Hot breath spreading across my skin, sending pulsating sensations to my inner walls. I'm pinned against the wall while his mouth explores the edges of my face before finding my lips again.

Screw him—Oh, I guess I am—what I mean is screw his need to control the situation.

My hands come down from the wall and find his shirt buttons that I fumble with. Deciding it's all or nothing, I give up and just rip his shirt open.

Take that, bootcamp training.

He flips me around and again places my hands against the wall, pulling my back to his front. He *knows* what he wants.

I would not expect anything but Josh Ives taking authority in the bedroom and my body responds to that thought with an inferno of pleasure growing between my legs and my behind pressing into his hard dick which makes me release an audible gasp.

His hands find my zipper and he unzips me before his hand moves under the loose fabric to caress my breasts. Roughly moving my bra fabric to the side, his hand palms my breast and I am nearly already breathless for him as it fits perfectly in his hand. His hands are skilled and not too rough, but not too soft. Our mouths find each other when I look back. I just want to get drunk on his taste.

This is good. So fast. So needy. Hungry, raw, we are two people in primal mode.

Turning around again, I let the dress fall to the floor and our kisses become frantic and hard. It feels so good, *too good* to not think. My hands find his belt, but before I can finish the job—he picks me up with my arms looping around his neck, body hanging against his, and he carries me to the bed.

"You really don't follow the employee handbook, do you?" I manage to gasp, and it earns me his hands firmly squeezing my ass.

"Screw you, Layla." I can hear the playfulness in his voice. It probably earned me a smile, but I would not know as my mouth is too busy exploring his chiseled chest.

"I hope you do," I counter.

Dropping me on the bed, he lays me down. A ruffle of rose petals touches my skin. Normally rose petals on a bed would be the image of a teenage girl's fantasy of romance. Now… these rose petals are a freaking obstacle in the ambiance for this hate sex scene that I most definitely have been fantasizing about.

But not enough of an obstacle, I do have needs after all.

Quickly he finishes pulling his belt off and his pants come down. Sweet mother of… his naked body is better than I imagined. The man obviously works out and is the right balance of slim and muscle to accommodate his mid-height frame.

Joining me on the bed, he quickly places a kiss on my mouth that is fast and hard before his eyes give me a warning as his head slowly moves down my body. His fingers tugging my red lace panties with him on his journey. My skin melting under his touch like butter. Shuddering from anticipation, and I feel a layer of wet silk releasing between my folds.

He drags his lips up my thigh, grazing me, teasing me as my pelvis tilts up to him. His five o'clock shadow toying with me. I moan when he reaches my center and as his mouth presses against my glistening slit, a thousand molecules in me scream. He stops short of my clit where he blows. My body buckles under him.

He looks up to me with a wicked grin. "Slow you said, right? Your perfect theory."

Fisting his hair, I cannot help it. I want his mouth on me, but I want his cock in me more. I do not want to drag this out. I need it now.

"No, not for this," I admit breathlessly.

He crawls over to me on all fours with the petals

bouncing around his hands and arms until he is caging me in underneath him.

"Say it, Layla," he urges me. His mouth finding my neck and sending glorious sensations all the way down to my toes. But that need between my legs is still too strong to ignore.

"Hard," I gasp as his finger dips inside me, and I arch into his touch.

"What else?" he whispers as he slips another finger inside me.

When his thumb begins to rub my clit in circles, I tremble. "Fast." It comes out slurred.

"Oh, so you want me to take you hard and fast?" He is taunting me.

My legs wrap around his hips tightly as my entire body curves into him.

"Hard and fast," I confirm through shallow breaths. My body totally surrendering.

His look of satisfaction far too sexy for me to even care anymore that he is getting to do this his way.

Quickly, he moves and flips me over to my hands and knees. I look back when I hear the crinkling of the condom wrapper and I am even more turned-on. My hand can't help it, and I reach for my clit to rub.

"You are so incredibly hot," he croons as he positions himself behind me. Taking over for my hand as he slips into me and I yelp softly. He is big and I want every inch of him, but it has been a while since I have done this.

He senses this.

His hand gently rubs circles on my lower back. "You okay?" Josh asks softly as he slowly moves in deeper as if he is reading my body language and waits for my body to tell him to push in farther. His question does not come across as the normal protocol in these situations. It sounds… tender.

"More than," I answer as I close my eyes and sink into the feeling with his hands gripping my hips. A few seconds later, I've adjusted, and he finds a perfect rhythm with me.

The sounds of both of us moaning and our skin hitting one another fills the room.

"You feel so good," he grunts as he pumps harder.

"I mean… I guess I can't complain," I breathe out.

He nearly growls as he stops, pulls out, and guides my hips to turn.

Turning around, I lay on the bed as he hooks his arms under my knees to hold me open wide. I'm very aware that we are now looking at one another.

He re-enters me and moves slowly.

"Look down," he urges. My eyes tilt down to see him move slowly in and out of me. "I think you really enjoy the sight of me inside you. Your body definitely enjoys me inside you. You are so fucking wet and it's all because of me."

I cannot help, but claw the sheets and let an overpowering O escape me as he moves deep inside me. The man has a point to prove clearly.

Our eyes meet. "Like I said, I guess I can't complain." I give a gentle smirk and he grins.

It makes him move harder, faster. A magnificent few minutes follow.

Soon we are both trembling over the edge to sated. Collapsing onto the bed breathless, almost spooning one another.

For a minute or two, his fingers gently brush along my arm in an almost affectionate way before he heads off to the bathroom to take care of the condom.

In that moment, I'm too smart.

I am numb from pleasure, but smart enough to know that this was a horrible idea.

As in brother's business partner, my somewhat boss and life's irritation bad idea.

I bounce off the bed and find my clothes and quickly throw them on. Before I get a chance to make it to the door. Two strong hands pull me back into the room at the waist and turn me around. Pinning me between the wall and his fine-looking body.

"Going somewhere?" Josh gives me a knowing look with the corner of his mouth curving up.

Trying to avoid his gaze. "Yes. This was not a clever idea." The tips of his fingers grab my jaw to lock my sight with his.

"No. You see, I think you have been dying to taste my mouth again." His gaze does not leave me.

"Geez, your ego never relents. We needed to work out some tension. Done and sorted," I inform him and manage to pass as confident. Managing to look away from his masterful fingers.

There is a pause.

His long finger tilts my chin up to his gaze. "You okay?"

For a moment, his deep eyes almost draw me in. As if we are in some out of world experience and he is really checking that I am okay. But this situation is a dead end.

"Okay. But I need to go back to my room and find my sanity in my suitcase. It got lost somewhere on our trip here," I snipe, which earns me that sexy grin on his face.

"Forgotten?" he asks and then I have a sinking feeling that he feels this was a horrible mistake and plans on forgetting it. And even though that is what I was thinking two minutes ago, I still feel disappointment.

"Sure." I break away from him and leave.

5

JOSH

Staring into my coffee as I sit at the breakfast table, I am completely screwed. There is a full spread breakfast buffet behind me served on antique china with the sun shining through the big windows of the indoor terrace. The ambiance pushing this hotel to cross to the lines of elegant chic. I should want to down a plate of bacon to restock my protein supply after last night, but I am not hungry.

What the hell happened?

First off, Noah is going to kill me if he ever finds out about his sister and me. The guy played college-level football and I only did a few boxing lessons. Something tells me the guy will be able to take me down a notch or two in a throw-down.

Two, yeah technically this was not a business-savvy move as on paper Layla does report to me... nah, I really don't care.

Three, why did I feel the need to take her like it is the only thing I have desired for the last few years?

She just... well, in her dress and her attitude... it was the combination.

Who the hell am I kidding? That woman has been on my mind a few times while jerking off over the years. The golden apple I couldn't have, which makes her all the more indulgent. Her feisty personality just does something to me. Last night I saw an opportunity.

Josh Ives does not miss opportunities.

She felt better than my twisted mind could have imagined. Soft skin, luscious breasts, sensual lips and she tasted like the only item I would ever want on the menu. Those red nails clawing the white sheets, well... on a loop in my head.

But it's Layla. She hates me and sometimes hate sex is the way to go. Right?

Now, I just hope we manage to make it through the rest of the trip in one piece. She already texted me to eat breakfast alone. My guess is she is avoiding me. She made it clear it was a one-off thing. As it should be.

Shouldn't it?

We have a late morning meeting with Trey, so hopefully she cools off by then. My phone pings and when I get the email, I see our meeting has been pushed back to pre-dinner drinks. That is good. Buys me some time to screw my head on and tell my dick to stop interfering with my brain.

My phone pings again and it is my sister Harper. I would consider us close. She is a free spirit, witty, and has no filter. A lot like Layla.

Harper: How is the big easy?

Me: Interesting.

Harper:??? Communicate with actual words please.

Me: Not thinking clearly, to be honest. There is an unexpected, complicated moment to this trip.

Harper: Complications can be good. What have I taught you?

Harper went to some hippy yoga retreat and came back as one of those pundits who spews words of wisdom.

Me: Really? You want to do this now?

The flow of annoyed emojis comes my way.

Me: Fine. The unexpected moment is always sweeter. Happy? My thumb actually typed that garbage.

Harper sends me a smile emoji.

Harper: Pinterest doesn't lie! Remember, spontaneity is the best kind of adventure...

Me: Stop sending me quotes. I've got stuff to do. Talk later.

Deciding breakfast is not going to happen. I push my coffee to the middle of the table and get up. Taking my leisurely time as I leave the breakfast area and head into the elevator and up to my room. When I get to my door, I stop and after a second of staring at both rooms, I debate if I should knock on her door to clear the air.

Quickly, I decide to be the guy that leads which has led me to success so many times.

Knocking on Layla's door, it is a few moments before she opens. When she does, she is...

Glistening wet.

Droplets of water sliding down her smooth skin.

Her dark hair dripping water.

A thick white towel wrapped around her and so easy to pull off.

"Yes?" she inquires with the bit of sass I would expect when we are in close proximity.

My eyes do not leave her. They are conducting an investigation of her body, retracing her every curve. "The meeting has been pushed back to early evening," I inform her as I clear my throat.

"Oh good, I have time to—" she begins, but I do not let her finish.

My hand reaches for the back of her head and my mouth finds hers. She pulls away quickly with her hands against my chest, but she looks at my eyes then my mouth and decides to slam her lips back into mine.

Good decision, Layla. *Excellent decision.*

Whatever remnant of a conscience I had while I tried to eat my scant breakfast plate has vanished. No, seeing her answer the door like that and there was only one thing to do.

Enjoy the forbidden fruit.

Again.

This unexpected moment is going to be sweet as honey.

Walking her back into her room and slamming the door behind me with my foot, I have her lying on the bed in record time. She looks at me with intrigue as she props herself on her arms as she watches me throw off my suit coat and crisp white button-down shirt that was on underneath until I am left in my dark jeans. Her bottom corner lip is getting attacked by her teeth as she looks like she is enjoying the view.

Because I am a damn good view.

"You have time for me to make your incredibly spectacular body come. We have time for that," I warn her and rip the towel away. Her smell of coconut and macadamia shampoo is making me dizzy with need.

Pushing her thighs apart with my hands is easy as her legs feel weightless and willing. My mouth finds her pink and ripe sweet spot. And it is the only thing I want. I'm desperate to taste her and to hear her express noises of pleasure. Her fingers grab my hair and when my eyes peer up to her, I can see her head is falling back in contentment with eyelids hooding closed.

"We really shouldn't," she manages to say through shallow breathing. "But—oh—don't stop," she purrs.

I go at her mercilessly with my hard tongue. Her body arching up to my mouth as I suck and lick relentlessly as she tastes of mellow sweetness and I want every last drop of her. Delving inside her with my tongue, I am not sure what I enjoy more. Her taste or her hips tilting up into my mouth from enjoyment. Returning to her clit, I circle her then stroke her, Layla's breathy moans accompany her visible smile. It does not take long for my magic tongue to send her seeing stars. She comes against my mouth and I don't let her go, I'm going to stay on her until she stops pulsing.

Fuck, she is gorgeous when she climaxes and lets her eyes shutter closed as she finds her hand laid next to her head to gently bite her finger. A relaxed smile forming.

I cannot help smiling at my accomplishment and I kiss her inner thighs. Just when I think I should give her a moment to recover before we go further with my plans for her, her eyes pop open and she looks at me, shooting up to sitting as if a jolt of energy came to her like a shot. Her eyes roaming me up and down. Before I can contemplate what is going through her head, her hands grab my arms and push me to lay on my back.

My head can't keep up as Layla is now straddling me, and it turns me on so much—it hurts.

Her moist pussy riding my jeans and my straining cock just wants to spring free. I groan as her hands guide my hands to her tits which seem extra perky this morning. I come up to sitting to take a nipple in my mouth. Sucking the hardened bud with force.

"Please tell me you brought a condom on your unexpected visit to my door?" Her voice is husky, and she seems lost in the feeling of our bodies ravishing each other.

"Layla, of course I brought one. I know you have been counting the seconds until I showed up at your door," I remind her sarcastically.

She gently shakes her head, slightly amused. But still on a mission. Assuming right, she hops off the bed to find my wallet from my suit coat and finds one. All the while, I take my pants and briefs off. Joining her to stand when she holds the square package in her hand. I take it from her, and she pushes me onto the chaise lounge chair in the corner.

A wild spell seems to have taken over Layla. With my length sheathed in a condom, she straddles my throbbing dick as I sit on the chair and she begins to ride me—even throwing in a spiraling motion which is a pleasant surprise. My arms wrap around her and pull her close as she moves up and down with determination. Her arms tightly looping around my neck.

"Damn, Layla. What has gotten into you? It's my big cock, isn't it?" I give her a cheeky grin.

"Maybe it's your expertise at irritating me that does a number on me," she bites back both in tone and literally biting my neck.

With that, I pick her up with my shaft still inside her and her legs wrapped tightly around me. I move us from the chair to the bed to laying us on the bed so I can show her how I can really do a number on her.

————

LYING in bed after having just had mind-blowing morning sex. We both stare at the ceiling as we recover our breathing. A towel tangled around us as we lay on top of the unmade bed of white linen.

This hotel is magical. Less than twelve hours here and I

got my wish of lying on my back on the thick high thread count sheets with a woman riding me with abandonment.

Two times together now and already I notice a behavioral change. When we are having sex, we are two different people. There is no putting on the brakes as we are completely involved with the other and wanting every last inch of each other.

"What happened to forgetting about last night?" she asks.

"That's what you wanted," I remind her.

Layla moves to rest her head on her propped arm.

"No, *you* asked, and I said sure," she counters.

"I asked to see if it was what *you* wanted. See, I am not an asshole. Besides, I just came to let you know about our new meeting time. I just so happened to make you come twice after, which is a very kind thing of me to do," I explain to her as I move to my side to look at her with my cheeks tightening as I try not to grin.

Her lips tug into almost a smirk.

Even after great sex, we are still playing a game of push and pull.

"Besides, what the hell was that? You turned into some mystical animal there." I have to compliment; I don't think I've ever seen a woman so eager and crazed. Wonder Woman from the Amazon doesn't hold a candle to the creature I just witnessed.

She hits me playfully. "Oh, so it wasn't your magical spell?" She shrugs. "I just needed it, okay? What now, boss?" Layla asks, almost intrigued. But I make a note in my head to figure out why she needed it.

A sigh escapes me. "I don't know." I am honest. Because this is complicated.

Layla nibbles her bottom lip and is lost in thought. "This is no big deal. I still see you as a jerk. Shouldn't we focus on the pitch?" She falls back and stares at the ceiling again.

"Sure. We can move past this, we are professionals. Heaven forbid you actually admit how much I turn you on and that you may actually find me a decent soul," I muse as that towel laying across us and around her breasts is teasing me again. My face must be giving me away.

Her foot gently kicks me on my leg. "Not happening again, like ever," she warns with a coy grin.

"Hmm, I've heard that before," I remind her and she growls in response.

Layla rolls out of bed, taking the towel with her, leaving me alone and naked.

"Okay, what's on the agenda for today?" I ask sincerely, as she is in the bathroom throwing on clothes.

Her head peers out from the door. "*You*—Mr. Boss, must have a lot of other work to do. *Me*—I need to go shopping since this trip is longer than planned."

"Okay, I will go with you. I want to stop at this other inn to check out their marketing. Field research and all." I throw on my clothes.

Layla appears in a blue wraparound dress that will be easy to play with all day, and sandals. "Fine."

6

JOSH

Sitting at a small table on a terrace with a fan twirling above us and green vines wrapped around the rafters of the architecture, two beignets are placed in front of us.

"Why am I here again?" I ask, although the coffee I just sipped is almost as orgasmic as this morning.

"Because apparently this is the best beignets in the city, and I am starving. Plus, you decided you felt you needed to tag along to piss me off at some point today." She smiles before diving into the donut type treat in front of her covered with powdered sugar. Almost letting out a moan that matches last night and this morning.

Taking a bite into mine, it is tasty, not going to lie, and yeah, I could use some real calories after—looking at my Rolex—the last twelve hours.

"This is really good. The best thing yet on this trip." She gives me a playful look that tells me she is teasing me.

"Right. Since we are forgetting the last twelve hours," I deadpan.

"Yeah, it's for the best. I don't want to be left scarred with nightmares that I have seen you naked," she says neutrally as she grabs her phone from her bag, swiping her screen.

"What about this?" She shows me a new design of the label of the Sweet Dove Hotel and it looks pretty impressive with bright color shading and font letters. The Dove almost looks like a jazz player—but sophisticated. Just like that, I am reminded that I need her to win this pitch and I cannot screw this up.

"I like it and it takes into account the theme of the hotel in terms of the colors they used to decorate. The Dove is good too. Different and I can tell you are into drawing characters." I cannot help but smile at that fact.

"Yeah, it helps now that we have seen the place first-hand. I think we should go for the jazzy and romantic feel."

"Why is it that you didn't want to work for us permanent-ly?" I ponder and I am serious as she is talented, smart and everyone in the office loves having her around.

A laugh escapes her. "A. I like having different clients and projects. B. You as my boss on a permanent basis would be a nightmare based on past experience and you know that too," she admits.

Leaning back in my chair. "Why is that? Why do we annoy each other so much?"

She shrugs her shoulders. "I don't know. Well, I mean, I have a list of reasons. Just nothing concrete. But we seemed to have found a way to defuse it just enough to last the next few days, right?"

"Next few days?" I have a compelling urge to test my luck.

She shakes her head no. "Not going to happen again."

"What, the rose petals aren't doing it for you?"

She laughs. "They really are overdoing the romance

theme. Did you notice the bottle of wine waiting in your room when we got back after dinner?"

"No, I didn't. I was kind of relaxed after you left and got some shut-eye. I needed it. I have not slept well in a few days. I was out west to visit my sister and it always makes me exhausted."

"Oh yeah—I met her once or twice. Seems like the life of the party. You guys are close?" she asks, genuinely interested.

"Would like to think we are. She would love all this voodoo stuff here in New Orleans. Really believes in all this paranormal crap. She is getting married soon to her realtor, which is kind of funny. They probably have a good story to tell over wine."

"Sounds like it."

After I settle the bill, we leave to walk along the streets of the French Quarter. She seems to be admiring the city, taking in the sights, and stopping occasionally to look through quirky shop windows. When we come across little art galleries, she compliments the owners on their work from the doorway. It is calming watching her get lost in sightseeing.

In fact, today is by far more comfortable, borderline enjoyable, than yesterday. Maybe sex is the answer.

All the while, I wonder why today Layla seems more bearable than normal, sweeter than normal, and incredibly breathtakingly beautiful in this moment.

My mind ventures to what it would be like to have her a few other ways. Admittedly, my mind may have ventured to those fantasies a few times. There may be a file in my brain worthy of a hard drive that should be in a locked drawer.

After a half-hour of walking, she looks across the street where there is a lingerie store and I cannot help noticing that seems to be her destination.

"Now if you will excuse me, I need to buy a few things *alone* since we are stuck here longer than planned," she hints.

Fuck me senseless, this must be her way of testing me. Especially as I see an olive green set with a lace bra and panties with matching stockings that would look amazing on her with those heels she wore last night.

As she is about to cross the street, I grab her arm.

"Layla."

She looks at me, slightly confused as to why my hand found her arm. Yet a subtle slant of her lips tells me that she isn't going to kill me either.

Progress.

"Yes, Joshua? Don't you have an inn to see?" she asks in an authoritative tone.

Looking away then looking back at her, I know I am a confident guy and I'm not afraid to say what I want, and I know my brain may slap me for this. But I don't think we defused us enough.

Giving her my best sexy smile that normally earns me luscious lips and puppy looking eyes from the female population. "The green lace in the window… it would look good on you."

I swear her eyes sparkle and her lips twitch, her face turning slightly pink. Her lips then part, borderline jaw about to drop.

"Good to know," she answers simply.

Letting her arm go, she heads off and I depart to do some market research.

———

SITTING across from Trey at the circular booth table. I purposely made sure to sit between Layla and Trey. Not only is she a knockout in a black dress tonight, but tonight she has a V-neck shape in the front. Trey boy hasn't picked up his dropped jaw since we ordered a new round of drinks five minutes ago.

Finally, I clear my throat and get this show rolling.

"Had a look at some of the other hotels and inns nearby, history of the building plays a key role in marketing, which isn't new. But the story to tell needs to be unique. That should play a key role in all your hotel literature both online and in the hotel room books," I explain.

"Look, Josh, I know you guys know how to nail this when it comes to the task at hand. That, I am not worried about. It is more about seeing if there is a chemistry match," Trey explains as he drinks from his newly arrived cocktail and his eyes don't seem to leave Layla.

Moving slightly more to the left next to Layla, I can feel she remains well-poised.

"Ghost stories, right? I love how some of the hotels nearby really capture the haunted craze of New Orleans, yet somehow make it romantic. It seems like a lot of couples come here for a honeymoon, but love that there is some crazy haunted story attached to the place where they are staying," Layla notes as she grips her glass.

"Add in some jazz and that is exactly what people want down here. So, Josh told me that you are dating someone?" Trey asks.

Layla looks at me with a neutral look, but her eyes say enough. "I don't know if dating is the right word."

"So, not serious?" Trey is pressing.

Layla lets out a hum. "Serious is a big word. I mean, it's not like I am picking up guys in your hotel either," she jokes.

It makes Trey grin. "A shame for me."

Closing my eyes, how could I not see this coming? She is

playing a game. At that very moment, I feel fingers walking up my thigh under the white clothed table that put my dick on full alert.

Clearing my throat, I drink some whiskey.

"That is sweet of you to say. The Sweet Dove Hotel is definitely the place where I am sure a lot of magic happens. Where chemistry combusts between people, if you will. Makes me really excited to be part of a potential collaboration." The way it rolls off her tongue is too scandalous for my thoughts.

It's going to be a long shower later.

I would put my hand under the table to tease her, but I can't risk this being too obvious. Layla removes her hand from my thigh and brings it up to rub her lips before she grabs her glass.

A really long shower.

"Did you try breakfast this morning? It is top-notch," Trey beams proudly.

"I did have breakfast here and it was most certainly fulfilling," I comment and roll my gaze to Layla, who understands that she was my breakfast as she bites her inner cheek.

"I will try breakfast tomorrow. I hit the gym this morning, which by the way is a good place for an excellent workout. The best possible workout," Layla remarks and gives me a knowing look as this morning we worked up quite a sweat.

"Great. You are checking out the sights as well? You need the full NOLA experience. Not just the French Quarter. Go see some gators, check out some shops, hell, even have someone read your cards." Trey genuinely seems like he loves the city, even though he is not originally from here.

Layla laughs. "I really love your enthusiasm and for sure I am getting my cards read tomorrow, I love that stuff."

"Go at night. It makes it more fun," Trey adds.

"I will. Tonight, I may need to call it in early. I did a lot of shopping and need to unpack some bags. Might even get a massage from the spa. I see couple massages are popular, but I will stick to a relaxing massage for one." Layla gives me the side-eye.

"I really like your willingness to play tourist, I think it is essential for understanding the brand," Trey remarks.

In that moment, I realize he is not that big of an ass and to be honest, he stopped goading Layla in favor of gushing praises for the neighborhood. The guy really wants to partner with someone who will respect the brand and history of the city.

"Tomorrow it is full-on voodoo, massages, and beignets then," I declare as my hand falls under the table.

Taking an opportunity to let my fingers find Layla's thigh.

How did my radar not pick up on it already? It must have malfunctioned.

Looking at her, I zone in on one area. Any area. Any place that will confirm what I am thinking and need confirmation on.

There. I see it.

The edging of her dress that meets the olive green lacy bra that matches the olive green panties and the stockings that my fingers are currently touching.

My body is about to combust.

LAYLA

As soon as the elevator doors close, we are on a mission. Our mouths finding each other and our hands scavenging. Pushing me against the wall, he has me trapped between the wall and his hard body.

Because yeah, somewhere today I decided that this would be a fantastic idea. Bang it out so we may actually be civil to one another for the years to come. I mean, let's be honest—this guy most likely will be at my brother's weddings—yeah plural—because if Noah proposes to his current girlfriend then he will be marrying twice. Not to mention, I cannot escape Josh who is at every freaking party for my brother, I run into Josh randomly around the city looking self-righteous. I even run into him in my thoughts and that is just darn right infuriating.

Yes, melting of tension is good.

And he is *really good* with his hands, his tongue, his cock, his everything.

I went into that store needing a few extra days of simple lingerie, yet Josh's comment before I entered the store hovered around my ear on repeat and my fingers could not help but reach for the lacy number when I saw it. An insane impulse came over me to do something to turn him on and drive him crazy.

I decided a few days of fun was a good idea. Pure physical fun. I deserve it. These few days will go into our vault anyway once we leave. Why not add some sexy material to wear to the mix?

"What are you trying to do to me?" he growls into my ear which creates tremoring sensations down my body.

The doors ping open and we fall into the hallway. Unable to detangle as we move down the hall to our doors.

When we reach his door, Josh keeps his hands on my waist as my hands find Josh's suit coat edges. He manages to pull away slightly to tell me, "This dress is effective, and I need this dress off you now."

That confession is the best present my ears could receive. But also, a complete contrast to a moment in our history. So much so, that I have to place a hand on his chest and push him back a little to allow our eyes to catch.

I feel my chutzpah coming up to challenge him. "Funny thing." My look must be burning him.

Josh pulls away and rubs a hand along his jaw as he dares to let a defiant grin spread across his face. "Ah, there we are. Is that why you can't stand me?"

"Logical, no?" I challenge.

A sexy scowl spreads across his face. "Let's hear it, Layla. Tell me what you think happened?"

"It happened like this. I was sitting in the office working on some designs. One of the coordinators came into the office panicked that the model did not show up and they needed to take photos for a campaign that day. Some idiot from the corner cubicle decided to volunteer my name as a fill-in. I reluctantly said no—because I am not a model—but I was convinced to help. One hour later, I found myself in a next to nothing black dress," I ramble.

I don't mention the fact that the dress had me oozing sex and confidence—plus heels, perfect hair, and makeup. Even I knew I was a complete fox.

"Then I came to check on you," he adds.

He saw me and his jaw dropped. He looked like I stole his breath. That strong hand of his rubbed his face and his marbled eyes could not leave me. I felt I was melting under his gaze. He even had the audacity to nibble his bottom lip as if he was trying to calm himself. His eyes almost undressed me. His lips parted and he stepped closer, so close that we were breathing the same molecules.

"You said nothing. Your body was sending mixed messages," I continue.

I could feel his hot breath and his fingertips found my hip and ribs. The touch sending goose bumps down my body. Our eyes daring each other. The man looked like he was about to drool, and I loved the way he was looking at me—because I was looking at him the same way. Our bodies were arching toward one another and our heads were in a dance because it seemed our mouths were trying to find the other's. My whole body was flowing with anticipation.

"Then you stormed out." I remind him.

He smiles. "Twenty minutes later, you returned the favor in full by storming into my office. We began our usual squabbling and then our lips met. It was the only way to shut you up, but damn, it was better than Mozart's sonata."

"Yeah, then you told the project manager that I wasn't model material. You were a complete jerk to me. Not to mention, you seriously lacked any traits of being a gentleman," I explain with annoyance in my voice. The pin had dropped for me that he was a jackass and disliking each other was the only way to go. I had one bad apple in my life to last me a lifetime, wasn't about to add another.

"Layla," he says my name firmly.

His arm engulfs my waist and the other hand finds my upper back. He presses my body against his. Then he walks us back into the door so I am pressed between him and the door tightly, and I shiver.

"You couldn't be farther from the truth. You were so incredibly sexy. So, unbelievably gorgeous," he whispers into my ear with his mouth dragging along my ear to my neck. Then his lips brush the corners of my mouth. "I didn't want anybody else to see you. It drove me insane with the idea that anybody would see you like that. Not after I saw you."

"So, you decided to be a moron?"

"I *was* a moron. But you made me lose my words and I could only think of how much your brother would kill me for the thoughts that went through my head when I saw you," he admits, and our eyes meet.

I don't need to search his eyes long. I believe him.

And even though he still rubs me the wrong way. He was too seductive just now.

"W-what were you thinking that would have been so bad?" I dare to ask with a gulp because I am far too captivated.

This man knows how to do damage.

That sexy grin comes back. "Which way I should have taken you—from behind, sideways, or under me so I could screw you until you went blind."

This man sells it to me, I'll give him that.

My lips collide with his and our frenzy of uncoordinated kissing and grabbing continues. Our mission to reach his room resumes.

Pulling my lips away from his neck. "This is just stress

relief and as soon as this trip is over, then this stops." It comes out ragged.

"Until then, I can fuck you as much as I want and any way I want?" he asks as he lifts me and my arms loop around his neck and my legs wrap around his waist where I can already feel he is hard as a rock.

"Yes… well, maybe we need to negotiate on the any way part," I gasp.

How he manages to get the door open to his room, I do not know how. But the man is gifted.

Once inside, we get to the bed where he sets me down on my feet in front of the bed. The hotel turndown service has done another number this evening. Fresh rose petals, mints on pillows, and the duvet slightly turned over on the corner. I really need to pass the memo on to the front desk that we do not need this added confusion. No, we are two people enjoying no-strings bliss.

He begins to undo his cufflinks as he leans against the desk. "Take the dress off," he orders with his eyes never leaving me.

Unzipping the dress, I let it fall to the floor in a pool at my feet that I step out of. A breath escapes his pursed lips and the way he looks at me makes me feel like I am the treasure he was looking for.

"You are so fucking beautiful," he tells me as he grabs my wrists and quickly turns me as he steps behind me. We look into the mirror that I didn't notice before but is now in front of us. I watch his lips drag along my neck and the back of his hand glides down my side as he feels the lace of my new bra and panties that I *may* have gotten especially for him. His fingers edging along my stocking lines and up toward my middle. Shivering under his touch. Watching this all unfold in front of us. Unable to distinguish if I am more turned-on from watching him or feeling him.

I am still in heels. Every guy's fantasy, right? The heels I *know* will be staying on.

"So incredibly sexy," he whispers as he brings a hand to my brown hair that is flowing behind my shoulders. His hand gripping some hair and slightly tugging me toward his mouth as his other hand comes to my stomach to press me against him.

In that moment, I am certain that I have never felt so wanted and it makes me tremble.

Turning around, our eyes meet. Both confirming we want to go down this path of error again. It's just physical lust.

Quickly, I help get his shirt open with my fingers and let the shirt fall to the floor before my hands unbuckle his belt. Dropping to my knees as I take his pants and boxers with me in the process. It seems to surprise him. But I have a craving for him that is surfacing.

My eyes look up at him as my mouth finds the tip of his shaft and I take him in my mouth without thought or hesitation. Normally, this is not something I would do. But with him, I want to do this. It is an unexpected urge that overcomes me. My strokes with my tongue move to take him fully in my mouth. His hands weaving in my hair to help guide me. He tastes so good and he has not even come fully, I just want his thick smooth cock deeper.

Yes, Layla. So good Layla. Oh Layla.

He grunts, moans, and encourages me.

It does not take long before he croons. "Layla, you have to pull away. I am going to come." But my mouth just goes firmer and I tighten my grip. "Holy fuck oh-oh." He moans until I taste a salty thickness slide down my throat. I pull away and lick my lips. Grinding my body up against him as I come back to standing.

"You are something and I need to show you." The corner of his mouth curves and his face is light with post-orgasm endorphins. Reaching behind me, he unhooks my bra as my eyes do not blink and stare at him with a satisfied look.

He guides me to laying down where his mouth finds my nipples and he takes his time with each one. Making me drip between my legs.

"So good, don't stop." I sound needy and it only makes his fingers find my clit.

"So wet, all for me, Layla? Tell me," he requests in between sucking my nipples and kissing the valley of my breasts, all the while slipping a finger inside me.

"All for you," I pant as my tongue catches between my teeth and corner lip with my body arching into him as he hits my sweet spot between my internal walls.

He ravishes me with his mouth everywhere. Before I know it, I cannot handle it anymore. I need him inside me, and I reach for the condom on the side table and hand it to him.

"You want me, don't you?" he asks before tearing the condom wrapper open with his teeth.

"I want you," I whisper and internally question why I am admitting so much.

"How much?" He grins as he sheathes the condom over his shaft and positions himself over me.

"Too much," is all I manage to say. Because I want him more than I should. This is purely physical.

Has to be.

He slips into me with ease and before I know it, he is making me shudder over and over again with one leg over his shoulder, my heels still on. Taking over my body as it submits to his touch and pushes. He knows what he is doing, and I've never been with someone who is as skilled and experienced as he is. It has *never* felt this good.

As if all times before were the minor league and I now just entered the World Series.

Time may have stood still, or the world may have stopped turning. I have no idea how long it takes before we are rocking our hips in sync together until we unravel, but we enjoy every second.

We are two different creatures when we are together in this way. He goes as deep as possible, but I want him deeper. Our bodies are close, but I want him closer. We are inseparable, insatiable, and impatient. We want it all at once, every touch and kiss and thrust.

That thought alone helps send me to the peak with him. An urge overcoming us that we want to look in each other's eyes as we both explode from this wave of ecstasy.

"Josh," I scream.

"Yes, Layla, so good," he roars.

Finally coming down from our high. He rests his weight on his arms, but he is still inside me. My legs now wrapping around his waist. Our eyes still locked.

Taking a moment to come back to reality.

And reality hits like a ton of bricks while he gets up to go get rid of the condom and then rolls back into bed.

"I should go now," I mention and begin to roll up to sitting, but his hand touches my arm.

"No. No, you shouldn't." It comes out warm and soft.

Lying back into the bed, his arm finds me in a hold, and he kisses the top of my head. Before I have a chance to think what this is, I am reminded.

"I need to be inside you again and then again in the morning. Somewhere between in the shower too. You're staying here," he informs me.

Because this is just sex.

"You packed a lot of condoms for this trip," I comment as the number of condoms we are going through isn't normal.

He snorts and squeezes me. "Layla, I stocked up while you were buying lingerie for me. No way was this morning going to be the last time."

"Well, that was presumptuous."

"*Right*... because buying lingerie isn't presumptuous either."

I cannot argue. "If you win Radnor over, you really should consider persuading the hotel to offer complimentary condoms in the bathroom with their logo. These rose petals and mints don't help people reach the finish line safely," I mention sarcastically.

He chuckles gently. "Not a bad idea. I guess their idea is that romance is needed to reach the finish line."

"Amateurs. Sometimes good old-fashioned pretending to be the other's disdain is the way to go."

"Pretending? You must be tired. Go to sleep, Layla, we need energy for later." His voice is drowsy, and he quickly kisses my forehead almost tenderly, then pulls me tighter to him.

But I cannot help thinking that it is completely true.

Because I don't sleep in the same bed with men, not often. In fact, rarely. No. I run as soon as the sheets cool. There are reasons for my policy; reasons I don't share with anyone. But it's safer for my body and my heart. I don't like to think about what could happen when my eyes close and someone else is there. Sleeping alone is the only way I can sleep in peace.

But right now, this man has an unexplainable ability to

make me feel safe and his searing kisses make me let go of all my inhibitions.

It's new to me, I've never had this feeling.

Which is all the more reason I remind myself that it's temporary.

LAYLA

My eyes flutter open and it doesn't take long for my brain to register where I am. The acknowledgment that I slept deep is a little strong. It could be a good old-fashioned O as the root cause, or it *could* be the man lying next to me. But that would be ridiculous.

The shuffling of a mumbling body lying behind me makes me glance over my shoulder.

Fuck me, how does he look like this at six a.m.? It is a sin, really. The sunlight peeking through the curtains only heightens his features to the extreme and the morning stubble on his chin, I want to rub against. That half-slant grin is enticing—to me at least. He lies on his side and he is pressed against me.

Josh is already busy opening a condom, which should irritate me that he assumes, but it just arouses me more. Because I know I am ready and I most certainly feel that he is ready. His morning glory is impressive.

I smirk. "No good morning?"

"No, I definitely will give you a good morning," he tells me confidently with a gravelly morning voice and when his fingers slide along my sex, I moan a long slow *Mmm*.

His hand lifts my leg slightly up under the knee so he has a wider playing field and his cock slides into me and I know I am already coating him with my juices. His arm wraps around me and his cock pumps in and out until I am singing a song of O's and ooh's. His mouth covers mine with a few blazing kisses before my eyes sink back and want to close as I enjoy the pleasure. Morning sex always sends extra tingles over my overly sensitive body, but these tingles are different.

He takes us there. We get to our morning Utopia that leaves us almost sedated.

And we don't stop there.

After a quick post pleasure snooze, we head to the shower. Immediately, the man is on his knees licking me up to Mount Zion before I return the favor. I even scored a back rub in the shower for my efforts and delivery. Then I kicked Josh out so I could get a normal shower in.

Walking out of the bathroom in a thick white towel robe, I admire the view as I go to lay on the bed. Now I am numb and sore as the morning sun comes through the room and Josh is on his phone talking with someone about business as he stands by the balcony door.

He is sexy when he is bossy, a walking GQ ad, really. His defined body and towel wrapped around his waist may also help with his image. Throwing his phone to the side, he comes to the bed and begins to pepper kisses up my legs.

"You are supposed to find me obnoxious, remember? Not treat me like the only item in your diet. You've been failing all morning," I remind him, amused.

He stops and looks up to me. "Temporary truce, remember? And if you're my new diet then I love this menu." He begins to trail his tongue up my inner thigh.

"No, I can't. I need a rest," I beg and laugh as he pins my arms down and begins to graze my neck.

"Tell me, Layla, you like to call me boss because it turns you on," he demands to know and even with his mouth dragging along my skin, I sense his smug look.

"Why, whatever do you mean?" I feign and that earns me his fingers tickling my stomach.

Not a fair move.

"Tell me, Layla," he demands again and does not stop tickling.

I am laughing so hard and find the feeling on my skin unbearable.

"Okay. Okay. Yes," I nearly shout. He stops tickling and he retreats back with a satisfied grin.

But then his mouth finds my neck and his teeth grab some skin. Pulling away slightly. "Tell me, you will keep calling me that after this," he requests and he is dead serious as his teeth find my skin again.

"Hmm," I pretend to ponder.

His teeth bite a little and I realize that he will leave a mark if I do not answer. The man knows how to play. "Tell me," he warns me with a full mouth.

I whimper under his teeth. "I won't stop," I admit and manage to push him away as I laugh.

After a moment, I think aloud.

"Is it strange that I don't really care that it isn't professional to sleep with my semi-boss? I mean, it must look bad if it ever came out, right?" I doubt myself.

I am good at what I do, I'm always professional and it's the reason I have enough clients to work freelance. But why don't I care when it comes to Josh?

"You mean because I sign off on your invoices?" He seems entertained.

"Holy shit, does that make me a prostitute? No, it is okay, I won't invoice *those* hours."

I grin and he lets out a deep laugh.

"Ah Layla, you are Noah's little sister. Either way, the cards are stacked against you at our office," he jokes, but something tells me he is serious.

"Oh God, do people really think I am there because of my brother?" I speak aloud the thought I have always wondered, but never really cared. I give my best work, even if it is my brother's company.

"No, I mean everyone loves your work, so nobody doubts that. But everyone does know to not mess with you, or Noah would kill them."

I can't think further as my phone rings. "Grab that, will you?" I motion to my phone in my bag on the chair. He reluctantly pulls away and obliges.

A deep groan escapes him and then he shows me my phone with my brother's name flashing across the screen. "Speaking of the devil."

Shrugging to Josh, I say, "I can't avoid him forever." I take the phone and answer.

"Hey Noah… yeah it's fine… I think Trey likes us, seems to be going okay." I try to push Josh away with my foot as he continues to crawl up my leg with his mouth. "My boss isn't so bad… we haven't killed each other yet," I comment as I give Josh an amused look and he flashes his eyes at me. "It's not a big deal staying longer. I just need to be back by end of the week as I do have other projects to work on… yeah well, we are doing our own thing. I went shopping, I think he went to the breakfast buffet," I tell my brother when he asks what we did yesterday. I talk a little more about the meetings with Trey. "Okay, bye."

Throwing my phone to the side, I let out a deep sigh.

"I don't enjoy lying to my brother," I admit, and lay there motionless as a starfish. Josh comes to open my robe and nibbles at the bottom of my throat.

"You enjoy it a little," he informs me with a mischievous grin.

Maybe I do. Do I? Does it give me a thrill to have a secret rendezvous?

"You don't have a problem lying to him about this?"

He stops for a second and looks at me. Debating what to say. "Is it great? No. Is it the end of the world? No. But he isn't going to find out, so what is the harm, right?" He seems sure of himself.

We are going to have to talk more about that at some point, but now I am losing my train of thought. Because he opens my legs and positions himself and I am not yet sure if he is going to take me with his mouth or cock.

Before I get an answer, my phone goes off again.

Josh groans. "You're in demand this morning."

Pushing him off me, I grab my phone. "No. This one is my alarm. I need to go back to my hotel room; I need to take my birth control pill."

He lies on the bed with an arm behind his head as he watches me. "Yes, *please* go take those. Take lots of them as if it is candy. Then come back here." He grins.

"Not coming back here. I actually need to work, and something tells me you do too. Plus, I need to eat, like actual food."

I grab my bag and clothes from last night to enjoy the world's shortest walk of post-hooking-up back to my room.

"Meet me for breakfast?" he asks as he grabs his phone from the bedside table.

"Sure."

THE PLATE in front of me on the table is filled with bacon, beignets, eggs, fruit and I managed to nab a biscuit too.

Josh laughs hard. "How does someone as tiny as you manage to eat all of that?"

"I have a night of marathon sex to boost my metabolism," I deadpan as I stick a fork into my food.

"Do that often?"

"No, actually," I admit honestly as I look at him.

Not that I don't have fun on the occasional basis, but my view of romance is a little jaded. It has let me down a few times. But sex is sex, and this situation comes at a good time. I was in a dry spell and honestly, I am more stressed with Josh around if he is not inside me. When he is inside me, I seem to be on a pure relaxation retreat.

"You?"

"Believe it or not. No," he admits, and it surprises me. I kind of figured him as the guy who picks up someone in the hotel bar as he travels so much.

He begins to attack his bacon and eggs, but his phone pings, and he scrolls on his phone. "We are alone today. Trey will meet us tomorrow for lunch with a decision. He wants a full report of what we did today," Josh explains as he places his phone down.

Arching a brow, I ask, "Full report?"

He chuckles. "The business version, I assume."

"Alright then. Massage this afternoon then voodoo and cards here we come."

Taking a sip of his coffee, he looks at me curiously. "You actually seem like you really want to do that. The tarot cards."

I must look like a child opening a present. "I do, I *really* do."

"Your wish is my command then." He smiles.

"Why thank you, boss."

"Now *that*," he says, tilting his head to the side. "I think your brother *may* kill me for. So, freaking ethical when it comes to work," Josh mentions as I look at him while sipping my coffee.

"And you're not? Is that how you both managed to leave the agency a few years ago? You played the hard way?" I ponder.

He looks at me taken back and sinks back into his chair. "*Ah*, there it is. You think I convinced your brother to do something shady in order to leave the agency and open our own?"

Debating what to say. "Not shady. I just… Noah is sweet, kind-natured, and yeah, wouldn't ever do something outside the lines. Suddenly, he did. I thought maybe you influenced him. I mean, making the employee handbook of rules for your office was like his life's work," I admit as I play with my fork on my plate.

A bitter laugh escapes him. "Have you ever thought it's the other way around? For the record, he suggested we leave, and I just found a loophole to make it happen. Also taking some key accounts with. It was all above line. The joys of having a solid lawyer who can rip apart a contract." It comes out very confident and cocky.

Studying him, I realize that he is not lying. To be honest, I probably was always aware of that fact. I just never wanted to give the benefit of the doubt.

"Okay."

"Okay?" he doubts me.

"I believe you," I answer him and our eyes connect.

I am believing him on a lot of things lately.

"Is that why I annoy you? You thought I was corrupting your brother?"

Shaking my head. "A little, plus our little incident plus many things, but mostly it is your cocky attitude with a broody smile that sometimes looks more like a scowl." I have to smile now.

"Anything else?" he asks, crossing his arms, entertained.

Yeah, this could never be anything permanent, and jabbing the other as a ritual is the only defense mechanism I know.

"Let's just focus on the day," I suggest.

9
JOSH

After both getting in a few hours of work in our separate rooms and each nabbing a massage from the hotel spa, we walk around the city. I got to leave my usual outfit behind for the day and opted for jeans and a light-blue Henley shirt, while Layla stuck to a green cotton short-sleeved dress and sandals. Walking around, we take in the sights and get lost on small little streets, stopping occasionally to listen to live music of trumpets and bass horns on street corners.

Layla emerges with a bag full of carnival masks from a store.

"Big plans?" I ask, amused.

She gives me a playful grin. "I don't know. Is it a fantasy of yours?"

I laugh. "No, not my fantasy. Yours?"

"No. Thought they would look good on my living room wall."

"Oh yeah, Noah mentioned you moved a few months back. Like your new place?" I ask, genuinely curious.

"Yeah. I do. Great neighborhood with some local gems of

restaurants and bars. You're still in the Gold Coast neighborhood?"

I nod. "Yeah. Have you tried Morelli's? It is near your place. The menu changes every week, but it is great," I mention.

"Hmm, don't think I have."

For some reason, a thought passes through my head that I should take her when we are back. But that is just batshit crazy. I mean, we are just a few days of fun, we barely managed normal conversation at breakfast. She has a list of reasons why I am the evil prince in any woman's fairy tale.

Walking along the street and taking in more sights, we keep to general conversation about New Orleans and the Sweet Dove Hotel. The afternoon fades to night with the sky getting darker, but the lights of the city more colorful. Groups heading into bars ready for a night of fun, music getting louder, and random laughter sporadically erupting.

She pulls my arm. "Come on, I need to find a voodoo doll, it's next on my list." Layla seems serious.

With a concerned look, I ask. "Plans?"

Giving me a dirty look. "Yeah. I may need it after this trip. Just in case…"

"Sounds like I am in trouble."

She gives me her signature I-love-to-tease-you look.

My tongue circles my mouth and I decide to switch topics. "Drinks or cards?" I ask, knowing either answer is going to be enjoyable.

Did I just use the word enjoyable? Am I actually enjoying this? Yeah, because that would be ridiculous. Walking around a city on a workday as if I am on vacation with a woman who can make me laugh and later will use her hands better than the magician we just passed. Nuts.

Her hands come together in excitement. "Cards for sure."

Nudging her arm, I lead her to the small shop on the corner with purple etched lettering on the glass window called Luna Ray's.

"Have you ever done something like this?" I ask her.

"No way, you?"

Shaking my head no, we head into the shop with the bell ringing announcing our arrival. A middle-aged woman emerges from behind hanging beads, and Layla grabs my arm as she is trying not to laugh. Luna Ray herself has feathers coming from her red hair and colorful necklaces around her neck with a purple velvety dress that seems like it is thirty years old. All we need is a parrot and Layla will be over the edge in hysterics.

Right on cue, a parrot flies into the room.

Layla lets her head and mouth dive into my chest to block her laughter, which is a nice feeling—the vibrations of her laughter against my chest, her fingers clawing my shirt, her nose nuzzling into me. I place an arm around her and decide to take this up a notch.

"Sorry, she is a little giddy today. Being a romantic getaway and all." I try to keep a straight face.

"Come, my children, come back to the room." Luna waves a hand.

Layla looks at me shaking her head and I do not think I have ever seen her so hysterically happy. It is infectious.

Heading into the room, we sit at the table that has a leopard print scarf thrown over it, a candle, and a deck of cards. An overpowering smell of sandalwood filling the room.

"Shall we begin?" Luna asks as she shuffles the cards.

Layla nods.

Luna clears her throat. *Ah of course*. I throw a fifty on the table for the pure fiction of our life about to be spewed out in front of us.

Showing me the deck of cards, Luna indicates for me to pull a card. I do and I place the card on the table.

"Two of cups. This is the card every couple wants, but rarely gets. The symbol of commitment. The high probability of love, marriage and a need for the other."

My cheeks tighten in the ridiculousness of this and I try to not laugh. Layla claws my thigh as she finds this so outrageous and is having trouble containing herself.

"Perhaps a wedding?" Luna asks.

"Oh, for sure. This guy has a ring hidden back in the hotel room and I am just waiting for him to ask," Layla plays along.

"That's good, as life will ask you to marry sooner than later. Something will bring you two together," Luna offers her sage advice.

"Oh? But the venue we want has a waiting list of like two years," I feign, and Layla's look is priceless.

Luna places another card on the table.

"The empress. Sign of fertility, cycles, love..." Luna lists.

Yeah, not feeling that one. Birth control works wonders.

Placing another card on the table.

"The emperor. It seems the masculine one of your relationship likes power and authority," Luna speaks.

Okay, maybe that isn't far off.

"Sounds like the way Josh enjoys sex," Layla mutters under her breath and I shake my head in entertainment.

The next card comes to the table.

"The high priestess. This card shows that you are both connected with your dream world or feelings. It also connects to fertility and sexuality."

Hmm, that is one worth pondering. The sexuality part at least.

"Finally. The hangman. Something unexpected will come your way. Soon. This card shows us that everything you know will be turned upside down."

The way Luna says this sends a shiver down my spine. There must be something in her incense that overpowers the room. Or she has rehearsed this line way too much and she deserves an Oscar. It came across... authentic.

"Deep," Layla states and I can tell she is amused again.

After an awkward silence. We quickly end the session and head out of the small shop. As soon as we hit the street. Layla and I look at each other and burst out into hysterics.

"Oh my god, that was so much fun," Layla beams. She nudges my arm. "Come on, Josh—even you had fun."

My hands go up. "Okay. Yeah, it was enjoyable."

She laughs harder. "So crazy. For sure, my future is so clear now," Layla mocks.

After another minute, we finally manage to calm down our stomachs that had laughter barreling through. I think my stomach aches because I haven't laughed this hard in ages. It's... refreshing.

We begin to walk down the street and I can't help wrapping my arm around Layla's waist as we walk, and she doesn't seem to push it away or flinch.

"Should we try a bar?" I ask.

"Sure."

It just means my arm does not have to part from her all the longer.

————

LOCATING a bar that has great live music was easy to find. The city has so many options. We settled on a spot not far from the hotel with the menu on a chalkboard on the wall. The blue ambiance light of the place adds to the vibe with a string quartet playing some upbeat jazz rhythms.

Layla drinks from my drink as we sit at the bar top.

My head resting against my propped elbow, I look at Layla and realize a fact.

"Can I ask you something?"

"Sure." She looks at me.

"As much as I know you love tasting where my mouth has been." I wiggle my brows at her. "You only drink if you watch the bartender make the drink or if it's my drink. Why is that?"

Her eyes look at me. "Do I?" She is not going to tell me.

"Yeah, you do."

She drops her shoulders and lets out a *huh*.

"Can I ask you something?" she asks again, trying to move us along.

I nod and touch her hand on the bar. Her eyes travel between my hand and my eyes.

"You said you never had an office romance. But didn't you date Amanda from project management?"

I look at her puzzled as I have no clue who she is talking about. "Sorry, you lost me."

"Amanda? A friend of Noah's worked in project management at your old company. You hooked up or had a thing."

Shaking my head, I am confused. "Really have no clue who you mean."

"My brother said that you both—" She stops mid-sentence. "Oh my god," she mutters under her breath.

Waving a hand. "Care to clue me in?"

"Noah really doesn't want us together," she sighs. "He

told me that you and his colleague had a thing and it ended because of your jerk tendencies. But I guess Noah said that because he knew I wouldn't go near you after thinking you are horrible with office flings and we need to work together." She almost laughs.

I let my fingers play with her dress strap. "Is that another reason why I annoy you? Because I apparently hooked up with someone I know nothing about?"

A smirk forms in the corner of her mouth. "And the fact you are a perpetual asshole with a broody looking scowl," she reminds me.

"No, being an asshole would be suggesting we try a three-some with this Amanda chick," I say as I take a sip of my Sazerac.

Layla rolls her eyes. "Been there, done that." She winks as she twirls on the barstool.

I choke on my drink. "Are you serious?"

Her shoulders bounce up and down. "Maybe. Maybe not." She must be trying to get a rise out of me. Finally, she shakes her head no.

"Good. I don't know who in their right mind would want to share you," I comment and she looks at me pleased.

"Are you trying to gain points for later in bed?"

"Maybe, maybe not."

We are bantering with each other and she shakes her head in enjoyment.

"I really love it here in this city. Such great vibes. Most certainly coming back." She plays with a straw.

"You will come back a lot if Trey agrees tomorrow," I remind her, but she shakes her head no.

"*Yeeeah...* so I have quite of a few projects the coming months, so I don't have time to save my brother and his asshole business partner whenever they need." She grins.

"Plus, I am not sure me working with you as my boss is the best plan going forward. What happens next time we are together on a business trip or alone in a meeting?" she questions and she makes a valid point.

"You said I only get to have you on this trip and then it's done. Have you been converted to enjoying sex and realize I am the guy to fulfill the task?" I give her a cocky grin, but I know why she asked what she did. "We are professionals, right?" There is a subtle tone in my words that we should end this conversation, and she doesn't press further.

Thank the no-strings-attached gods because I do not want to think when I am with her. I just want my forbidden fruit even if it is a potential poisonous apple, no cherries... because she tastes like fucking cherries. The kind you find in a pie, not the cheap ones in a jar used for drinks. No, Layla is full-on organic baked cherries. Including her personality, which is sweet yet tart enough to give you a constant kick.

Christ. My head has been spinning that thought around for the last few days.

The music changes and the strings are joined by a sax and jazz singer. People move to the center of the bar to dance and Layla flashes her eyes at me then grabs my arm and drags me away from the bar.

She guides me to the dance floor. "You are not going to tell me you are one of those guys who don't dance." She gives me a stern warning.

My hands go up in surrender. "No way. I think I may impress you." I grab her hands and begin to lead the way. Twirling her around and pulling her in. Her laugh getting louder on each tilt back and sway.

"Okay. You are right. I'm impressed." She glows as we continue to sway.

I press her body closer to mine.

In that moment, our eyes play a game of searching into the other's. It takes a few moments to transition to our next move as we are lost in a moment.

And when I finally tilt her back on our next move, my lips find hers for a very public kiss. Pulling her back up, not letting our lips part.

Her lips taste of sour lime that I was drinking and her body presses into mine as the music blares.

Pulling away, she looks at me with swollen lips and twinkly eyes.

"So boss, what's on the agenda?" she asks softly.

Most certainly end public affection because that was a dangerous move on my part. I wonder where to take this night. "Dinner? We could go somewhere or room service?"

She licks her lips. "Room service." She does not hesitate. Layla grabs my hand and drags me away.

JOSH

In our room, we are taking advantage of the excellent quality bed linen with a fan twirling around on the high ceiling and lights still on. The French doors are open to the balcony to let in the evening heat and the sound of locusts buzz in the air. Jazz music plays in the distance from the street.

Lying in bed, Layla rests her chin on her propped fists as she lies on her stomach with her hair brushed to one side of her bare back. The back that I am drawing a map in my head on as I am sitting halfway up with the sheet hanging at my waist.

My eyes drinking in the view. Her eyes. They draw me in and then get me lost in her world every time.

I'm a smart man. I know something shifted somewhere in the last day or two. I just can't figure out what or when. Or what the hell to do about it.

She breaks my daze. "This was your easiest pitch yet, no?"

"You mean a few drinks and exploring a city? Or having sex while doing both of those things?" I slide my finger slide up her arm, and she gives me a playful slap. Turning serious I answer, "Yeah it is, but also because Trey isn't shopping around so we are the only ones he is discussing a change with."

"What are your other projects?" I'm curious.

She laughs to herself. "A cake company, two romance novels and a finance software. The full bag."

"Romance novels? Really? Like the kind my grandma would read?"

"No, the kind that would be too scandalous for your grandma to read." She is dead serious.

I flip her to her back and cage her underneath me while I nibble her neck. "Hmm, maybe we should try some of those scenes if you need to conduct market research."

Her hand grabs my jaw and forces me to look back at her face. "A break, please," she pleads with a low voice and half-smile.

I return to my back, because in truth I could use a break—I haven't had this much sex in a two-day period since I was in my mid-twenties prime.

"Shall we open tonight's wine bottle the hotel left?"

She comes to leaning on her side to look down at me and nods.

I throw on some briefs, go to the table and open the bottle of red, pour two glasses and bring it to her in bed where she is drawing on hotel paper with a pen. I drink from the glass and hand it to her. Then take the other one for me. Clinking the glasses, we drink.

"Thanks." She leans back in bed and studies me. I feel like she is considering telling me something.

We both end up leaning on our sides in bed with drinks in hand. I enjoy just looking at her and I don't think I have ever not enjoyed looking at her. Attraction isn't our problem, right?

"What are you drawing now? My impeccable ass?" I try to make her smile and it works when I see her upper lip twitch up.

"Nah, the drawings I made of you naked when you slept are locked in my room so I can share it with the project management department on Monday."

I laugh and take the paper from her to look at the drawings. It's an animated version of Luna Ray and a cat playing jazz in the corner. "You're really talented at this stuff. Do you have more?"

"At home, I guess a lot."

"You should do something with it. Noah and I know publishers."

Layla shakes her head softly. "Nah, it's just a hobby. Some people use tennis balls to destress, I use drawing."

My finger brushes some strands of hair behind her ear. "You noticed my balls?"

"Yeah, the tennis ball on your desk is your biggest asset. Does it help you destress?"

My head slants to the side as my lips purse out. "I guess it keeps my hands busy when I am stressed—yes."

"I could think of other things to keep your hands busy." She gives me that sexy look of hers.

"I told you, I have been a well-behaved soul in the office. So, I keep it innocent," I counter.

She takes the paper back that I was holding and places it on the bedside table. Layla looks at the center of the bed between us as she plays with the sheet.

"Why did you notice my drinking habits?" Layla wonders.

"Uhm, I don't know. Easy to notice."

"No. Noah never noticed. In fact, nobody ever noticed."

"Is it a big deal?" I drink more of my drink.

She bites her lip as she thinks. "I guess not. I just had a bad experience once, that's all."

My body immediately stiffens and I try to catch her gaze. "What do you mean?" I pry.

"In college. I was on a date with a guy... well not just a guy, someone I had been dating for a few weeks, and well let's just say there wasn't just alcohol in the drink he gave me."

Rage takes over my blood and already I want to kill the man wherever he may be. Before my mind thinks the worst, she continues.

"It's okay, I mean my friend—Lauren—figured it out really quickly and got me away just as he was taking me upstairs. I just don't remember anything from that night. So yeah, I am a bit cautious with my drinks. Noah doesn't know, so please don't tell him."

"You don't want to tell Noah? And the guy?"

Layla sighs and looks away from me. "It happened around the time our parents had their accident. Noah had enough to deal with. It was hard to prove it was my date that put something in my drink, so the police couldn't do anything. No clue where he is in the world now."

Placing my drink on the side table, my long finger finds her chin to tilt her up to my gaze. The knuckles of my other hand slides along her cheek. An overpowering urge comes over me to protect and comfort her. And something tells me that no matter what happens after these last few days that the wish to protect her will never go away. It's a new habit that I unwillingly volunteered for, but wouldn't have it any other way.

I tell her knowingly. "So, you only drink if it's been in

your view the whole time or if someone you know is drinking it?"

Layla nods and clarifies in a gentle voice. "Yeah. Someone I trust."

I'm taken aback with that logic and her history of stealing my drinks than it would mean she has always trusted me. "You've been stealing my drinks for the past few years."

She nods and she does not need to tell me more. I'm too smart to know that despite it all, she trusts me and that I shouldn't make a point to highlight that fact.

"Can I ask you something else?"

She reluctantly nods her head yes.

"Is it the reason you haven't had a boyfriend in a while?"

Her eyes roll to the side and she lets out a breath. "You mean why I don't have a boyfriend? No—I don't think all men are assholes or I can't trust them, if that's what you mean. Am I hesitant around guys? Maybe. I haven't found someone to fall in love with and even if I did—it doesn't mean much. My parents loved each other and ended up dying together. Nothing is happily ever after."

There is a peculiar silence in the room. I want to comfort her, but she seems at peace with her remark. So at peace and it is admirable. Instead, I decide to change the topic as she has admitted enough.

My mouth curves up. "And fear on airplanes?"

A cheeky smile spreads across her face. "That is just freaking horrible. I imagine a pigeon getting stuck in the motor or something. Crazy, right?"

"Pigeons are pretty evil." I laugh.

"You are fearless, probably would jump out of the plane to save the pigeon."

Shaking my head, I move to trap her under me. "No way, I hate heights. Total confession. I hired a therapist to help me deal with the fact my office is on the seventeenth floor overlooking the lake."

Her face turns to glee and her eyes are almost energized. "That is a great confession."

"Another confession." She grins.

"Go on."

"Noah's girlfriend, Rachel. What do you think of her?"

She studies me. I look at her and can tell we are on the same wavelength.

"Not a fan," I say bluntly.

"The worst, right? I mean, she is uptight and dull. I hope he doesn't ask her to marry him," she confesses, concerned.

"We will have Operation Stop That. I promise. I actually think your friend and Noah would be good together."

Her head cocks up to look at me. "You mean Lauren? Yeah, I've been wishing that for a while."

"Okay then we have Operation Stop That and Get That."

We both laugh and when it dies down, we take a few moments to just take in the moment, because she is still under me and that new current moves between us that we both are not sure what it is.

"*Sixteen Candles* or *Pretty in Pink*?"

"That is a tough one. But *Pretty in Pink*. You're a John Hughes fan?" I inquire, impressed.

"I can't live in Chicago and not be. Let me guess, you are a Ferris Bueller fan?"

"Absolutely. And confession—*Home Alone*… sometimes I watch it in July." I smile.

"Me too. Sometimes on the rare occasion I cook—I throw that classic on."

My eyebrow furrows. "You cook?" I am skeptical.

She playfully slaps me. "Not often. Sometimes meatloaf, this recipe from my mother. But that's the only thing I cook."

I realize it must be sentimental to her.

"I cook. But only when I need to impress." I offer her my charming grin.

"Oh, you mean when you need to get laid?"

"Nah, then I just find a witty piece of fire who calls me boss." I look into her eyes as I say that, and something resonates in our eyes. Maybe, just maybe this could be more than a few days.

There is a moment as we maybe both realize that we are enjoying a conversation without jabs and comebacks. In fact, all day it has felt like this. There is definitely something moving between us, and I can't seem to shake that feeling that this won't be easy to forget.

And maybe that clicks in her mind too.

Layla's legs wrap around my waist.

"Hey," I say tenderly.

She smiles as she slowly tips her pelvis up to mine.

"I think we are ready for our next round." Her voice sultry and her mouth giving me a sexy slant.

A voice in the back of my head reminds me this is temporary and this is our last night, but I turn that reminder off. Pinning her arms down, my lips find hers and we fall into another round.

11

LAYLA

We sit outside on the porch of the hotel with a spread of crawfish and jambalaya. The sun is shining, but we have enough shade from the overhang of the porch. Everything is antique from the table and chairs to the dishes and drink glasses.

Trey smiles as he drinks from his iced tea. "Tell me. How was your day yesterday?"

My smile must be uncontrollable. "It was fantastic, Trey. We had massages, walked around, went shopping, checked out some live music, and yes, we had our cards read."

Trey laughs. "That is great. Is your future looking bright?"

"My guess is many people are leaving NOLA with the same future and it does involve a wedding, kids, and lifelong love. Really, I came thinking Harry Connick Jr. was the best thing about New Orleans and now I know it's Luna Ray's tarot cards." I glow with my hands going to my heart because I am completely honest about that.

"Have to say the tarot cards were a nice surprise on this trip," Josh chimes in as he adjusts his watch on his wrist.

"I understand why your honeymoon and romantic weekend packages complete with a tarot card reading and a ghost walk are a hit. Throw in the massages, romantic breakfast for two and it's the complete package," I tell Trey.

He looks at me, impressed. "It is. We are even going to start conception moons and babymoon packages," Trey offers.

Josh nearly spits out his iced tea. "A what moon?"

Trey laughs. "I know, crazy. But apparently it is all the rage. A romantic holiday to get pregnant and then a romantic holiday when pregnant. So basically, we are covering all our bases from the romantic weekend where you propose to the honeymoon to the baby-making. Genius."

"I hope they get a discount if they do all of that at your hotel," I joke and grab my iced tea.

"I will consider it. But Layla, you should come back with the boyfriend and do the whole romantic weekend here with breakfast, cards, the whole shebang." Trey sticks a fork full of food into his mouth.

I stop drinking my iced tea and look at Josh and swallow. Ironic? I guess I did the whole experience already, with him —my non-boyfriend. I say nothing.

"Next time, I want to check out the musician's quarter and a few museums. Maybe even a riverboat up the Mississippi," Josh adds.

Trey looks between us and claps his hands together. "You two are almost radiant with positivity about the city. Must have really had a good time," he notes.

"It was a fantastic few days. Exactly what I didn't know I needed," Josh reflects, and the way it floats in the air, I can't help wondering if he means me.

Crazy, I know. But he is looking at his plate as if he is lost in thought. His hardened business look has been replaced by something softer.

"I will miss this when I get back to Chicago," I remark and for me, it means exactly as it sounds.

Josh glances at me.

"I won't keep you two waiting. You know I have no doubts about your capabilities as an agency to get the job done and now that I see you both respect and enjoy this place, then it's a no-brainer," Trey confirms. Holding his iced tea out for a toast.

A victorious look spreads across Josh's face and that hint of cockiness that wins him deals appears. "This will be a great partnership," Josh declares.

Our glasses clink. They discuss a few business things for a few minutes before Josh and Trey shake hands. "Contracts will be sent by end of day," Josh mentions.

"Look forward to it. Now if you two will excuse me, I have to fly to Aspen. Stay as long as you want before you head back to Chicago," Trey offers.

We all stand, and Trey kisses my cheek goodbye. Leaving Josh and I staring at each other.

"Congratulations, boss." I slide my fingers along the white steel patio chair.

"Pretty sure you were key in getting it." He tries to catch my gaze as he glides a few strides in my direction.

"It's your company, not mine. It's your win."

A stunted laugh escapes him as he licks his lips and his hand finds his hip. "Now you want to play modest?"

My eyes roll to the side. "Anyhow. We should probably get our stuff and head out. We have a plane to catch."

Josh studies me and then looks at his watch.

"No. We still have an hour to kill and I think we need to celebrate." It is not him suggesting, it's him informing.

"Last time," I warn him with a smirk.

———————

THE REALIZATION that I am going to have to return to a normal workout regime tomorrow is not a thought I want to ponder. I am enjoying this workout way too much. The kind that involves me straddling Josh naked as I ride him without a conscious thought. An unexpected world we created where only we have the key.

His hands hold my hips as I get utterly lost in the feeling. "You are good at this. Really good at this, Layla," Josh moans in pleasure.

"This feels... ohhh." I can't keep it in anymore. Any moment I am going to shake like an earthquake on top of him.

"Come for me, Layla," he requests.

A smug look must be slapped across my face. "Whatever you say, boss."

When he moves his thumb to my clit and thrusts his body up into mine. I'm done for. I shudder and shake on top of him with the quality of a quake with a high number on the Richter scale.

I barely can move, and he takes over my body. With his strength, he holds me in place and flips us over, so he is on top. I am underneath him and my eyelids struggle to stay open as I am completely lost in this experience.

"Watch me, Layla, look at me," he instructs, demands, wants. I don't know, but when my eyes flutter open to meet his eyes—everything multiplies. Every molecule of me becomes extra sensitive and his eyes have a conversation with my own. We are lost in lust, yet so aware that we are entwined with each other.

Moving in and out, speeding up until he reaches his high and it takes me to another wave. The melody of yesses and O's fill the room. Both completely gripped by our peak of pleasure.

His head dives into my neck and my hands find his hair. Our bodies syncing in mutually fast breathing.

A pinch near the area of my heart sends out a message to my brain. We crossed the line from physical to real intimacy somewhere in the past few days. It is very apparent now.

As we come down, he strokes my hair, kisses my cheek and I kiss his shoulder softly. The afternoon sun being a reminder that it is our last time here and the moment we step on the plane, this is all over.

Leaving us with the memory of a few good days. *Exceptional days*. A diffusion of tension and reaching our destination tolerable.

Josh gently moves off to go take care of the condom then returns to bed where I lay dazed. He lies on his side, staring at me and tucking some hair behind my ear.

"Layla. When we get back to Chicago, maybe we could —" His sentence which begins to re-spike my pulse is interrupted by Josh's phone ringing. He groans as he grabs his phone from the bedside table, it is the middle of a business day and he has to answer.

A deep sigh fills the room as he bites his lip. Swiping the phone, he answers on speaker.

"Hey Noah." Josh looks at me.

My stomach feels sour as I pull the sheet up to cover me as if we have been caught. Yet there is a thrill in me that I should question more. I adjust myself in the bed, creating space between us. Deciding to find my clothes to re-dress.

"Great news! This is definitely a win. We will have to celebrate," Noah exclaims from the other end.

Josh grabs his shirt and throws it back on as he speaks to Noah. "Maybe tonight we meet for a drink?"

"Sounds good, man, maybe bring Layla along? It was her charm that probably sealed the deal," Noah says on the other end of the line. I can imagine him walking along the street on his lunch hour.

Josh looks at me. "Sure. I will see if I can convince her."

Noah laughs. "Oh no. Are you still about to strangle each other? I was hoping you both would maybe call a truce. You are both too important to me for anything to be screwed up. We need to be one team, friends. Then we can have an easy road forward."

Guilt spreads across Josh's face and my own. My guess is he feels the similar sinking feeling in the pit of his stomach.

Clearing his throat. "No. It's, uh, been fine," Josh manages to say as our eyes hold.

"Good, and I hope you are watching out for her. Actually, I can't seem to reach her. I tried her phone a few times," Noah speaks. Josh indicates to me to grab my phone. I do and see I have four missed calls. I curse under my breath and let a hand go through my hair.

"Strange, she probably went for a last-minute shopping trip or didn't charge her phone," Josh lies.

What a lie too as I just put my phone on silent so I could have a final roll around in the sheets with my brother's business partner.

"Okay. Well, I trust you, so if you say she is fine then she is fine. I was also wondering if you could handle the Basil Grapes account, that new wine line out in California in Napa. You would need to go tomorrow, and it may take a few weeks. We are in the start-up phase of promotion. I could go out occasionally, but I have too much in Chicago to be away that long," Noah continues.

Josh softly smiles to himself as he finishes buckling his pants. "You mean you have a girlfriend and that's why you can't be away too long?"

There is a chuckle on the other end.

"Yeah, sure. I can get on the red-eye tomorrow and be gone for a few weeks." Josh looks at me as he nibbles his bottom lip. "Yeah, see you later."

He presses the screen of his phone and looks at me. I'm leaning against the French door to the balcony now fully clothed again. I am not sure what to say or do. Josh slowly walks toward me with his eyes piercing me.

"Noah can't find out about our work methods," I mention.

Josh closes our space and he is leaning now against the other side of the doorframe to the balcony with his hands in his pant pockets and one leg bent leaning against the doorframe, looking straight at me.

"Not my plan to tell him, *at all*," he reminds me.

I nod and let my tongue slide along my inner cheek. "Sounds like you are busy. Lucky me, the city is free from you for the next few weeks," I attempt to make a jab, but it comes out weak.

Josh nods. "So how do you want to play this going forward?" He scratches his cheek.

I make a sound with my tongue clicking as I consider, but I know the right answer. "Despite what the tarot cards say. I think we know what happens in NOLA stays in NOLA is the best approach. Right? I mean, this can't go anywhere. We had fun. We are excellent at sex together. *But* you and my brother own a company together… too many risks. I respect Noah too much to take the risk, I owe him that at least."

He places his fingertips on my rib cage as he looks at them and that tingle surges up and down my body again. "We are excellent at sex. *Together…* you won't bring back a voodoo doll to use on me?" A sneaky smile forms with a raised brow and I cannot help feeling slightly more at ease.

"Hmm, tempting. Maybe it depends on your level of being a jackass on the plane later." I grin.

"Okay, I will take my chances." He smiles as he leans in to kiss my forehead.

After a few moments, he pulls away and we look at each other.

There is no more stalling.

"Come on, boss." I gesture with my head to the door.

LAYLA

W e managed to keep it quiet and civil on the flight
    back. He offered me his hand on take-off and land-
ing. Of course, he had to try his luck on asking if we could
join the mile-high club to which I shooed him off quickly. We
were then both in a world of our own work. Josh worked on
emails on his laptop and I aimlessly looked at my laptop
screen and pretended to work. My mind was a little rattled, to
say the least.

Arriving back in Chicago, we hopped in a cab and headed
to a bar on the near north side of the city to meet Noah. He
was waiting for us at a trendy corner bar with high ceilings,
light wood bar tops and mint green furnishings with hanging
bulb lamps.

"The dream team is back." Noah grins. A bottle of champagne seems to already be waiting for us on the table. I give
him a hug before sliding into my seat, and Noah pats Josh's
shoulder.

"So, tell me?" Noah is far too curious as he pours us
champagne.

Grabbing a glass from Noah, Josh speaks as he scratches

the back of his head. "You know, the usual. Dinners, drinks, the guy really wanted to show us the city. You may be getting a tarot card reading on next month's expense form claim."

In no time, we all clink our glasses then drink.

Noah begins, "Josh took good care of you, Layla?"

Looking at Josh quickly then focusing my attention on Noah. "Yeah. A perfect boss."

Move us on, Layla, move us on.

"Good, because you both work well together when you put your minds together," Noah comments.

I nearly choke on my champagne. Then decide to finish my glass in one go. Noah looks at me, confused.

"Still recovering from those flying nerves, it was a rough landing," I try to justify my move and help myself to another glass from the bottle.

"Oh shit. Hope it wasn't too bad." Poor Noah expresses concern.

Josh decides to chime in. "Nah, other than the landing, she enjoyed every part of the trip. Really seemed to love breakfast." He is secretly grinning.

My eyes shoot him a warning look. The man is trying to mess with me.

"Anyhow, happy to have been of service. I gave my best performance on all fronts." This time I shoot the undertone to Josh who seems to enjoy it. "But I am quite busy the coming weeks, so you may need another designer, I can give you recommendations."

"I don't know, Layla," Josh expresses with doubt, but he is trying to get his way. "Trey really was keen on you working on the portfolio."

"Josh is right, you were key. If you could help us out, then I will find a way to make it up to you. I mean, Rachel even mentioned she may have someone for you. I just need to approve the guy," Noah jokes and it is a harsh reminder of why Noah may one day kill Josh.

A vein seems to emerge on Josh's neck as he swallows his drink through gritted teeth.

I laugh. "Uhm solid pass. I don't need a blind date arranged by your girlfriend, and it would not tip me over the line of making it worth my while to work more. But I will work on some of the things when I can from my home office."

Because I do not want to be in their office. Not when there could be a desk and Josh in the same sentence. Add my body to the equation and my head is a frenzied mess.

"Sure," Noah answers.

"*But* my team does have team meetings occasionally that you would need to attend in person," Josh cleverly mentions as he drinks from his champagne flute.

A huff escapes me.

"Okay, I am going to take a wild guess that the tension I am experiencing means you two still want to strangle each other's throats?" Noah comments with a hitched voice as he looks between us.

"No." "Yes." Josh and I say in unison, both with a different answer. I roll my eyes.

Noah holds his hands up in surrender. "Come on guys, for me? Please. Can we just get along? It would mean the world to me. I don't want anything to come between us, so please put your differences aside," he pleads.

Josh and I look at each other and after a moment both nod.

That reminder that my brother doesn't want anything to come between us twists me the wrong way. I excuse myself to go to the ladies' room, because I am going to go then fake a headache and get the hell out of here.

The ladies' room is on one side of the shared sink and sitting area with the men's room. Hand towels nicely folded in a basket and a waterfall going down a rock slab.

Looking up from the sink and into the mirror, my frustration skyrockets when I see the devil himself appearing behind me. Spinning around, I face Josh.

"You are an absolute asshole," I spit out. "What was that out there?"

A haughty look appears on his face as he comes and places a hand on each side of me on the sink. "What? You and I are normally like fire and ice, just making it clear to your brother that it hasn't changed."

"Please," I huff. "You were trying to mess with me after we *explicitly* said that we return and move on from the last few days." I'm livid, boiling, and he seems to be enjoying it.

"True. But it was so much more fun out there, no?" Josh seems overly satisfied and that cocky grin tells me this game is turning him on.

"I only slept with—"

Josh places a finger on my lips while his devilish smile remains strong. "Shh," he instructs.

Blowing his finger off my lips, I continue. "It was to defuse the tension. Now you just re-filled that supply to the brim," I mutter, angry and annoyed.

A fake gasp escapes him. "Oh dear. Maybe we will need to go back to our methods to bring that tension level down."

This man is taunting me, and his body is slightly pressed against mine.

I am so incredibly turned-on.

A growl leaves me as I step away from him. "You really are a piece of work. Did you not hear my brother out there? He will have a meltdown if he ever finds out. Even I know you care enough," I fume as I cross my arms.

He takes a moment to look away and then his hand finds his chin.

Something changes in him and he rolls his head to look at me. "You are right." At last, that decent guy I got a glimpse of the past few days comes out tonight.

"Please. Just please," I beg once more.

He holds his hands up. "Okay. I'll keep my promise. We forget and move on. I am out of town for a few weeks now anyhow. So, there is no chance we will invade each other's bubble."

This is good news. Great news.

Nothing like distance to make the heart grow colder.

I turn to leave, but he grabs my arm.

Rolling my eyes. "Geez, did we not just establish the new protocol?" I tell him as he is now irritating me to the max.

This time a warm smile spreads across his face. "I'm behaving, I promise. Can I just say one thing though?" he asks innocently, holding up one finger. *It's convincing.*

"I guess *one last* well-behaved thing won't hurt."

Oh crap, that sexy slant of his mouth is back. I overestimated his innocence.

He pulls me to him, and his mouth finds my ear as one hand stays on my arm and the other snakes around my waist.

He whispers, "That olive green bra and panties set that you wear so well. Make sure nobody else ever sees it on you. It was for my eyes only, Layla."

I'm molten.

Not only is his breath and whisper steamy. The words are hot. The idea that a thin piece of lace would symbolize so much control and desire, I'm soaked.

I should be seething at his move, but I am flattered. He makes me feel craved.

My reflexes should be shooting out a jab, but all I can do

is let a little giggle escape me and a soft smile form on my mouth for him, which makes him pull away satisfied.

"Go on your business trip and come back an even bigger jerk, please," I request and grin. It makes him chuckle.

In truth, I really do need him to return even more of a jerk. It makes it easier to forget our blunder of the last few days, because right now, I really feel like I don't want to forget at all.

We head back to the bar and the rest of the night act normal. All saying goodbye like three normal humans. I head to bed, relieved that Josh is going away for a few weeks so I have a chance to get him out of my head. Because he's overly occupying it at this current moment.

13

JOSH

The last few weeks, I have been in full-on beast mode with fifteen-hour days in Napa. Finally, we can say our client is on the road to a successful ad campaign from print to online media. Flavored wine with basil and herbs coming your way at your local organic supermarket, because clearly, it is what you never knew you needed.

I was working on a high, partly because a few days of an excellent portion of sex prior to my arrival in California helped. It put me in a good mood, gave me some extra doses of oxytocin, and I needed the distraction of work to try and forget what had transpired in New Orleans.

While our sessions of tension releasing are on a constant loop in my spank bank. I know there is a list of reasons why nobody can know about what happened. Okay, nobody is Noah. There is also the reality that tolerable is not the keyword to be the driver of going further with someone. And *maybe* Layla passed my line of tolerable and was heading into the box of enjoyable to be around—but she made the message clear. It would go nowhere.

That's why I have been a perfect gentleman and haven't

once reached out to her. Respected her wishes. Prince Charming would be so damn proud.

Prince Charming *may* question my willpower.

A few times my thumb grazed the screen of my phone. Even getting as far as typing a message or eight.

Miss my cock?

Your vibrator just doesn't compare, does it?

Thinking of your beautiful face when you come.

I had a really good time; did I tell you that?

Maybe you want to grab dinner when I am back?

What's the harm of another night?

You're thinking of me, aren't you?

How are you?

But I never sent them.

An odd phenomenon took over me the last few weeks. When a busty brunette stranger approached me in the hotel bar, I was not interested. When I enjoyed a stiff drink at the end of the day, I missed a particular pair of lips that would steal my drink. And when I heard a random woman laugh, I was reminded of Layla and that night together after Luna Ray's.

Forgetting our transgressions is nearing impossible. But I drag on.

When I notice a new email arrive in my inbox as urgent, I open it up to find a panicked message from HR and a project manager. It seems Mindy—our in-house designer—needs to cut back on work before her maternity leave and the project team is having a freak-out as there is some key work still to be done. Looking at the trail of emails, I see someone asked if Layla could help us and Noah suggested I contact her as it is one of my projects.

Five minutes later I pace my hotel room floor creating an imaginary hole in the carpet. Phone to my ear, I wait for

Layla to pick up. I was supposed to be on a full Layla detox, but work threw a wrench into that.

After two rings, she picks up.

"Hi." It comes out simple from her end.

The sound of her voice already spirals pleasure in me. "Hey… sorry to bother you, I'm not sure if you saw the email?"

Freaking hell, I want to tell her that I want to take her six ways to Sunday.

"Yeah, I did."

"I know it is short notice, but it seems Mindy needs to cut back on her work early due to a complication with her pregnancy and it would help if you could pick up one or two things that we have a deadline for." I'm wanting so desperately to break through the phone to see her face.

I know her body enough now to know that she is standing on the other end contemplating while biting her lip.

"I'm not sure—"

"Please," I beg, but I don't even care about the work. I want her to agree so I have an excuse to speak to and see her more.

"I guess… I guess I could. Will need to work from home as I do have other clients. If someone could just send me what is needed, I have a general idea but need more specifics."

"Of course," I assure her.

There is a pause, yet if listening to her breathing and knowing she is on the other end, then I think I would listen to this silence all day.

"Is there… something else?" she asks, and I sense curiosity in her voice.

"No, I guess not. I will have Stephanie email you. Probably will have a team meeting sometime in the next few weeks. Might expect to see you there."

That beautiful silence is back and I'm certain our pulses are spiking. It's as if we both don't want to hang up but can't admit it. Holding on to a rope to the very end.

"Probably won't be able to go. I think I will have a headache that is too bad." She is actually teasing me.

"There are ways to relieve that." It comes out neutral from my end.

"Your cell is a company cell, no? I get the feeling HR isn't going to like this conversation." I can hear the playfulness in her voice.

"Good thing I own fifty percent of the company." Now I have to grin.

"Yeah and the guy who owns the other fifty percent may just kill you if he knew we were having this conversation."

"What conversation are we having? The one where you listen to your boss and come to the office? Sounds legit to me."

"As an external consultant, normally I would never attend such meetings. So why now?" she volleys.

"Because you like to listen." Came out a hundred percent frisky from my end and I hear her laugh.

There is a long pause.

"Layla?"

"Yes, Josh?" There is renewed energy in her voice.

"It's good… it's good to hear your voice." I swallow and something in my body floats.

In my head, she is gently smiling and touching her chest for comfort.

"You too… to hear your voice, I mean."

I'm almost certain that soft smile is in her voice.

That lingering silence floats between us.

"I should probably let you get on with your night," I mention.

"It's-it's okay. I am actually having a quiet night in. You?"

My lips twitch from her continuing to speak. "Long day on an account, so just taking it easy in my hotel room alone, maybe ordering room service." I made a point to say alone.

"No bottles of wine waiting for you with roses on the bed?" I can hear her smile.

"Nah, only a cold white bed. You?" I go to lie on the bed and look at the ceiling.

"Poor soul, such a hard life. I just took a bath and going to go to bed soon." Her voice is soft.

The oxygen supply to my dick just cut off. What a view she must be right now.

"So, we are both in bed, it seems," I comment.

"Just not the same bed."

It is like we are thinking the same thought and both not blinking as we speak to each other.

"A shame." My words float in the air.

"It's the way it is supposed to be," she reminds me, but I don't hear confidence in her voice.

"Right… hypothetically if it wasn't supposed to be. Then what would it be?" I have to take us down this rocky road of curiosity and what-ifs.

"Josh." She almost purrs my name. But then surprises me when she continues. "This is a dangerous conversation. Next thing I know, you will ask me to send you a photo."

"I never gave you credit for your good ideas," I tease her.

"I'm going. Have a good night."

"'Night Layla."

We both hold on the line for a few extra beats before hanging up. A deep sigh escapes me as I lay motionless on the bed. After a minute, I hear my phone ping and I bring my phone into my eyesight.

Holy fuck.

Layla sent me a photo.

A photo of herself.

A photo of herself in just a towel with her hand looking like it is gliding up her thigh.

I don't see her face, but I know it is her. I know because her thigh is etched in my mind in detail, every freckle and every smooth curve.

Is she lying in bed? My mind can't comprehend.

A caption under the photo **if it was supposed to be, it would have been me sending you this.**

A smile spreads on my face and a string tugs in my chest. What I wouldn't do to get her under me again. But tonight the ceiling and my hand will be the only witnesses to what that thought does to me.

I text her back. **Yeah HR, isn't going to like this conversation or the thoughts in my head right now. I'm back in a few days by the way...**

I don't get a reply, but I don't care. I know she is mulling it over.

———

As soon as I get back to Chicago, I head to the office. It's the first time I've seen my dear colleagues in a few weeks since landing the Radnor account and being a master at jump-starting the promotion for the new account out in Napa.

Everyone says hi to me as I make my way through the hall to my office.

"Hey Josh, nice flight?" Karen, my assistant, greets me with her typical cheery smile that sometimes is too over the top. Her glasses, pulled up black hair and library sweater reminds me that although a lovely lady that the highlight of her week is watching someone else play *League of Legends*.

"Yeah, can't complain. No crying babies and a half-full flight."

Noah joins me as I enter my office and compliments me as he pats my back. "The legend himself is back. Well done, nailed that down in record time."

I proceed to my desk.

"Another successful trip in the pocket," I tell him as I take my laptop out of my bag and set it on the desk.

We quickly dive into a few work-related matters, then spend time talking about Tom Kane, our next client we want to put in our books.

"Don't worry, Noah. I will handle the first meeting and then we will charm him over dinner. We will land Tom Kane as a client," I assure Noah as he leans against my office door.

"It would be a good one," he says as he knocks on the wood of the door out of habit for luck.

I give a satisfied look. "It would, wouldn't it?"

"We got this." Noah grins before walking away.

I lean back in my chair and play with a pen as I look at my screen that is filled with facts on Tom Kane. He took over his father's real estate company and needs a rebranding. The man has the looks to be the face of the brand—I'll give him that. Hearing that he enjoys a good dinner and drinks, it was a no-brainer to book a table at a small invite-only restaurant nearby. The chef will bring us what he cooks and we will have a good bottle of old country French wine on hand. Noah and I have this, just like all the other clients we have been picking up in the last year.

Clicking on my computer, I continue to read his history in real estate, his recent vacation house purchase and the line of girls that change at every public function yet they all share the same common denominator of blond hair.

Hearing a knock at the door, I look up.

"Hey Josh. I have a budget for you to sign." Lauren smiles as she comes into the office. Her blond hair is up in some strange blob with a pencil. She is focusing on her stack of papers in her arms and places one paper on my desk. "It's the one from the email, just need a hard copy signed."

I briefly remember that she is Layla's best friend and she probably knows more than I care for her to know, but it doesn't bother me. Lauren found this job because of Layla and she is a really good accountant too.

"Sure." I glance over the numbers on the page before I commit to signature.

"Why are you looking at his profile?"

I look up at her and see she is looking at my screen. "He is our next client."

"I really hope not." She gives me a conflicted look.

Puzzled, I ask. "Why is that?"

She rolls her eyes and contemplates what to say.

Twenty minutes later, and I know what to do. Noah is going to kill me when he finds out and I won't be gaining points with Layla either, but I need to tank this potential client.

14

LAYLA

Sitting at Red Fox, a cozy lunch spot with farm-to-table food and antique furniture with little jars and candles, I speak with my client's publicist about an upcoming book launch. Feeling mighty fine in my tailored fitted gray dress and black heels.

"We could use this shade of blue, but then we need to change the font color," I explain as I show Natalie my tablet. She is in her mid-thirties and well dressed. I've worked with her a few times and we gel nicely on the professional front.

"I don't know, I really like the font color."

"No problem, then we keep the original color options." I put my tablet down.

"Really love the work on the last book. The cover was great for social media. Looking forward to seeing the outcome of this one." Natalie smiles and it makes me feel proud.

"Thanks."

I notice Natalie is looking across the room.

"Sorry, I recognize that guy. Doesn't he work with your

brother?" Natalie asks and I do not even need to turn my head.

Of course, in this big city, it has to be this tiny restaurant that Josh Ives finds himself at. To be fair, this place is within two blocks of his office, but still!

"Why yes he does." There may be a slight disdain in my voice that became a natural reaction over the years. Secretly, I am lapping up this opportunity to see him again.

While he was away, the guy managed to stay in my head. Unescapable almost. The memories of what we did, the way we had fun walking the streets of the city and the marketing guru himself may even have persuaded me that he isn't as big of an ass as I originally thought.

We had a pull.

Then we spoke on the phone and something in me danced. I had fun. I did things I never would do, such as send a photo—nobody would know it is me—but it isn't something I have ever done.

Turning my head, I see Josh and my pulse rate picks up, the butterflies in my stomach flutter and his smile I want to admire as we lay in bed talking. It's so painfully obvious that it will all be hard to forget those few nights.

…but facts are facts.

I turn to look at Natalie who speaks to me. "I used to work with him a few times before they broke away from their old agency."

Her smile widens and by the way my body begins to race, I already know he is walking our way.

Natalie stands up, which means I should stand up. Of course, a smug and canny look is slapped across his face as some guy stands by his side.

"Natalie, long time no see." Josh throws on the charm and kisses her cheek.

Natalie seems like a superfan, *lucky me*. "Yeah, I was just telling Layla."

Josh comes and kisses my cheek; except he throws an arm around my waist to pull me into an additional hug. A possessive hug that lets me get a whiff of his cologne, his smell. The smell I want to be bathing in.

"Layla, looking gorgeous," he mutters my name and combined with his touch leads to my inner walls clenching for stability.

"This is Logan Jax, an old client," Josh introduces the man at his side who gets a few points for being easy on the eyes.

I stick a hand out.

"You must be Noah's sister?" Logan asks.

"Guilty." I smile and notice that Josh's hand is resting on my lower spine as if he has territorial claim to me.

"Seems to be the place for working lunches," Logan remarks and his gaze does not leave Natalie's.

Natalie almost giggles. "We are almost done actually."

"Oh, so are we. We were just stopping in for a drink. Maybe we can join you two gorgeous ladies for a drink before you need to go?" Josh's eyes do not leave me, and I know his look. It's trouble—for me.

It's a game like he played that night in the bar with my brother.

"Great idea," Logan beams.

Before I know it, chairs are pulled up to our tiny table for two and we have two guests who ordered a round of gin and tonics for us. My guess is within two minutes, a warm hand will find my thigh under the table and I think I would not complain.

When the drinks arrive, without thought Josh drinks from

his glass then hands it to me without anyone noticing. But I will not drink it, not today.

"You're back, lucky me." I'm sarcastic as I speak low in our own bubble.

"I am. Missed me?"

"Could barely breathe." I roll my eyes.

"Oh? That's concerning. How are you feeling now?" He fakes concern.

"Better, but I may feel a migraine coming on now brought on by you." I give him a warning look.

Natalie and Logan seem to be in deep conversation and take no notice of us.

Josh leans in but looks forward. "Looking extremely stunning today, your dress would look great on my bedroom floor."

A sound escapes me softly. "Can't happen. I need this dress on a hanger or it is ruined." I smirk.

"You can send me the dry-cleaning bill, hell, I will buy you a new dress."

"Tempting," I deadpan. "But not going to happen."

He lets an audible exhale escape. "Fine, just thought I would try my luck with another bonus this week after that photo."

My head makes a sharp turn to look at him head-on, my eyes warning him. "I was in a giving mood that night. Clouded by my brain on a hiatus. Hope your right hand doesn't get a strain from its extra exercise."

"Deeply touched by your concern for my hand. Are you still in a giving mood?" His brow arches and his head tilts slightly as his eyes assess me.

"Nope. Nada. Absolutely not."

Clearing my throat and speaking up. "I really hate to have to run, but I have a meeting to get to and I don't want to take any more of your time as you two seem to have business to discuss," I speak to Logan.

"Actually Josh, I think I will stay and talk with Natalie, we have mutual friends it seems," Logan comments and even I know that those two are heading to a hotel for a little afternoon delight.

"Sounds like a good plan." Josh gives Logan a knowing look.

After saying goodbye to everyone and paying my bill from lunch earlier, I head outside. Knowing very well that in 3,2,1...

His hand grabs my arm and spins me to him.

"Yes, Josh." There is an obvious indifference in my voice.

He moves his face low in order to look up into my eyes. "Hey, I am just being the jerk you wanted me to be when I came back. That's called listening."

Sighing, I say, "I am not in the mood for games."

"But your body is saying something else." He gives me a coy look and looking down, I see that I have two buds on my chest that have come out for a show. They must be conspiring with the man in front of me.

Damn it, I want to pounce on him like an animal.

I snap and wave my long finger from side to side. "Tsk tsk, boss. We said no more. We had some fun, but it gets us nowhere."

"Exactly, sweetheart, nowhere. All the more reason."

"I am not having this conversation."

But then my stupid mouth turns off its filter and speaks. "I'm stopping by your office tomorrow for a team meeting my boss is adamant we have. *Maybe* I will find you after."

As I walk away, there is an unguarded smile that spreads across my face and a flow of anticipation rushing through my body, making me dizzy.

———

"HERE. Got you that croissant with chocolate you love so much," Lauren offers as she slides into the seat across from me.

We are sitting at the coffee shop Beans on the ground floor of the skyscraper office building where Ives & Wells have their office. The coffee in the office is good, but nothing compared to Beans.

"Uh, thanks, not really in the mood for one right now." I push the plate away.

Lauren drinks her coffee and leans back in her chair.

"Yeah, you look a little rough. I mean, not like a few weeks ago. Then you were glowing. Like I wanted to know the name of every anti-age cream you use glowing."

I laugh. "I don't use anti-aging cream and I wasn't glowing."

"Uhm yes you were. My guess is it has something to do with a certain man that works with your brother whom you sometimes call boss." Lauren gives me a knowing look as she puts her mug down and I also wonder how she immediately guesses it has to do with him.

I pour my coffee into a to-go cup to the side. Lauren has been my best friend since college. She knows all my secrets and has been there for me at the most challenging of times. What the hell, I could use an ear.

"I need to pull in the secret vault card," I request quietly as I lean into the table so only her ears hear. One thing about a great best friend is the secret vault card is solid even if she works with Josh and Noah. I know she will take it to the grave and not tell a soul. Just like I am the bearer of her secrets, which is currently she is on a dry spell of two years. I'm almost traumatized for her.

Lauren's hands come together in excitement. "I knew it. You slept with him, didn't you?"

I sigh. "Nobody can know. I mean, like no one. It's bad, Lauren."

"As in the sex? Because Josh strikes me as someone who knows what he is doing." She's puzzled.

"Oh no. That, he is really good at. The sex was ahh the best. But it's bad because Noah can never, ever know. He would go through the roof. Not to mention, technically Josh is my boss sometimes. But mostly, it's Noah. I owe it to him to not screw up the relationship between his business partner and him. Noah has done so much for me," I explain.

"I get where you are coming from, your brother in a way took on a role of parent when your folks passed. But you are now a grown adult and what if Josh is the one?" Lauren offers her advice.

I start laughing. "No way is Joshua Ives my one. We may have great sex, but we still struggle to be in the same room together."

Lauren starts to eat my croissant. "Really?"

"When did you see him last?"

"Yesterday, before that, it was a few weeks ago. He was away for work."

"Okay, and you guys communicated while he was away?"

I look at her, puzzled.

"You know. Phone, email, even maybe old-school style by letters in the mail?"

I shake my head no. "Nothing except one call for work. The space was good. We have to forget what happened. It can't go anywhere."

"He hasn't reached out any other time while he was away? What a jackass."

"Nah. I mean, why would he? I made it clear we should

move on. It was really a few days to be kept a secret. Hmm, did I just accidentally find myself in a secret tryst? Oops." I shrug my shoulders with a humorous look.

Lauren shrieks and lets her knees bounce under the table. "I remember seeing him at a holiday party at your brother's condo. You had fuck-me eyes for each other already then. This is awesome. It must have been so hot. Did he pin you against a wall? Tell me he pinned you against a wall. He seems like somebody who would do that." Lauren is giddy.

I have to laugh and nod all at the same time.

"So, do you really think it isn't going to happen again with Josh? I mean, if it is only sexual, then what is the harm? Get a few extra O's in."

"Maybe. I mean, he irks me except when we are well… then he relaxes me in amazing ways. I kind of let go when I am with him in that way. The guy has this ability to make me feel safe. I feel like I can do anything with him, things I normally wouldn't do—"

Lauren shrugs a shoulder. "No, it happens sometimes with sexual partners. Did you guys just always do the deed, or did you also have the occasional pillow talk?"

I smile to myself and tilt my head to the side. "I guess we talked. In New Orleans, we were pretty stuck with each other."

Lauren smiles. "Interesting. Heaven forbid Layla Wells falls in love one day. But I am happy to see you like this. Normally you are apprehensive around guys and I get it."

I contemplate her words. "Strange, but I am not that way around him." I tap the table and debate how much information to divulge. "I actually told him what happened that one time. He noticed the way I drink and I eventually explained. It just flew out of my mouth without thought."

There is a pause as Lauren studies me almost as if she is carefully considering her words.

"Layla, that's… something. You never tell anyone. You trust him. This is big." Her face stays neutral. I'm taking in her words, because my heart muscle twists with a reality check of truth.

I brush it off. "It's not. We had a good time, but we can't go anywhere. It would be like sitting on the Titanic waiting for the iceberg to hit us."

Lauren hums in doubt.

Taking a sip of my coffee, I have an urge to spit it back out. "Have they changed the beans or something?"

"Not that I know of. But let's head upstairs, I think you have a Radnor team meeting soon."

I nod in agreement.

———

HALF AN HOUR LATER, I emerge from the ladies' room after trying to calm my dizziness when the sound of two arguing men fills the office. Quickly, I recognize that it is Josh and Noah. Panic hits me, but as I walk toward Noah's office, my own panic fades. Instead, I hear them arguing about business. The door is closed, but it doesn't stop a few others from listening nearby pretending to be making copies at the copier.

I go to stand next to Lauren.

"What's going on?" I whisper.

"They have been arguing for ten minutes."

I join her and listen in.

"What the hell!" Noah yells.

"It had to be done," Josh replies.

"You had the meeting at two and now we aren't continuing on. What did you do?"

"You need to trust me on this."

"Trust you? This is crazy. Can you at least tell me why the hell you would ruin our chances?"

"He isn't the type of guy we want to work with. Just please trust me." Josh sounds adamant yet frustrated.

"I'm furious," Noah barks out again.

"I know."

Deciding this may be my cue as a peacekeeper, I take my chances and walk a few steps then open the door to Noah's office and walk in uninvited.

"What the hell is up with you two? The whole office can hear you both grumbling in here."

Noah and Josh look at me, surprised I am there.

"Josh decided to piss me off today," Noah snipes as he turns to look out his window, standing with his hands finding his hips.

I immediately look at Josh with panic in my eyes. He shakes his head no, and I know nothing about our recent indiscretion has been mentioned.

Josh sighs. "We are going to go in circles, man. Let's just end this conversation. I did it and that's that." He seems to be trying to wrap up this conversation.

"I really don't want to see you for the rest of the day." Noah is still livid.

"You guys need to calm down." They both ignore me.

"No problem, Noah. I have shit to do. I'll stay out of your way and you stay out of mine and we will see each other tomorrow." Josh sounds irritated before turning, then barging past me and out of Noah's office.

My usual instinct would be to stay with Noah. But for some inconsolable reason, without thought, I follow Josh.

15

JOSH

Heading straight to my office, I am a little pissed off, to say the least, and may have taken it out on the intern —poor guy—as I headed into Noah's office earlier. This is not my day. I knew tanking Tom Kane was going to get me into trouble.

The look on Layla's face was a low blow too. As much as I would love to beg her to trust me on my decision to piss off her brother, I know she has loyalties.

Admittedly, I am a man unhinged. Layla found her way into my every thought when I was away and seeing her yesterday didn't help. Even more crazy, I do not know if it is my cock or actual mind doing the thinking. Then there is the bonus of her image imprinted in my head with a photographic souvenir.

Arriving in my office, my body has an odd sensation and it only takes the corner of my eye to let my body know. I forgot that I seemed to have developed a radar for that woman. To my surprise, Layla has followed me here.

Turning my head slightly, I am faced with a sight for sore eyes. Layla standing in my doorway. And despite my fuming state, I notice the minor details. Such as her plaid dress that flows out mid-thigh with ankle boots. The dress has a trail of a zipper, and I think my mind already mapped it out in my head.

My thoughts are broken when she calls out my name and comes to meet me standing in the middle of my office.

"Josh." She tries to grab my arm and it sends a buzz through me.

"Now isn't the time, Layla." It pains me to say as I pull my arm away.

"I know, but—"

She is interrupted by the arrival of the Radnor account team that quickly finds a home on my sofa and chairs. *Ugh*, forgot we had a team meeting today. I need to re-think my managerial style that is so adamant on these meetings.

"Team meeting it seems is now," Layla informs me with a click of her tongue. Her eyes tell me we will be having a debate later.

"We have some deadlines to go over," Stephanie, the project manager, begins as she poses her pen to her paper pad. Her look displays her uptight personality and the tight blond ponytail isn't doing her any favors. Rumor has it that she is as uptight as a librarian going over late fines. But she does a good job at what she does. I may just ask HR to discuss her shitty timing skills at her next review though.

"Go for it," I say as I perch on the ledge of my desk and unbutton my suit coat, trying to not let my eyes find Layla.

After a half-hour of outlining the rollout of the new campaign for Radnor, especially the Sweet Dove Hotel. I try to wrap this up.

Layla was quieter than her normal feisty self. I didn't get any push back from her when it came to work. In fact, at one point she looked a little pale. I did my best to be a professional, but now I just want to get on with my day.

"Okay, if someone can just put everything in an email to recap the meeting and just update me on where you are next week. We can plan another face-to-face in a few weeks," I speak as everyone packs up. "Layla, can you stay behind, and we can discuss the designs, please."

She reluctantly looks at me, but after everyone leaves, Layla lingers behind casually and closes the door to my office and turns to me.

"You were saying?" I ask monotone.

"I can't be in the middle of you and Noah. What happened earlier is the reason why you and—" she reiterates but can't finish the sentence and seems to be stuck on her words.

It only makes me shake my head in annoyance.

"Clear. Now can we discuss actual work please?" I'm a bit snarky and it catches her off guard.

"Yes." She returns the snark and crosses her arms as her hip tilts out.

I go to sit behind my desk and open my laptop. "Can we have a look at the layout of the brochure for the hotel literature?" I maintain my business-like manner. But it's for show.

She comes to stand behind my desk to show me the screen. Leaning over, she clicks away on my laptop, invading my space and her smell intoxicating me. My eyes enjoy the view and draw a line up and down her body. It would be so easy to pull her onto my lap. She would fit perfectly.

But my glass desk and glass door essentially cock blocked me from any possibilities in this corner office. Only confirms that I should have fired our interior designer.

She hits a few keys on the keyboard with vigor then returns to standing yet remains close. Close enough that my body feels like our bodies are knitting into one and I'd be lying if I said my cock wasn't twitching.

"There. It was in the email from the other day, as I am sure you already know." There was a twinge of attitude there.

A deep laugh escapes me. "Yeah, but it was so much better getting it this way," I admit and she curses under her breath as her eyes blink slowly closed and open. She is a little cranky today. "But actually, that's not why I wanted to speak. I am not sure about the design. I think we can do better."

I see fire on her face.

"What do you mean? This is the design that we have been bouncing around in the group email for the last week," she snaps.

I place a hand behind my head as I lean back and slightly twirl in my chair, as I am relaxed. "Yes. But I was not caught up yet and now I am caught up and think you need to relook at the design, the cover page for sure."

She really doesn't, but I needed *something* to sound legit.

Her face hardens. "So, you are saying you don't like the design?" She crosses her arms and tries to maintain her anger.

She isn't used to people criticizing her work. She is good at her work.

"Maybe I am." I get up from my chair and ignore her as I walk toward the door.

"Anyhow. I've let you know, and now I need to head home. This day requires a scotch in my hand." I grab my jacket from the coat stand. "I would invite you, but something tells me you need to work on those designs tonight and you made it clear our methods of destressing are not on the menu." I throw that into the fire.

Her engine is starting with eyes glaring at me and if there was ever such a thing as a sexy dragon, then her flaring nose would make her a dead ringer.

"Close the door, *now*!" she demands sharply through gritted teeth and hands on her hips.

A satisfied grin forms on my face and I oblige, taking a few steps closer to her.

"Don't use my work to get me into bed. Unbelievable. You really are a piece of work." She is angry and admittedly, I was hoping for this. Her hand even claws some of her hair.

I'm a sick bastard sometimes.

I cock my head to the side. "It got your attention, didn't it?"

"I know you like the designs, so don't pretend you don't," she informs me rather sternly with her eyes not blinking.

I shrug a shoulder to my ear and confirm. "I like the designs."

The wheels in her head are moving as confirmed by a tight-lipped smile forming on her mouth.

"Trust me when I say, today is not the day to piss me off."

Crossing my arms, I study her. "I don't want to piss you off. I want to do the opposite to you in case you haven't figured it out."

She looks at me and debates what to say, but her breathing is intensifying. Her finger jabs my chest and I quickly grab her wrists.

We have been here before.

"Like I said, don't piss me off, Josh, really. You are on a fine line of being a real asshole today. I mean, why the hell did you have to go and have a fight with Noah? It makes this more..." She is frustrated and again struggling for words.

I step as close to her as possible without the rest of the office being able to see our exact proximity through my glass door and I release her wrists. My fingertips graze her thin scarf around her neck. "More what? This is what is going to happen. I am going home; I would say we leave together, but let us not make this too obvious to the office watching us argue in here. You will meet me at my place. We can discuss, fuck, whatever as long as it calms us down."

"Fine, give me an hour to do something. You are in luck; I need to destress today, and it seems like you are the only option." Her look is brazen.

"Ah Layla. You know that I am a make wishes come true kind of guy."

16

JOSH

Gazing out my floor-to-ceiling windows overlooking the city—I am grateful my ridiculously priced therapy sessions helped me overcome my phobia of heights—a rainy late afternoon sky in Chicago is almost mystical. Lights of the city peeking through drops of rain that run down the glass window as clouds hang low and blend with the tops of buildings spiking through. The scotch in my hand is equally splendid.

Now, I am positive my demeanor today did not put me in Layla Wells' book of gentlemen. But this playing hard to get scenario was testing my patience and it feels like I am battling in the trenches with blue balls. It's ridiculously effective, and I now understand why men and women have been playing this game for years.

I am a man of action, so I took action.

Admittedly, goading her into an argument is a wild card. It could backfire on me. But this woman has me at my wit's end and that's never happened to me.

It took a few sentences and I know the last hour she has been mulling over what will go down and my guess is that she still has not cooled down from my antics. When I hear banging on my front door, I have my answer.

Knew putting that little vixen on my approved anytime list at the downstairs door was worth it.

Taking one last enjoyable sip of my scotch, I set it on the white counter in my modern kitchen on my way to the hall and the door. I begin to unbutton the buttons of my sleeved wrists to loosen my shirt, because I feel we have a little battle coming on.

Opening the door, I throw on my best self-assured look.

Layla's eyes look at me then she lowers her gaze to my hand that is finishing unbuttoning my shirt sleeves. Something tells me women love that move like men love women in heels with their legs around their neck.

It's effective.

Her eyes shoot back up to my face. "We really want to go down this road?" She barges in and walks past me, stopping in the middle of my hall. Layla seems riled and even with a jacket and thin scarf around her neck, I can see her chest heaving up and down from her agitated breathing.

"We do," I confirm as I follow her in.

Her hands find her hair that she grabs as she lets out a sound of aggravation. "What planet was I on to actually have slept with you?" She seems to be talking to my ceiling.

"More than once," I add. "We slept together more than once," I clarify with a cocky grin.

Another frustrated growl escapes her.

We are now standing where the hallway meets my living room.

After a pause. I decide we need to change the course to get us where we need to go. Because it is a fucking marvelous destination.

I close our space and my fingers gently glide along her

thin black scarf that must be more for style than to actually keep her warm. Cotton yet strong. Perfect for how the next ten minutes are going to go.

My hands unbutton her jacket and she watches what I am doing but does not stop me.

"You are irritating," she mutters, quite feistily, yet a droll smile begins to form on her beautiful mouth.

Her eyes narrow in on me as her jacket falls to the floor. My hands move to her scarf to unwrap it from around her neck and my lips curve up into a slight smile. "I irritate you? We have so much in common, it seems. As you are not exactly gracing my good books this week with your teasing."

Layla shakes her head before letting her hands push against my chest. "Why in the world would I want to be in your good books?" That droll smile not fading.

With that move, I grab her arms and manage to turn her around so her back is to me. Walking her forward a few steps to the back of my sofa.

My mouth comes to her ear. "Oh, Layla. Enough of the back and forth. We both know we want you in my good books, so let's work through this."

Our bodies press and her breath hitches as I grab the unwrapped scarf hanging around her neck.

"Fine, but boss only because I have to face your night-marish face again and I really need to destress and you have an uncanny knack to be able to do that."

But her body eases into mine, and it seems she is eager for me to touch her as her body sub-consciously presses into my hard cock. It earns her my hand gently touching her ass before I grab her wrists and guide her hands in front of her and I stand tightly behind her.

Bringing her hands together, I tie the scarf around her wrists with an extra strong pull to tighten it. She is a willing participant as she shows me her wrists can't break free after I complete a strong tug.

"So that's a yes boss, let's work through this?"

"Yes."

"Tsk tsk, Layla, you didn't say boss," I hiss into her ear as I place her arms on the back of the sofa and my hands guide her hips, bending her body into a ninety-degree angle. My body merges against her from behind. There has never been such a perfect position as what we are standing in now. It's physics and beauty combined into one.

She glances behind her shoulder and gives me a playful half-smile. "Yes, *Josh*."

It makes me smile and her saying my name is better than any boss bullshit any day. Because it means she is acknowledging that this is going to go down between us and not some pretend scenario.

My upper body leans forward so my mouth can find her ear and my hands find her breasts that I palm through her clothing. "Item one on the agenda, Layla. I have a strange inkling that you really want me," I tell her.

She lets a moan escape as my fingers find her taut buds that popped through the fabric of her dress.

"Shall I feel you to find out?" My hands slide down the front of her body and hikes her dress up before finding the edges of her tights that I pull down. My finger rubs along the satin fabric of her panties that have a pool of thick juice underneath. A pool I want to swim in. No, I want to drown in. The sounds she makes turns me on more.

"This isn't fair. It's a one-sided interrogation," she manages to argue as she gets lost in my touch. I can almost swear that I hear a smile through that sentence.

A chortle escapes me as I press my hard bulge against her ass. "Do you have your answer if I really want you?"

"No. So kiss me," she requests firmly.

With pleasure, I turn her body around and let the sofa support her as my hands cup her cheeks and my mouth hungrily kisses her lips. Breathing her in like oxygen. Finding her tongue, brushing her lips, sucking her bottom lip. I am kissing her harder than I have ever kissed anyone. And it still is not hard enough. Because she is about to break my scale of how much I want her.

Pulling away slightly, I make sure our eyes meet because I want to witness her eyes as they glimmer with satisfaction. "Does that answer your question?" I ask softly as my thumb rubs her bottom lip.

She nods her head with swollen lips and her eyes lighten.

"Good. Now item two—I think you missed me. You miss everything we did together," I say to her as my hands encircle her waist, pulling her closer and my mouth finds her neck that is hot to the touch. I can feel her bound hands resting on her stomach between us.

A sly smile forms on her mouth. "I *may* have missed you a little," she admits as my hand glides through her hair and pulls her head gently back so my mouth can tease her neck better.

"D-did... you... miss... m-me?" She is struggling to speak, and her hands try to reach for my belt, but they are restricted.

I turn her around again and press her forward against the sofa. My hands pulling down her panties. "You were on my mind, non-stop," I admit with a husky voice.

And Christ, it is *completely* true.

I dip my finger inside her warm center that is better than a warm pot of honey.

She tries to break her hands free but can't. "I need to touch you," she begs.

"Uh uh, Layla, we need you to stay tied up while we work through this."

My other hand circles her hip as her body moves around my finger. It feels as though she is moving of her own desire and getting what it needs from me.

"Please just… just…"

I lean over to hold our bodies close together, if only we could be closer. "Tell me, Layla. Tell me you want it again," I demand.

"I-I do," she confesses, breathless.

The sound of my swooshing belt buckle makes her tremble and an audible gasp escapes her. I cannot slow this down, not with her. There is a point to prove, a craving to fulfill.

In a new personal best, I get the condom on in record time and my tip finds her soft folds to slide along the slippery line that gets me to the destination we both want.

We both moan as I dive slowly deeper into her. She is snug, which almost makes me delirious that she has been waiting for me while I was away. But still, I need to ask.

"You feel amazing. You okay?"

"Mmm, don't stop," she murmurs through harsh breathing.

Her head nestles into her arms that rest on the edge of the sofa and her moans are continuous as I find our pace. She is tightening around me, meeting my every thrust, and it makes me groan in absolute pleasure.

There is never a concept of time when I am with Layla, but we enjoy our rhythm. Me going deep and steady, her moaning with every pump. Finally, I tilt my upper body forward and pull her toward me to hold her close against my body as we reach our final stretch. She seems to be almost light-headed or her legs have gone weak, but I feel her body losing its stance in my arms.

"I've got you." It comes out ragged.

"I need to see you. Turn me around," she pleads desperately with an almost urgency.

I quickly turn her around so the front of our bodies are against each other. I re-enter her as she adjusts to leaning against the sofa and her bound wrists rest between us, yet her fingers manage to grip my shirt.

Looking into her eyes she appears like she may be in another world.

"I've got you," I remind her again. But I can't help thinking that it wasn't what I meant. She's got me in more ways than one.

I want to cradle her face except I need to support her hips and our hold as her leg wraps around my hip.

Maybe it is my words, or maybe I am just fucking magnificent at my talent, but she starts to pulsate around me and lets out an almost high-pitched soft scream. My mouth captures her so I can feel the vibrations of her scream in my mouth. She almost rips my shirt with her intense grip.

It takes me over the edge too. Energy coiling under my navel, building until I burst and release. "I'm there." It comes out breathless.

It's a release of frustration, waiting, and desire all rolled into one.

I let go inside of her and she hums into my neck.

Taking a few moments, I let our bodies breathe as we hang off each other. Her hair is thrown across her face and her dress skirt crumpled at her waist. The smell of sweat and sex gently tingling our noses.

If I could take a photo of her like this and put it on my wall, I would, but I do not flaunt my conquests. And I think she may be too beautiful for my wall. Too beautiful for anyone else to witness. And she is not a conquest, not by a long shot.

I gently brush her hair out of her face and let her body lean against the back of the sofa as her eyes are fixated on me.

"Destressed?"

"I-I'm..." She cannot seem to complete a sentence.

I pull out of her. "You okay? I need to get rid of—"

"Don't leave me here tied up and barely able to stand." The look on her face is a drowsy grin. It makes me slightly laugh.

"Okay, okay." I untie the scarf around her wrists, yet still she does not seem to move. I kiss her cheek and she lets out a pleasurable mmm, which tells me she actually enjoys my affectionate gesture.

Deciding I will let her enjoy her temporary bliss, I quickly go to dispose of the condom in the kitchen trash. My mind quickly drives down a road that I was not expecting.

Maybe order in late dinner for us? Open a bottle of wine and put on a movie? Entice her with another round? It is quickly apparent to me that I don't want her to leave. It comes down to that. Has nothing to do with sex.

Walking back to her, I see she already re-straightened her clothes. She is almost frowning.

I don't give frowns to women.

"For someone who just came, you look a little down. Do I need to try again?" I rezip my jeans then grab the scarf that was hanging off my couch.

Layla does not respond at first and she seems lost in thought. That, or she is thinking of a way to rip me to pieces in thirty seconds because it's well... Layla.

"Josh. I'm… I'm…" She does not finish the sentence. Suddenly, she snaps back and looks at me.

She jerks the scarf from my hands. "I should go."

"No, you shouldn't. Stay." I realize that was a plea.

Her mouth opens and it seems like she may actually agree. "I don't th—"

I place my finger on her lips to quiet her and she does not blink. Her eyes look at me, warm and vulnerable, almost as if she is longing for something. God, I hope it's me. But then she roughly removes my hand from near her mouth.

"No more games. I am serious. This shouldn't have happened like this," she tells me softly.

Right away, I can't not ask as I gently touch her shoulder. "Do you regret it?"

She gently shakes her head no. "No. But I'm… this is more complicated than you think. Can we meet tomorrow night?" She is not playing; she is dead serious. Her being serious about us meeting again… I like that mindset.

"I hope you have big plans?" I'm hopeful.

Something in her turns again. She gives me a look that drips sensuality and tilts her head to the side and informs me, "Big plans? Well, I am sure I can think of something to send your body into shock." The way she says this tells me she is half-serious.

My eyebrow arches in interest. "Oh yeah? What does it involve?" I want so desperately to tease her neck with my lips in that spot that makes her squeal my name.

An unusual expression spreads across her face, one that I have not seen on her yet. "Tomorrow night. Can we just meet? I am sure I can surprise you then."

Crossing my arms, my eyes roam her up and down. "Sure, but feel free to move that date up in your calendar. I can make some room for you now."

Her eyes don't leave me. "I'm... I mean. No. I need to go." She finishes buttoning her jacket and adjusts her scarf. "Just promise me no more games."

Okay, the vibes she is sending are chilly again. I may be getting whiplash from how this week is going. But I need to let this go, so I simply nod in agreement.

————

THE NEXT DAY, I am sitting in my office. Admittedly, my morning coffee did not snap me into clarity. I still have no idea what just happened with Layla. Hot then cold. My head is spinning, because I know what I want, and I'm not nearly done with her yet. And the crazy part is... I want more. There is something about that woman. You never know what is going to come out of her mouth and she keeps me on my toes, it feels rejuvenating. Gives me a thrill. Even when she is ready to murder me, it is still a fun scene that unfolds.

I have to smile to myself as I am busy typing an email when there is a knock on my door.

"Sorry to bother you, but I need you to sign off on these invoices so I can have it booked before bank closing today," Lauren explains as she walks into my office.

"Sure. No problem," I tell her as I finish typing my sentence then grab the papers from Lauren. I do not pay much attention to her as I quickly glance at the invoices and start signing.

"Heard about your fight yesterday." Lauren mentions and I look up to see she is giving me an understanding look. But we say no more.

I'm not in the mood to discuss any more with Lauren.

Luckily, Noah knocks on my door with his girlfriend in tow. He must be in a better mood today.

"Grabbing lunch, anybody want anything?" Noah offers. Okay, he is clearly taking the professional approach after yesterday.

"No, it's fine. I have a lot to do."

Lauren smiles at Noah, which I cannot help observing that uptight Rachel—his girlfriend—does not seem pleased. "Thanks, but I am actually going to stop by Layla's."

That piques my interest.

"Is she still sick? She has been battling something all week even when she came to the office yesterday," Noah mentions.

Lauren quickly looks between Noah and me. Rather uncomfortably. "Uhm, I guess so. Must be a flu or something she picked up at bootcamp." She is trying to brush this topic under the table.

And I am utterly lost, as I saw Layla yesterday and she seemed different, but not sick.

Noah looks to Rachel. "Didn't your sister have the flu the other week when she was over for dinner and Layla was also there?"

Rachel laughs. "You mean my pregnant sister? No, that was just morning sickness."

"Unlucky. Okay, well, we will see you both later," Noah comments before he and Rachel head off.

My pen stops mid-signage and I am almost frozen. Only awakening when Lauren begins to tug the paper from under my pen.

"Josh. I kind of need that back," she requests awkwardly.

I finish my signature and then throw my pen across the desk before leaning back in my chair with a deep sigh.

I do not even notice when Lauren leaves and she must have left in a hurry, knowing I would ask.

My heart begins to race as my brain works in overtime.

When my smart head and well-trained legs finally share the message. I storm out on a mission.

When I reach Layla's building twenty minutes later, I manage to stop the elevator door just in the nick of time by placing my arm between the closing doors. Immediately, Lauren looks at me with surprise and oh-fuck-he-realizes eyes.

My hands motion for her to hand me the tray of coffees and the bag of food she is holding. "*I* will be taking this to Layla. Don't think your services will be needed right now as my lucky guess is I need to have a little chat with Layla." There are no hypotheticals in my tone.

Lauren reluctantly, after a few tugs from me, lets me have the tray and bag.

"Just be nice," Lauren states before walking out of the elevator with her eyes not leaving me, as if she is inspecting what frame of mind I am in.

Which is, I am the guy who is way too smart. That racing heart rate and brain turning over works again. When I look at the tray of coffee, a scoff escapes my mouth. Unbelievable.

Dots in my head.

Layla sick – A half-dot.

Layla acting cagey – A dot.

Layla saying she can shock me – A double dot.

Layla wanting to speak – A triple dot.

A coffee cup that says momccino.

All. The. Dots. Connected.

LAYLA

I hold a mug of ginger tea in my hands, with my knees to my chest as I sit on the sofa and stare at the colored pencils on my desk across the room. I've been trying to relax from my day of the earth opening up. This required candles lit and Billie Marten playing on my speakers. It has been raining outside which just adds to this scene, which would be fit for an intense confession or intense entanglements that involves no words.

Fitting. Really, fitting.

Last night added a slew of more complications to my already complicated predicament. How he used the scarf was like winning the lottery. He unlocked a fantasy of mine that has been floating around in my mind.

I walked right into his trap. But my mind and the inferno between my legs needed me to do something to detonate. There is something about angry sex that is therapeutic. I was boiled, but not for the reasons he thought.

He probably was reveling in his mission accomplished of getting me to his place and having his way with me. Fine. I will let his ego think that. In reality, I needed to not think and wanted one more time before reality may hit me in the head. One more time to be wild, and be desired for just being me.

And he wanted me to stay. I should have. I should have stayed and laid with him to talk, which is something we are good at. I would have told him about our complication. But maybe it is a false alarm and then I freak him out for nothing. Those tests can be wrong. Plus, we were safe. Freaking double safe. This is just not possible.

…or it is, and now I am incubating the child of my semi-boss and brother's business partner who knows how to use a scarf.

I am startled into the present when I hear a knock on my door and remember that Lauren was going to stop by with supplies for me—food.

Swinging my legs off the sofa, I walk to the door in my soft Teenage Mutant Ninja Turtle pajama pants and a tight black tank top. Because even I have a respect for retro.

Throwing a smile on my face, I open the door expecting to see Lauren. My smile quickly disintegrates.

And there is my frog who turned into a prince somewhere along the way.

"Expecting someone else?" Josh is standing with a bag of food and a tray of two coffees. "Lauren got called into a meeting." He walks into my apartment without waiting for me to speak—because truthfully—I am speechless. I was not expecting this turn of events mid-day.

There is literally an unexpected guest in both my living room and body.

He walks in like he lives here.

"You are like sand in my beach bag—I never can get rid of it," I mention as I follow him to the kitchen and quickly get a glance of my phone on the charger with a message on the home screen as he sets the bag and coffees down.

Lauren: Sorry. He hijacked your delivery as I was about to go into the elevator to yours.

Fucking fantastic.

"Josh?" I ask with slight disdain, and I cross my arms. "What is up with you? Your annoying streak seems to be back since you came back from California."

He does not blink. Instead he steps to me and in a swift movement his hands grip my sides and he lifts me until he sets me on the kitchen counter. *Kind of hot.*

A short laugh escapes him. "What is up with me? Don't you mean you? Something you want to tell me?" His eyes close in on me and his face tells me he is waiting.

My face freezes, because I have an odd impression that I know where this conversation is heading. It involves Luna Ray and her ludicrously crazy advice and warning signs.

He hands me a to-go coffee from the takeout tray. Then he holds a finger up, indicating to me not to speak. Grabbing his phone, he speaks into his phone to use voice search.

"Enlighten me—what is a momccino?" he asks as his eyes pierce me with his gaze, yet the corner of his mouth is hitched in amusement.

I really need to talk to someone at Beans to not label the freaking to-go cups with its contents. The smartass must have seen the label on the cup. I look at the cup and yeah, big black letters display my secret. Momccino.

The phone answers us with a delicate feminine voice. "A momccino is a decaf coffee, dairy-free milk and normally ordered when pregnant or breastfeeding."

I'm not amused with his antics, because, A. not amused with his antics, and B. That phone voice pisses me off even on a good day.

Josh puts his phone back in his pocket. "Always so *very* informative. Thank you." There is sarcasm in his voice.

I decide to play ball and I take a sip of my momccino and lean back on the counter. Relaxed and casual.

"When were you going to tell me you are pregnant?" he asks firmly.

I draw in a breath and look away briefly.

He steps closer to me and his hands find each side of my body to cage me in on the counter. "Was this your way to shock me later?" His eyes grow large.

"I don't know a hundred percent, okay? Wasn't going to bother you until I knew for certain."

He looks like he is about to go into action mode with a million thoughts flying around. "Okay. We will go get one of those test things. Because I need to know. As in now. Already. As in fifteen minutes ago when I connected the fucking dots." There is a slight roughness yet nervousness in his voice.

"That's not needed. I took one."

"Okay? And?"

How has he still not blinked?

"Positive," I admit simply and he seems to be studying me as he lets out a sound of disbelief.

"Shouldn't you take another in case it was wrong or something?"

My eyes squint and I look anywhere but his gaze. "I might have taken more than one... or five," I inform him with an awkward hitched voice as I scratch the back of my head. "I'm waiting for the doctor to confirm at my appointment later this afternoon."

His hands run through his hair and he lets out a deep sigh. "Five tests?! Five positive tests? You took *five* positive tests?"

Surely, he is a bit louder than he intends to be. His voice admittedly sounds like a teenage boy who is going through changes.

"Shh. Keep your voice down. I am trying to not freak out."

"Layla! I had you tied up last night. I tied up a pregnant woman!" he exclaims and seems to panic.

I find that part hilarious.

A mischievous grin forms on my face. "Cross that fantasy off your list then."

He shakes his head at me. "You knew you were pregnant, and you let me tie you up?!" He is both parts horrified and entertained.

"Relax, Josh. And I kind of may have known I might be pregnant. I may have taken a pit stop to take a test somewhere between your office and your apartment yesterday." I hop off the counter and head to my living area. I grab a book from the table that I received today in the mail and step on the ladder of my bookshelf.

I watch him rub a hand across his face. "Fuck. How did this happen? We were careful every single time."

Turning on the ladder, I look at him. "No clue. But maybe I am not pregnant, those tests can be wrong."

His hands come to each side of me on the ladder.

"*Sweetheart,*" he responds in his condescending voice. "You are either in denial or really want to believe it. I'm going with you to the appointment," he demands, yet it's soft and his eyes try to hold me.

"Not necessary," I say softly, but I do not really mean it.

Clearing his throat, he gives me a glare. "I'm going." He remains firm.

"Fine," I let out, disgruntled, but truthfully there is a lightness in me that is relieved he wants to come with. I am not sure I want to be alone.

"Maybe it's a false alarm. I mean, it's not like we signed

up to the Sweet Dove's conception moon package. You are determined, but that doesn't mean your sperm is." I cannot help but jab him. It is my defense mechanism for dealing with him when the man either softens me, arouses me or pretends to irritate me.

Shaking his head his hand rubs his temple. "This is unbelievable. How are you so calm that you manage to still insult me?"

"Because I may be limited on my options to cope until I know for sure, so I'm using alternatives to let out my frustration," I deadpan.

An inviting grin forms on his face. "I could think of better ways to let out your frustration. Last night seemed to help you."

Trapped between the ladder and his body, I admit, "This news may be a roadblock to our methods."

"I like a challenge," he whispers.

Something tells me you really can't like this one.

But I do not need to think about it now. It is too soon.

I become a little breathless and his fingers touching my skin will have me submitting to anything.

"How do you want this, Layla? Right here?" he asks and warns me at the same time. I can hear how turned-on in his voice he is.

Gosh, against the ladder is new for me but *yes please.*

"What are you doing to me?" I give a lazy smile because I am becoming boneless.

Our eyes meet and I think my body is about to move in for a kiss, even though this latest development is a wrench. This is crazy, but this man has a gift to relax me.

But he pulls away. "Get off the ladder, Layla," he orders through gritted teeth. His hands help me off. "No more ladders in your condition." He returns to a normal voice.

Well, that was an unfair play.

I shake my head. "Is this a preview of what the next nine months look like?" I cannot tell if I am annoyed or excited about that prospect.

Yet it breaks any tension we may have had. We both look at each other for a few moments.

"You were trying to tell me last night, weren't you?" His eyes narrow on me and his hands stroke my arms.

I lick my lips before biting the corner of my mouth. "I *may* have thought about it, yes."

He gently nods.

"I'm sorry if it is wrong that we—well, and I didn't tell you. I just really needed to not think."

A soft smile forms. "Ah, destress. I get it now."

I nod and then we have a thick few moments where the air feels humid. Something grows between us in the air, it isn't sexual either. A magnetic pull, but we don't act on it.

My hands find the pockets of my pants and I step back. "So… my guess is you need to head back to work and I really need a nap before the appointment, *so…*" It drags out and hopefully he gets the hint.

"You're right. Wait, how are you feeling?" The concern in his voice sends a flicker through me. Fueled more by the fact his fingertips come to touch my arms again gently.

"Not great. Or maybe I am allergic to you. So many options." I give him a reassuring grin. "Five p.m. I'll send you the address. Meet me there?"

"Absolutely." His lips twitch into an almost smile.

He pulls his phone out again and types something as he walks toward the door.

"Are you searching what the fuck to do? Because I already did that," I offer with my lips curving.

As he is about to open the door. He turns to look at me

and sarcastically says, "Yeah. The interwebs tells me that home pregnancy tests are 99.9% accurate, which means I should be looking at cribs to buy and weapons to defend myself from my possible upcoming murder that Noah may be guilty of... I guess Luna Ray was 0.01% more accurate than the five pregnancy tests you took."

I cannot help but smile at his sentence. Somehow making me feel relieved in the process.

18

LAYLA

This is not how I envisioned my weekday. I should be enjoying a yoga class after still recovering from a weekend fueled by coffee and the sensations of my vibrator. Instead, I am in a paper gown that rips at every movement with Josh sitting in the room watching me like a hawk. To top it off, we have been given the doctor who is far too cheery for my brain running on decaf coffee to handle.

"Okay Layla, let us have a look, shall we? Ooh, exciting, a baby. Have you two been trying for long?" Dr. James—who looks like she just graduated—asks. She seems like she is quirky in spirit with black-rimmed glasses and dark hair.

Josh lets out a disgruntled laugh from the chair in the corner that he is sitting on. "Can't say we were trying for this one."

I roll my eyes.

"Have you two been together long?" Dr. James asks, still too cheerful.

"No. We are not together," I clarify and look at Josh who seems to be enjoying this awkward situation.

"Oh. Well it takes only one time." The young doctor smiles.

Josh clears his throat and gets up from his chair and comes to stand next to me. "Can't say it was one time only either."

I huff as I fall back onto the table.

"Oh? Well I don't understand." The poor doctor tries to grasp our situation.

I jackknife it up back to sitting. "Look, Doogie Howser," I begin. The doctor looks at me confused. "Neil Patrick Harris pre-*How I Met Your Mother*." She tries to smile at me, but still seems lost. "This wasn't planned at all. We used birth control. A lot of birth control. I mean, we were good at that, right?" I glance at Josh.

He shrugs a shoulder. "I would say we nailed down that protocol," he comments with a confident look.

I continue, "So it would be great if we can just get that confirmation that this guy's" —I point with my thumb to Josh — "Sperm didn't knock me up."

"I see, well what makes you think you may be pregnant?" she asks.

A deep exhale escapes me. "I'm a little late. Stomach not doing so great. This guy seems to edge me a little more than he normally would today—"

Josh interrupts, "She is moodier than normal and took five positive tests. I'm going to go on a wild whim here and say this one" —he points his thumb to me— "is in denial."

My death stare must be strong.

"Well those are all good signs for pregnancy. But I am picking up some crazy vibes between you two. Not sure if this is good news or if Layla wants to be alone, but how about I just check?" For once, the young doctor speaks with reason.

She turns to me. "I'm going to do an ultrasound and it's your choice if you would like to be alone as the options for the pregnancy are yours."

The mood in the room changes and I look to Josh whose face turns serious. He doesn't like the decision I have to make. But there is no hesitation from me.

"No, it's fine—he can stay, and I don't need to know my options. I know what I want," I admit and I realize I never actually asked Josh what he would want.

My choice was made the moment I peed on a stick. I knew I would want this baby, no matter how much of an unexpected turn to my life it may be. Caring for a little piece of me. I am a grown woman who can do this no matter what role the father will play. I've lost enough close family, no way would I take away an opportunity to bring a little soul into my life that will be my family.

I'm snapped back into the present by that way too cheery voice.

"Well then. Shall we check to see if his sperm succeeded?" Dr. James smiles again and puts her hands together.

Growling, I fall back to the table again.

"Okay, Layla, this is going to feel a bit cold and I am going to start on your stomach as you are quite small. Normally I need to do an internal but like to avoid those if I can," she explains.

Letting out a deep breath as the cold gel hits my skin, I feel my hand being scooped up by a warm and strong one. Looking, I see Josh interlaced our hands. There is an odd sensation near my heart as if it is aching to explode and I'm not sure for what reasons. I squeeze his hand as I look away to catch a moment for myself.

My mind lets different thoughts float in and out. A baby?

A baby with Josh? Whose birth control failed? I mean, I took my pill, right? His condom wearing skills seemed like a solid A+ too. This is crazy. Oh, but with Josh's nose and my eyes then the kid may have struck gold. Geez, who paints a doctor's office gray? They really need to freshen the paint color in here...

"Layla." I hear my name being whispered and my head turns slowly to Josh who has a soft smile on his face, and he indicates to the screen in front of me with his head. My sight draws a line from his eyes to the screen.

"There you are, Layla. No question about it. You have a little baby." The doctor smiles as she presses a button on her machine and the room fills with the sound of the swishing baby's heartbeat that beats fast. My own heart jumps at the sound.

My hand squeezes Josh's hand, a force he returns. Tears well in my eyes and I'm overwhelmed with a plethora of emotions that I have never felt before.

"A baby," I barely manage to whisper. Josh kisses my hand that is interlaced with his and our eyes meet. Even we know that with everything aside—that this little baby is from us.

After a few more minutes, the young doctor prints off some photos and turns the machine off. Josh and I let go of our hands.

"These are for you, Layla." She hands me the photos. "Does Dad want one too?"

"Yes, he does," Josh answers and holds out a hand.

"I will put it in the app too. Welcome to pregnancy these days. Everything is via an app except pushing the thing out," the doctor jokes. My face just turns to terror. "Oh, I mean. It's super informative and fun," she tries to assure me.

Really bad save, I feel like I am now carrying a baby on Planet Mars.

"Okay, so based on your cycle and the ultrasound, you are around eight weeks pregnant. The two weeks before your most likely ovulation and the weeks after—"

I cut in. "Whoa, are you saying that the one week I decide to have copious amounts of sex was the week I was most likely to get pregnant?"

"Seems like it."

"Well, that was bad planning," I remark to myself and it explains a lot. I'm always extra frisky around my ovulation.

"Right. Prenatal vitamins and rest are key now. If you continue to have really bad morning sickness then call the office and we can write a prescription." The doctor puts the pen of her tablet in her pocket and shakes our hands before leaving.

Josh calls out to the doctor. "Quick question. Is it bad if you are pregnant and get tied up during very excellent sex?… *asking for a friend.*" His eyes and mouth flash me a trying-to-rile-me-up grin.

The doctor looks between both of us. "Uhm, you can tell your friend that the internet probably would answer that. But as long as the position is right for the stage of pregnancy and open communication between partners, then it should be okay. Nothing too tight." The doctor looks at us oddly before getting the hell out of there.

I shake my head at Josh before laying back on the table and I exhale a sigh. After a moment, I feel someone watching me.

"You okay?" Josh asks as he leans against the wall with hands in his pockets, his foot playing with the floor.

"Yeah, just… overwhelmed maybe?"

He comes up next to me and passes me my sweater with a reassuring smile. "Come on. Get dressed and let's get out of here."

"Where are we going?"

"Somewhere to talk."

LAYLA

The entire ride back from the doctors, we were quiet. Arriving at Josh's place, he throws his keys to the table near the door as I follow him in.

I flop onto the big dark leather sofa where I never actually got to sit last time I was here. *Fun times*.

"Want something to drink?" he offers. I shake my head no as he comes to sit next to me.

There is an awkward silence.

"So," I drag out as my fingers pat my thighs.

An exhale escapes him. "This is crazy," he mentions. I look at him and can't for the life of me figure out where his mind is at.

"Look, you don't need to be inv—"

He cuts me off, "Whoa there, sparky. Don't even say that. I'm involved."

Truthfully, relief hits me like a tsunami.

"Okay."

He takes my hand in his. "Everything, okay? Pregnancy, baby, next eighteen years. I think you are kind of stuck with me for life."

"Okay." My eyes do not blink as I look at him.

"Are you going to keep saying okay to everything? Because this is going to be an easy conversation then. I should probably throw in—do you want to give me a blowjob?" He tries to make me smile.

And I do want to smile, but I also erupt into tears at the same time. *Damn hormones*.

"Crap. I already made you cry."

I hold a hand up. "No, it's the hormones. The world is royally screwed with me pregnant," I sob.

After a minute of me sobbing and Josh not sure if he should poke me, prod me or hold me—our conversation resumes.

"Noah is going to kill us," I hiccup as I wipe tears away with the back of my hand. Josh offers me his sleeve and I use his sleeved arm to dry my face then let go.

Josh sighs and lets his fingers rub the bridge of his nose. "Let me worry about that," he tells me.

"After your argument with him, not sure now is the best time to tell him. Maybe we wait to tell him? I mean, it's still early. Or does it make it worse if we wait?" I wonder aloud.

Josh rubs the back of his neck. "What do we tell him exactly?"

Leaning into the back of the sofa, I rub my forehead. "That you had me begging to scream your name during a four-day marathon of sex?" I say monotone.

Josh looks at me with a look of panic before realizing I am trying to lighten the situation.

"You are in marketing—you're probably going to have to maybe spin that a little," I add on.

His thumb rubs his jaw. "Give me some time to figure it out. I guess I need to put a spin to sleeping with my direct report too?" Now he gives me a soft grin, because I know he doesn't care.

I sink into the couch. "We are an HR nightmare, really."

It makes Josh laugh as he sinks back into the couch too. We both just sit in silence for a few moments.

I don't want to, but I have to ask. "How do we" —I motion between us— "do this?"

He looks at me and debates what to say, I can see it written on his face. A deep exhale escaping. "I don't know. I'm the jerk, remember?" Yet he delicately tucks some of my hair behind my ear as he speaks. His fingers sending me on a time travel to those few nights lying in bed.

"And I push you into near insanity, remember?" I counter blankly.

Josh studies me for a second as his hand touches my arm. "Lately, we've been doing okay, right? I mean, we found a great method to be around each other."

A scoff escapes me. "Sex we are good at."

"Maybe we were on that path to something anyway," he suggests.

"That would involve a lot of tolerance," I state, but I am not serious. I just want to give him a rise.

He rolls his eyes. "You really are not a fan of me, huh."

I bite my inner lip and sigh. "You're growing on me. More than I would like to admit. Sometimes I even have an odd sensation that resembles that I may find you likable. Maybe even enjoyable," I tease as I give him the side-eye with mouth slant. "But the stakes have kind of changed now. It's just…" I stop for a second.

Before it was Noah finding out, but there is no way he will not find out now. So, what is it?

"Yes? Go on," he asks, amused.

"I don't know. I didn't want to come between you and

Noah. Now it is inevitable. Actually, I think we should take a break from whatever we were doing. Let the news sink in, things for you and Noah to settle."

Josh adjusts himself on the sofa to look at me and lets his fingers graze my arms. It seems like he is about to protest.

But my stomach really swirls.

Holding a hand up over my mouth, I run to the bathroom.

Five minutes later, I am sitting on the bathroom floor with the world spinning. Josh sitting next to me, as he held my hair up as I vomited my breakfast, lunch, and dinner—*lovely*. I feel horrible. I would say embarrassed, but this is his doing.

I point a finger at him as he hands me a warm washcloth. "This is all your fault. You knocked me up. It's your swimmers that broke through a condom and told my birth control that it's a useless science."

He swallows and tries not to laugh. "I can't even argue with you now. Guilty. One hundred percent guilty. But it could also be some voodoo from Luna Ray. I mean, she seemed pretty pissed we didn't take her too seriously. Maybe she did some witch doctor spell on us," he jokes.

"Maybe you are right actually." I am more serious than I should be. "Oh, my goodness, that card. The unexpected card. This is kind of hilarious now." I laugh to myself.

Josh laughs too. "Hangman, right?"

Oh no, that wave… it is back. Turning over, I vomit again into the toilet. Josh's hand rubs my back. It is comforting and in a strange way makes me feel supported.

After finishing this round. Finally, I feel able to drag my body off the floor and he guides me to his bedroom.

"I have no idea what twisted fantasy you have. But this lady can't even contemplate the idea of sex after vomiting half my weight," I admit.

A half-smile appears on his face. "Sleep. You need to

sleep. Lay on your side, it will help," he tells me as he brings me a T-shirt.

Without thought, I throw my dress off and Josh puts a hand out to stop me from putting the shirt on.

"Whoa there, mama. Have you been wearing that under your dress all day?" he asks, very curious and satisfied. Looking at myself, I forgot I am wearing a black lace bra and panties set.

Shrugging. "I didn't know how naked I had to get at the doctor's. And truthfully, if I wasn't pregnant, then I may have celebrated using a method that we can't use anymore." I realize how ridiculous that sounds and even I have to join Josh who is chuckling.

"I really like the way you want to celebrate, but did you really think you weren't pregnant?"

I shake my head no. I knew. Just denial was strong. This is a big deal. An unexpected big deal. We have a lot more to talk about. But my head is spinning again.

Throwing his shirt on that drowns me, I go to lie on my side on his bed. Realizing I have never been in his room, yet we have slept together before. Funny.

Not sure if the episode in the bathroom is affecting me, but his king-size bed with gray sheets and black bed frame feels like a cloud in heaven. I do not want to leave.

Josh comes to kneel next to me beside the bed to align his eyes with my level.

"Can I ask you something?" he requests gently and I nod. "You said you would have celebrated if you weren't pregnant. But since you are?"

True, I did say that. It would have made life easier. But easy was literally not in our cards. And—I think I still feel like celebrating.

"I'm surprised. But there is a little girl or boy who will

have their parents' attitude joining the world and that is pretty cool, right?"

He smiles at me. "Yeah. Yeah, it is."

Josh begins to leave, but I grab his hand. "Why do you seem to be taking this news so well? You seemed more concerned you tied me up than the fact that your baby is in me," I ask because he hasn't freaked out the way I expected him to. He is overly calm and almost seems excited.

"We'll talk about it another day. But there are not enough reasons to make this not good news. Never understood the phrase written in the cards until now."

I smile softly at his reference.

"Sleep Layla, you look exhausted," he instructs.

"Geez, you know how to compliment a lady. But where are you going?"

He stands in the doorway with a soft smile. "To get you some water and yes before you even say it, I already know the next months you are going to be an absolute boss. Water and fresh cloth coming your way."

His look adorable, his card reference cute, his ability to take care of me surprising. Not wanting to kill each other—in fact, wanting him closer—surprisingly… right.

———

WAKING UP, I feel heavy. As if the world stopped and I deeply hibernated. Fluttering my eyes open, I remember I am in Josh's bed. Rolling over, I see that he is not there and slowly I stretch out my body and begin to sit up.

Looking at the clock, I realize I slept a solid twelve hours. I missed the fact he came into bed with me because I was out like a log.

Then it dawns on me that we slept in the same bed and

did not do anything as in not sending each other into the universe of O's—the only reason we shared a bed before. Okay, I wasn't exactly sporting my best look having just thrown up.

There is a shuffle in the kitchen that I hear.

Getting out of bed, I slowly walk through the bedroom to the hall. Rubbing my eyes as I am still groggy. I arrive in the kitchen to find Josh ready for work in his signature fitted jeans, dress shoes, button-down shirt and suit coat. He looks up at me as he drinks coffee.

"'Morning. You okay?"

Hopping on the kitchen counter to sit, I realize I am low on coverage on the leg front as his shirt is still on me. "'Morning. Yeah, I think I am okay."

I grab his coffee cup, but he immediately grabs it back. "Nuh-uh. It's not decaf."

A growl escapes me. "This kid is testing me," I agonize.

He leans against the sink and I feel like his eyes are examining me.

"You slept pretty deep. I had to check you were still breathing a few times."

Pulling my hair into a messy bun, I yawn. "Really? I guess I do not remember you even coming to bed, which is a comfy bed by the way. Magical."

He wiggles his eyebrows. "Yeah, a lot of magical stuff does happen in my bed."

"Walked into that one, didn't I?" I smile.

He nods. "You did indeed… I need to head into the office as I have a meeting. Stay as long as you want. Want some breakfast?" He sets his coffee cup in the sink.

"No. Just the thought of food makes me eww." I nearly gag again. Then the thought of biscuits comes to mind and suddenly my mind is focused only on that, it's craving it.

"Biscuits, I need buttermilk biscuits or maybe beignets. That is what I am going to do this morning. Find biscuits."

Josh starts laughing as he grabs his phone from the counter.

"You are messing with me, right?"

I look at him confused.

"Really? Our child is making you crave the foods you ate when he or she was conceived?" The look on his face tells me he is entertained.

"I didn't think about it like that, but the cravings don't lie. Hey, you said our child." It comes out sentimental and feels as though the back of my heart discovered a new door.

Josh shrugs like it is nothing. There is a long pause.

"Josh, what I said yesterday about cooling down."

"You're right," he simply answers as he grabs his keys.

M y tennis ball is facing my wrath as I lean back in my chair at the office. On the outside, I am calm as a clam about the pregnancy. Some may even say I appear peachy these days. On the inside, I am flipping out. I arrived at the doctor's office fueled on a double espresso and even Motown was not calming me down—how messed up is that?

I have read articles on pregnancy, all the while wondering why nobody has done a statistical study on the link between tarot cards and getting knocked up—something tells me it would be staggering. I would get on that bandwagon of crowdfunding in a heartbeat.

To be honest, a future with kids was not on my radar. But Layla Wells in my bed or shower was not on my radar either. This baby is completely unforeseen and a complete bombshell. But there is an overwhelming excitement that keeps jumping up inside me and that is also a shocker. I am going to be a dad. *Wow.*

Not many guys in their bachelorhood would admit it as it ruins the hard to tame persona, but kids? I love them. While I am not going to spin some bullshit that they make the world go round. They are fun little creatures. I just was not planning on one in the coming few years. Still, there is no hesitation in my mind.

We are having a baby.

Layla and I are having a baby.

My vague recall of high school Spanish keeps bringing the word *loco* up in my head on repeat. Crazy this is.

Yet, if I had to plan a very unexpected baby then I did it well. Layla is no stranger and our lives already intertwine in some way. She seems like someone who will step up to the mom role in a heartbeat and do it well.

Me? I would like to think I was raised well enough to be a responsible man, and unlike my old man who traveled a lot for work—I want to be the guy who is at every soccer game or ballet class of the little me.

There is also that one factor from childhood that may affect my reasons for jumping on the baby train, but I brush it out of my head before it gets too deep. No instead I focus on Layla.

A few days ago, I had sex and Layla on the brain. Now I have pregnancy and Layla on the brain—okay, sex is still there too—I just feel the tables turned. Don't get me wrong, an app I downloaded told me to be ready for the side-effect of the female being extremely aroused while pregnant and I am fully ready to be at her beck n' call to help with that issue.

But there are other priorities in figuring out our road *together* in handling this, and I could use a fucking clue of how to approach that. Because together sounds like nirvana right about now.

Tapping my desk with the ball, I give up in defeat that my brain will not get any work done. Rubbing my hands over my face, I hear a knock on my glass door.

"Hey boss." Layla's soft voice greets me and immediately I look up to her.

Quickly, I get up from my chair and come to meet her in the middle of my office. She had not planned to be here at the office today, she works her own hours and has other clients too.

"Feeling better?" I ask, trying to catch her eyes with mine.

She shakes her head side to side.

"We still have a lot to talk about," Layla mentions gently and I nod.

With impeccable timing, Stephanie skips human communication and interrupts us. "Oh, good you both are here."

Layla and I look at each other, but our eyes agree to go with it.

"What is it, Stephanie?" I ask, not entirely enthused. Stephanie comes into my office and all three of us go to my sofa and chairs.

"Radnor is asking if you both could travel a few times in the coming months to view some more hotels?" Stephanie asks.

"Uh. I gue—" Layla begins hesitantly.

Immediately, I cut in, "I can. Layla needs to stay here." They both look at me, a little taken back by my abruptness. In truth, there is no way in hell I want Layla to be traveling on a regular basis while pregnant. "What I meant is, Layla mentioned she has quite a few other projects here and wasn't sure she could stay on this account."

Layla looks at me with a neutral face and I am not entirely sure she understands my logic.

"Can I get back to you?" Layla smiles to Stephanie.

"Sure. No problem." Stephanie nods. After a few more questions, Stephanie goes on her lively way.

Layla looks at me with crossed arms and an inquisitive look. "I need to stay here?"

Walking to my desk, I perch on the front of the desk and grab the tennis ball—I need it.

"I don't think you should be traveling in your condition," I explain.

Layla stands up and it looks like I lit a fume. "My condition? You mean you knocked me up and now I can't eat because I am a carrier of a souvenir for a nine-month condition?" She raises her voice as she walks toward me with a pointed finger.

Agony sweeps through me. Geez, here is my first experience with Layla pissed and hyped up on hormones. *Lucky me.*

But she is kind of adorable when she is annoyed in this way and adorable doesn't exist in my vocabulary.

"Just being a protective jerk," I inform her with the corner of my mouth slanting up.

"Right. Because you get a say in what I can and can't do now." She crosses her arms.

I begin to squeeze the tennis ball due to my stress from trying to calm her down.

"Not saying that. But yes, shouldn't I have some input?"

"Really. This is why people shouldn't sleep with their boss/brother's business partner. It turns into a hot mess," she huffs.

Now I cannot help but grin. "Hot mess? Happy to hear it is at least hot."

She grabs my tennis ball and throws it across the room. Most certainly, there was anger in that throw.

I hold my hands up and laugh. "Easy there, tiger."

A hopeless look flashes in front of me on her face and I can see something is bothering her. "Layla?" I let my hands find my pockets.

A deep audible sigh escapes her. "What are we going to do? Especially when I start to show?"

"You mean Noah, or what people may think?"

"Both."

Thinking about it a few moments, there is no hesitation in my mind. "I don't care what people think and Noah, well it's tricky, but not impossible. We just found out, let us give it a few days before worrying," I suggest and reach for her arms. Noah and I have cooled down enough that we can wait in peace to tell him.

"You're right. What about you and—"

Geez, I need to get a do not disturb sign for my door.

Noah comes barging into my office and Layla instantly pulls her arms away to create space between us. "Hey guys, I thought I saw you both here. Want to grab lunch?"

Layla and I look at each other. Panic in her eyes.

"I think I have a meeting," I lie, and Layla looks like she is also trying to figure out an excuse.

"Sorry, I really need to get home to work on some things," Layla tells him.

Noah does not seem to pick up on the unusual tension in the room. "Okay, next time then."

Layla grabs her bag and heads toward the door.

"Let me walk you out Layla, we need to discuss Radnor's request that Stephanie mentioned." That came off logistically casual enough. So much so that Noah does not blink an eye.

Walking to the elevator, we reach the doors and I press the button. I wait with her as the elevator needs to come up from below.

Putting my hands in my pockets and slanting my shoulder up, I attempt to make conversation. "Do you really have work to do?"

"Yeah. I do. Between your offspring making me sick and

recovering from your offspring making me sick, I need to catch up," she berates.

"Will you at least stay at mine or let me come stay at yours?"

She looks at me a little surprised as she straightens her posture.

"I don't like the idea of you being alone when you're sick," I clarify.

Layla taps her fingers against the strap of her bag. "Right. Because I am now just your problem to take care of." She seems annoyed with me again.

I am not going to win today.

Touching her arm gently. "I don't see you as a problem, so what is with your sudden attitude?"

Oh no, her eyes rage again.

"I don't even know where to begin."

My eyes bulge at her. "Talking. It is a great method. You should try it sometime." That came out a little harsh.

The elevator doors open, and she storms into the waiting car with a sulk.

I give up. Really. Today is not going to be the day we reach any milestones.

———

RETURNING to my office and sinking into my chair, I dial my sister.

"Big brother, what's shaking?" Harper has her usual bubbly tone.

"A lot," I admit.

"Do tell. I hope it has something to do with a woman. You really need one of those." I can already imagine Harper saying this as she lies on her couch with her legs in the air in some odd meditation position.

"I have found myself in a crazy situation. Need to pull the best sister in the world card. The one that includes the bonus of keeper of secrets," I request as I throw my feet on my desk.

"Absolutely," Harper confirms with excitement in her voice.

"Right, so Noah's sister. I think you met her once or twice," I begin.

"Yeah. I met her… wait… did you? Oh please tell me you did?"

Sighing. "Yeah, we did. Noah doesn't know."

Harper squeals. "Awesome. Forbidden romance—so hot."

"Whoa. Remember this is your older brother you're talking to," I remind her, because she tends to talk about everything including what she and her fiancé get up to. Can be quite traumatizing.

"Okay, but sounds like there is more?"

"Yeah. *So…* looks like you're going to be an aunt." It rolls out of my mouth with ease and I realize she is the first one I have told.

I swear the phone nearly drops.

"Shut up! Really? No! This is awesome. You're going to be a dad!"

Looking around the room, I check to make sure there are no hidden cameras, spies, or further surprises for this week.

Allowing a good minute to pass of Harper's excitement, I continue. "Yeah, well, the mother-to-be seems to despise me and my business partner may throw me out my office window. But other than that, I think it's actually special news."

"This is awesome. The golden boy knocks someone up out of wedlock. I am no longer the wild child. But Mom and

Dad are going to love it, they are crazy about kids. I will not tell them, but yeah. Why does Noah's sister despise you? You are a real catch if you want to be."

Rubbing my neck, I ponder. "Layla and I didn't exactly start on the right foot. Or maybe it's the morning sickness. She is throwing up a lot. Like a lot a lot."

"Hmm. I can imagine her head is a wreck. This wasn't planned, right?"

"Absolutely not," I make it clear.

"Give her some time, just be patient. Really patient. My friends who are pregnant, I swear morph into pregasauruses which are part dinosaur and human. It's no joke." The way Harper says this, I know there is not a humorous grin attached to her face the way there should be.

"Yeah, the app mentioned something about that," I joke.

Harper laughs. "Ahh, you already downloaded an app," she coos. "What a twenty-first-century daddy to be."

I feel like patting my shoulder that I am already taking steps on the daddy to be train.

"Just keep trying to be open with her, patient, and use your Josh charm," she reminds me.

"I'll do my best."

We talk a little more about her wedding and our parents who are on holiday in Mexico. I promise her that I will be there for her whole weekend of wedding festivities and when she asks if Layla will be my plus one, I have to take a pause. We have not yet discussed what happens after our cool-down period. But I say to keep it open for her. I mean, either way, she will be part of my life, right?

After keeping conversation simple with Josh during the last week, I find myself back at the Ives & Wells office. This time avoiding him and heading straight for the open office of desks where blue exploded everywhere. Mindy has her last day in office, which means there is cake and blue balloons for the upcoming arrival of her little bundle of joy. Since I am taking on some of her work, I stop by for any last-minute notes.

Sitting with her at her desk, we finish going over her overview that she made and right when we finish, colleagues arrive with cake and presents. Someone mentions party time and I smile at Mindy. She seems to glow in excitement.

I cannot help thinking that this will be me in thirty weeks. It hits me more and more every day that my life is about to change.

"Almost there, Mindy. Must be excited." Noah smiles as he hands Mindy a piece of blue-colored chocolate cake on a duck designed paper plate.

"Yeah. I am just so happy it's almost here," Mindy tells us

as she puts a hand on her belly that is bigger than her actual body.

Music is now playing in the office and people are in office party mode with various conversations happening.

"You have some nice gifts, Mindy. You got a really big box from Josh," someone mentions.

"Sounds about right. Outshining me on the gift front," Noah tells us then sets his plate of cake down and heads off.

"You are going to have a really long maternity leave. That is nice. Are you using vacation?" Lauren asks Mindy as she passes me a plate of cake.

"No actually. I am getting a longer paid maternity leave." Mindy smiles as she continues to rub her belly.

"Oh? That's nice. Didn't know we did that here. Did Noah arrange that?" Lauren raises. I'm also intrigued as maternity leave these days is sometimes a battle to receive anywhere still.

Mindy shakes her head. "It was actually Josh. A few months ago, he said that I shouldn't have to worry about rushing back to work and said that they would arrange paid maternity leave and for longer. I even can start back part-time when I come back," Mindy explains as she dives into her cake.

My heartstrings tug and I look at Lauren who flashes her eyes at me. Because Josh Ives is more of a prince than I thought. In fact, he has been growing on me for a long time now. But that could just be the mixture of icing and pregnancy emotions.

Powerful stuff.

Speaking of which, a freaking crying violin decided to start its warm-up inside me. Really f-you hormones.

Blinking my eyes to hold in my tears on the verge, I decide I need to find a cure. Deciding the cake is the best option, my fork nabs a big piece of cake. As soon as it hits my mouth, sunshine fills me again. This is a rollercoaster.

Stephanie decides now is the time to ask a line of questions to poor Mindy.

"Are you happy the little big guy is almost here? You were sick a lot," Stephanie reminds Mindy, and I cannot figure out if she means to be bitchy or it is her genuine way of trying to relate to people.

"I didn't stop vomiting for like the first half of pregnancy, the nausea was the worst, then the cravings—well, that is just crazy. I craved French fries in ice cream. Now I am so big, I don't even have room to eat."

"But it's not like you were sick all the time, right?" I ask as an internal freak-out begins.

"Hmm yeah it was all the time," Mindy confirms.

My face drops.

"But it's fun getting all the baby things, no? I mean picking out the bed and toys?" Lauren tries to throw in a positive and looks at me like she knows where my mind is heading.

Mindy gushes, "Yeah, that is the best part. We picked out the stroller and car seat early. That stuff is like buying a car, so many options and models. My husband loved it."

That violin in me is warming up again with a thought of Josh doing that. He seems like someone who would overthink the model of a stroller.

"Sounds fun," I say softly. "But is it really uncomfortable the farther along in the pregnancy you get?" Because cozy thoughts aside, my body is going to have to push out this thing.

"It's not exactly a picnic, no. I'm freaking out over the delivery. My sister was in labor for twenty-six hours," Mindy mentions.

My stomach sinks. "Twenty-six hours?" I gulp and my look of fear must be strong. Thankfully, someone ushers Mindy into opening some gifts.

In that moment, I feel it is all too much and I do not know if I want to throw up or faint. Cake. Cake is the answer.

Grabbing another plate of cake, I decide to get some fresh air. My legs decide to walk me to Josh's office, because that is apparently a forest of fresh air. Knocking gently on his door, he looks up from his laptop.

"I brought you cake, figured blue cake and music wasn't really your scene." I walk to behind his desk and flop the cake on a duck covered paper plate down. Then decide to perch on the edge of his desk looking at him as he sits in his chair.

He leans back and looks at me, slightly puzzled. "Why is that?"

I shake my head side to side. "Just figured you are more the party with champagne as opposed to parties that revolve around diapers," I admit.

"Right, fulfilling the evil prince profile to the max," he breathes out.

Biting my inner lip, I know the next minute may boost his ego slightly, but I can't help it.

"…it's really sweet of you. Looks like you bought her a giant gift. The baby present, I mean."

"Hey, even I know Mindy deserves butterflies and unicorns the next few months. That baby sounds like it is going to be a monster to push out." He grins to himself and I can't help but smile.

"Do babies run big in your family?" I wonder aloud.

He gives me an odd look. "Do you really want that answer?"

My face sinks, my stomach drops. *Oh great, just great.*

There is a pause.

My foot nudges his leg. "And it's also incredibly generous of you… the maternity leave."

He looks away like it is nothing. His modesty is doing a number on his sex appeal.

Josh rolls his gaze back to me. "Anyhow enough about my staff. How are you feeling?"

Propelling myself off the desk, I walk toward the window. "Considering I am going to throw up a lot, get really fat and have twenty-six hours of pure hell then I would say I am handling today quite well," I say blankly and his mouth forms a grin. I look at him and it makes me irritated that he takes pleasure in this.

"Don't laugh at me. I am serious."

Josh gets up off his chair and walks toward me. "I am not laughing. I am trying to keep up with your changing moods, which is nothing new for me. But now there is actually an explanation for your crazy attitude."

My face must give him a warning. "No. Before it was you and now it most definitely is all you and your little prodigy that found a habitat in my body."

It only makes him laugh more, and how I manage to keep up this facade of back and forth is even making me laugh at my mental state. Because looking at him, I see something different. My resolve for the man is weakened. Hell, it was weakening the moment our lips crashed onto one another all those weeks back.

Speaking of which, I look at his mouth and it looks like it may be extra soft today. Extra delicious with a taste of buttercream icing lingering. His hands I bet would show me a lesson or two about me barging into his office and telling him everything is his fault.

Wait a second—a week ago he wanted to do just that. I wanted that too.

There is a tingling running up and down my body that decides to form that desirous aching feeling between my legs. The upper two buttons on his shirt that are loose are screaming at me. *Come play, come play...*

The tautness of his shirt is highlighting his firm chest.

"You okay there? You look a little light-headed," Josh inquires as he gently touches my arm. I snap back into the moment and hope I wasn't drooling.

Get. A. Grip. Layla. Get a grip.

But his chivalrous move of concern means he is now in my bubble and it sends quivers up and down my body.

My fingers begin to play with his loose buttons. "Yeah, just was thinking." It comes out airy and playful. "I'm disappointed, that's all. I didn't get to see you without a shirt on the other night when we slept." *Whoa*, I threw on my flirty voice with a fake pout there.

Screw getting a grip and cooling off. I have needs and wants to fulfill.

His cheeks tighten as he tries to hide a grin.

"I know my body does do a number on a woman's satisfaction scale." He is brash, yet I love it. My other hand finds the buttons along his stomach.

As I am about to let my body press into his, Josh steps away and lets a hand glide through his hair as he clears his throat.

"I have a meeting in two minutes," he mentions.

Okay. Message received.

I begin to strut my sexy self out of his office, but he calls my name.

"Layla. Maybe take some rest this afternoon? You have

had a lot of commotion today already." He looks at me with eyes that are all parts concerned and dictating.

"Right. I am just the carrier vessel." I snicker then storm out. Positive, I heard an audible grin form on his face again.

———

LAUREN SITS on my sofa drinking wine from a glass.

"Shouldn't you be at the office?" I ask her, amused as I clean up colored pencils and my sketch pad on my desk in my living room.

"Nah, I put in extra hours last week during end of quarter financial closing. Plus, I need to drink your wine supply since you now have no use for it." She adjusts her body to lie on her side.

"Right."

"How is it going with baby daddy? He seemed a little on edge at the office the last few days," Lauren comments, and I look at her curiously.

"Yeah, well, I am sure I am partly to blame for that," I admit and flop on the big lounge chair. "That man irritates me sometimes."

Lauren comes back up to sitting with a questioning look.

"But he is supportive, right?"

"For sure. He is almost calmer than me about the baby news. But now I feel like he sees me as his responsibility and nothing more," I divulge. Lauren raises an eyebrow to me, and I continue. "Before the news, he was trying every way to get me into bed again. Made me feel like I was the only object of his desires." *And he would bang me into oblivion over and over.*

"And now?"

"Even though I said we need to cool off, take a break. He

hasn't tried once, that's not him. Normally, he would ignore what I say and still try to persuade me. Now, I'm just the pregnant one. He wanted me to stay at his place the other day so he could take care of me while I vomit. I mean that isn't yelling let us have sex," I say this and realize I may be borderline ridiculous. Confirmed by Lauren's laugh.

"Are you saying, you want to have sex with him again? This isn't a hormonal thing, right?"

Looking at her, I cannot answer. I want him again. *A lot.* Now, I feel extra sensitive and my brain cannot think clearly.

"Why do you need to wait for him? Before, you had no problem telling him like it is, definitely don't stop now. Tell him you want no-strings sex for the sake of the baby," Lauren advises as she drinks the last morsel of wine in her glass. "And I think it isn't just sex. I think you really like him."

"I-I maybe find myself liking him, yes," I slowly draw out my confession.

"And backtrack a second. You two slept in a bed and did not do anything? Doesn't the guy have a guest room that one of you could have slept in? Something of the emotional nature if flaring between you two."

I look at her and my brain registers her reflection. Because it is true. "I guess it's no big deal. I mean, we are going to have a baby; nothing gets more emotional than that. Plus, he was just taking care of me," I try to downplay the reality.

"I know sometimes you struggle letting guys in, but if there was one person that you should let in than it's the father of your child. It sounds like you don't mind at all he is taking care of you. It's the first time I have seen you let a guy do that for you."

Before I reflect too deeply, my door buzzes. Heading to the front door, I have no clue who it could be as I'm not expecting anyone. The doorman from downstairs hands me a box and I say thanks. Returning to the living room, I place the box on my coffee table and Lauren helps me open it.

"Well looks like baby daddy sent you a gift. But this is unusual?" Lauren states as she examines the contents.

But to me it is perfect. "No, it's exactly what I need." I smile.

A box full of buttermilk biscuits.

22

LAYLA

Just my luck, my brother has his birthday party a few days later. This means I need to stop by his place to fulfill my sister of the year duties. It also means I must face Josh, who I have managed to render away from my bubble for a day or two. The man has a protective streak, I've learned. It's a little overbearing at times. Stuck to the basic check-in texts of how the morning sickness is going.

It's not that I am avoiding him, I am just trying to figure out how to play this going forward since he obviously lost any attraction to me since we found out he has super sperm and I decided to set the rule of cooling down. Sounds like a lose-lose situation for me and for some reason it bothers me.

Noah's living room and kitchen are flowing with people. Everybody has drinks in hand as the music plays. My brother has a great place on the twelfth floor on the near north side with a place a lot like Josh's. Big windows, clean finishes, no chance of finding a candle anywhere. It screams bachelor pad. Working my way from the front door, people say hi to me as I head to the kitchen. Once in the kitchen, I set the white box of birthday cake on the counter.

"Hey Rachel, here is my brother's cake. His favorite," I beam because I do love bringing him his birthday cake every year. Rachel, his girlfriend, opens the box and a look of disappointment washes across her face. Her tight frown is almost as stiff as her outfit and hair in a bun.

"Hmm. I was hoping it would be a red velvet cake," Rachel comments rather dissatisfied.

Oh geez, just what I need when I am battling nausea and raging emotions.

"Well, *Rachel*. My brother loves giant chocolate chip cookie cakes and it's what he has every year," I explain rather curtly.

Rachel touches her necklace then heads off with her face looking like she sucked on a lemon.

I shake off my annoyance and grab a fresh glass from the cupboard and a can of unopened club soda in the fridge then pour it into the glass. All the other options are looking bleak.

Because well… alcohol… baby… a no-go.

"What the hell!?" My favorite man of the week hisses through gritted teeth and comes to lean against the counter next to me then leans closer to me so nobody can hear. "Are you drinking?"

Looking at him, I give him a glare. "Relax. It's just club soda," I justify sharply. Then I throw on a forced smile and continue to talk through my teeth. "If Noah asks, it's filled with vodka. Since appearances are key now for my brother not finding out that… well… you know."

"Yeah, I know. I was there. For the creation and the news," he reminds me with knowing eyes.

Seems like he is on a roll this evening of being that itch that I cannot seem to scratch.

Josh steps out to look at me in full view and as he is about to speak, my brother comes to join us.

Noah gives me a quick hug. "I am so happy to see that you both are not ripping each other's throats off for my birthday. Couldn't have asked for a better birthday wish." Noah smiles.

Josh and I look at each other.

"Nah. I may need him around for a while. Work and all," I say blankly, but my gaze stays on Josh as my lips slightly quirk, which earns me a warning glare from Josh.

Noah nudges my arm. "Actually I think Josh may have finally found someone."

I gently cough and wonder where this conversation is going. "Oh?"

"Why would you think that man?" Josh asks with an amused smile and his forehead forms lines.

Noah points his drink at Josh. "I don't know. You seem different lately. A bit cagey. It's been a while, so you are due for someone to have some fun with."

He is going to regret that sentence one day.

I cannot help but slightly laugh to myself.

"Right," is all Josh manages to mutter.

Noah then nudges Josh's arm. "Plus, I caught him looking at a photo of some chick in a towel on his phone."

I nearly choke and turn my choke into a cough into my fist. Josh gently rubs his face with a sly smile he is trying to hide.

This is not cool.

"Something tells me that you shouldn't be looking at his photos, Noah." I sound a tad judgmental and my eyes don't blink at Josh who finds this quite a thrill, I am sure.

"Relax. At least he is getting some action, right?" Noah mentions and I gently shake my head to myself.

"Who says he is getting any action? Maybe Josh isn't

actually delivering on his policy of making every female's wish come true." My piercing gaze hopefully rattles Josh.

Noah shakes his head as he walks off as Josh scratches the back of his neck.

"Well, that was fun," he states, amused.

"Was it?" I slide my gaze around the room while I take a sip of water from a bottle.

"How are you feeling?" he asks genuinely.

Rolling my eyes. "The same and you don't need to ask me every time you see me."

Annoyed clock about to go off.

He is about to say something, but a brunette with big blue eyes and a big bust arrives and steps between us.

"Josh, it has been such a long time. So good to see you. Crazy that you are here." The brunette smiles and gives him the I'm-down-for-anything slanted look.

Not in the mood to witness this.

"Hey Miranda. Not *so* crazy as Noah *is* my business partner. It's been a year or two, right? Listen, we can catch up later. I'm kind of in the middle of something," he tells her, but his eyes stay on me.

But I have been in this place for ten minutes and already I need out. My stomach is reflecting my mental state now and both are not looking too promising.

"It's okay. You two mingle. I need the ladies' room anyhow."

Oldest escape line in the book and well—yeah, I am feeling a little light.

Five minutes later, I am emerging from the guest bathroom in the guest room. Everyone forgets about this place. Except, Josh—who is waiting as I open the door from the bathroom.

Walking past him toward the closed door to the guest room, I am stopped by his hand managing to grab my wrist and wheeling me in, so I am within a breath's distance of him.

"Clue me in, Layla."

"Nothing to clue you in on."

"Really? You seem a little off and I am quite certain I was picking up some classic Layla annoyance undertones via text."

He begins to rub my arms and the feeling is soothing. His magic touch.

"I just... I was."

He gives me the entertained waiting smirk.

"Ugh, I'm not your responsibility. I am not just someone you need to check up on," I begin.

"You kind of are," he returns and I give him an annoyed look.

"Can't I just be the one you wanted to sleep with?" I admit, looking up at him.

A laugh escapes him from the back of his throat. "You wanted us to cool off and take a break."

I groan at my own doing. "I know. But it just feels like, I don't know... it's harder than I thought and I thought you would still be persistent. I don't know. I really am not thinking clearly right now."

"You think I don't want to be persistent?" he asks with his eyes narrowing on me as he slowly begins to walk me back toward the spare empty dresser in the room.

I shrug a shoulder. "I kind of feel like you don't see me that way anymore since the baby news. You have not tried once and in your office, you brushed me off. And if you don't want me that way then fine—but I may have some needs." I do not even know how that sounded other than I was maybe challenging him, but I allow myself to get trapped between the dresser and Josh.

His hands firmly rest on my hips as he presses his body to me and his mouth within inches of my face. "Whoa there, sweetheart. No way in hell are you screwing someone else with my baby inside you if that is what you are implying. If you have needs, then I am here," he informs me rather sharply then one hand finds my hair and the other hand allows his thumb to rub my cheek.

His sense of protectiveness and ownership for me, weakens that spot between my legs.

"This has got to be hormones or some test. Is this a test? Because it's a little crazy."

"Is it?" I nibble on my bottom lip.

"Yeah. It is. You set the cooling-off rule and now you seem to be changing your mind. Do not think I don't want you. Of course, I want to do everything to you that you would let my mouth or cock do to you."

A mischievous grin forms on my mouth. "But not your fingers?"

He has to smile. "And my fingers. But you were right, we have a few extra factors to think about now. It's complicated."

"I know this is a bucket of complications—wait a second. Since I am not allowed to sleep with anyone else due to your territorial rights you seem to have expressed, does that mean that…" It drags a little and I hope he can finish the sentence for me.

He seems to be entertained with me. "You mean if I will sleep with someone else?"

My eyes look at him impatient as I just want an answer.

"Wasn't planning on it," he confirms.

Miracles.

"Okay." It comes out bluntly.

"If you did not have our unexpected news floating in your head, would you have stayed after I tied you up?" His fingers tuck some hair behind my ear and a thumb rubs my bottom lip.

"I think I would have, yes. What would you have done?"

"You would have had a long night ahead of you." He smirks.

"That sounds fun."

"But fun isn't going to help us right now. Not when we have a baby factor," he explains.

I have to smile. "I am impressed that you can keep your very big dick in your pants. Because I am basically throwing myself at you."

He laughs softly. "Well my very *big* dick knows we have to keep our head in the game for our little baby that is coming. Plus, I have a photo on my phone to look at when I get desperate."

My forehead rests under his chin, but still, I slap him gently on the chest for that comment. "It was a weak moment. Just guard it with your life, even better delete it. And you're right. So, I guess that means a break on the sleeping together front?"

"Never going to delete it. Not a chance. And sex—yes, at least until we maybe know it won't be an added complication. Sleeping—not on a break. I don't like you being alone when you are not feeling well."

"Okay."

I realize we are holding one another. It feels natural. It feels like I am floating. And not because he has cast magic on me.

Pulling away from his embrace, I run to the bathroom again. This kid is turning my life upside down. Luckily, this time I do not need to throw up. Instead I need water on my face as I am dizzy. After a minute, Josh rubs my back.

"Come on, let's get you out of here."

I laugh. "Not so easy, Houdini. It's my brother's birthday. If you and I go missing then that screams red flags that we do not need right now. I will suck it up for the cake then head out."

We begin to walk toward the door, and he stops me again to let his hands encircle my waist. "Okay. But I am going with you. Don't think for a second you are going to play the stubborn as a mule card tonight and ignore me."

"I think I am debated out with you for the week. You win. I will find you and we can discretely leave."

He nods as he gives me that signature side slant of his mouth that even makes the corner of my toes run wild.

I like this perseverance he seems to have with me. The way he wants to take care of me. I have never had someone be this way for me. It softens me and I am not used to that.

———

AN HOUR LATER, we are at mine. After changing into a soft black cotton short jumpsuit with lace edging, I head to my bed where Josh is laying in his boxers.

"Really? This is what you usually wear to bed?" He gives me a distracted grin.

"It is and it's comfortable. Sorry you have only seen me naked or in your shirt in bed," I answer as I get adjusted in the pillows.

"Oh, I'm not sorry I've seen you only naked or in my shirt in bed. But this is a new look that has me telling my big dick to behave," he admits as he lies on his side to look at me.

"Apparently in the second trimester, I will be like a rabbit," I state randomly.

"Yeah, the app did say that."

I laugh and swat him with my arm. "You downloaded an app? Wow, you are really into this. Does it tell you what size the baby is?"

He nods as he drapes an arm around me, and I am not sure that move was part of our rules.

"I actually told my sister the other day. Sorry if I was supposed to keep it a secret, but she lives in Colorado and will keep her lips sealed."

"It's okay. Lauren knows, but you probably figured that already. You're close with your parents?"

"They are good parents and we speak on a regular basis. My dad worked and traveled for work a lot when I grew up. So, we didn't see him much, but when we did, then he was a hundred percent there."

I realize a possible thought. "And you wouldn't want that for the baby?"

He squeezes my arms. "You don't beat around the bush... but yeah, I don't."

"I get it. When our parents passed, you realize what you miss when they are not around."

"You were in college when they passed, no?"

"Yeah, I just had started. They were killed when their car spun on an icy road. It was unbearable at first, but now it seems so long ago that sometimes I forget it happened. Noah and I managed to make life go on."

"Are you sad they will miss the baby?" he asks tenderly as he pulls me tighter and kisses my forehead.

"Geez, we are going deep. I haven't thought about it that way. I had a good eighteen years with my parents and of course I wish they were here. But they are not. I got used to that reality already years ago. Sure, I have extended family, but Noah is my close family and he has done a lot."

"Is that why you feel indebted to Noah?"

"A little. He paid for my college and took care of everything related to our parents' death. Sold the house. Did everything a twenty-three-year-old shouldn't have to do. Because of him, I am doing well now. Hope he isn't disappointed with this unexpected news." I look at Josh and realize he has been staring at me intently.

Josh looks at me with a puzzled look. "I don't think he will be, it's not like you are a teenager. You are an independent woman now. You definitely are strong-willed."

"Oh, and you are not? Isn't that why you and Noah had a fight? You went with your own tune for a client?"

There is a pause.

"It doesn't matter, Layla. It doesn't matter."

I can't help but sense that there is something more to it, but I shake off the thought.

I am exhausted from the last few weeks. In fact, between finding out there is an unexpected souvenir in me and throwing up like an erupting volcano, I have not had much chance to think about what I want. It was only supposed to be sex when we had those few days and here we now are about to embark on parenthood together and being just parents together also doesn't feel right. It feels like something is missing from that equation.

23

JOSH

Sleeping together just to sleep—it's new in my book. There have been a few nights when our little creation made her throw up for hours, and there was no way I was going to leave her alone. Plus, my eyes really enjoy watching her lay in my bed with her legs on display and sheet tangled around her body. Feeling her warmth next to me and hearing her subtle breathing.

I deserve a medal for behaving though.

Noah is away on business and it is one of those non-productive days at the office. I decided to leave the office at three which sent Karen my assistant into a tailspin, but some-times you have to throw some extra excitement her way. I head to Layla's where she is probably working or sleeping. It is either one of those two these days.

Arriving at Layla's, I use my key. The key happened because one day she was so sick she couldn't leave her bed. Not even biscuits were a saving grace that day.

When I open her door, I am taken back by the loud music. Walking toward the kitchen, I slow my pace. Then take a casual lean against the kitchen counter with arms and ankles crossed, my face very much enjoying the view.

Not only is she in cute little shorts that barely pass as shorts, but she is swaying and singing at a hundred percent effort. Is she singing along to Drake on the Bluetooth?

She sings as she moves her body standing behind the kitchen sink, her back to me.

"Somebody is a good girl," I offer with a smirk and she turns around startled and lets out a gasp for air.

"Where did you come from?" she asks, surprised as her hand is still on her heart overcoming the fact that I am A. here, and B. witnessed her solid interpretation of Drake's *Hold on, we're going home*.

I let my winning grin spread across my face. "Your dreams of course."

She shakes her head at my response as she turns down the music. "Funny. Hey—I heard from that early pregnancy workshop today. The one with a long waiting list. They said I could join as a spot opened up. It's a little early, but it is for early pregnancy."

I grab a bottle of water from the fridge. "Sounds good. Is that the one that my sister recommended?"

Because Harper has been sending me a barrage of texts with pregnancy information including what rocks and crystals should be left around the apartment and pregnancy yoga classes to attend. I showed Layla the texts the other day and she laughed for five minutes straight. We agreed that laying crystals with essential oil under our pillows was a hard no.

We had enough voodoo magic with Luna Ray and her tarot cards.

"Yeah, and it's actually… also for you… if you want to come with?" she hesitantly asks.

No reluctance from me. "Absolutely. Sign me up."

A wide smile spreads across her face. "Good. Because they actually have a workshop tonight."

Drinking from my water and smiling to myself. "Let's go be top students then."

———————

SITTING in a room with a few other couples who are also first-time parents to be, we find ourselves on a yoga mat with a few pillows and a ball that you can probably bounce on. Dim lighting and candles with soft Tibetan music in the background add to the ambiance of the room.

I am beginning to doubt what we signed up for. Everyone is barefoot and the teacher speaks in this delicate voice that I am positive is not her normal voice. It can't be. Who is born with that voice? I already forgot her name, so my mind just calls her guru lady.

Before we start, there is an introduction round. It is awkward, almost excruciating.

Layla tells everyone our names, and then the interrogation begins.

"How long have you two been married? Sperm-doner? One-night stand like me?" A pregnant lady who seems quite quirky smiles.

Layla brings her hands out to indicate to stop. "Not married, definitely not the sperm donor and not my one-night stand either. He is the father of my child; we are doing this, and we have had amazing sex in the process."

There is that feisty woman I adore. Proud of her too.

"Shall we keep this show moving?" I ask guru lady.

Guru lady adjusts her sitting position and smiles.

Guru lady gives her words of wisdom on healthy eating for pregnancy, classes to do later in pregnancy, when to start having a birth plan and constantly reminded us that connecting with the baby already starts now.

"Okay, now if the partner will take the mother between their legs."

I should never have doubted guru lady.

Looking at what other couples are doing, I realize they mean Layla needs to lean back against me as she sits between my knees. Layla gives me a look that says 'this is interesting,' but she obliges and finds her way to sitting on the floor and leaning back into my body then resting her arms on my legs.

"Great, and now you are going to take time to connect with the baby. You are all early in your pregnancy, but already your baby can pick up your energy. It's important to take moments each day to connect with the baby and each other creating a supportive and loving bond. Now if you both place your hands on the mother's belly, we will practice breathing and connection," the guru lady instructs us.

Looking at the other couples, I am relieved to see that other dads-to-be are also doubting this. Like *really* doubting this.

My arms loop around Layla's body and my hands inter-twined with Layla's. Our hands rest on her tiny little bulge that is beginning to change ever so slightly. Her body presses more against mine as I feel her breathing. I am holding her, touching her belly and we mold together.

"Don't laugh," Layla murmurs softly to me, but I think it is more to remind herself.

Guru lady speaks again. "Great. Everyone is connected to their baby. But really now is about connecting with each other to be there for the other as the pregnancy progresses. Take the next few minutes to breathe, talk and hold each other but never let your hands leave the belly."

Everyone focuses in their yoga mat bubble. I feel Layla

move slightly in my hold and she sinks more into my body. My nose breathes in her coconut smelling hair that is half up.

A sigh sounds from the back of her throat. "This is comfortable," she notes softly.

I kiss her hair, it comes naturally.

"I'm not complaining," I reflect softly and her fingers tighten with mine.

"Should we try breathing together?" she asks, then slightly turns her head to look at my face. Her face tells me she finds that idea ridiculous.

"Uhm, yes?" I ask, puzzled because I am not sure if this is another test.

But soon we find our breathing syncing as I hold her with my arms wrapped around her and our hands on her belly. After a few moments, I cannot help myself and I kiss her cheek and linger. I can feel her cheek muscles move from a smile forming.

"Josh."

"Yes."

"Is it really bad if I say that I think I want to skip all of this pregnancy prep stuff and just go straight for an epidural?"

I laugh softly. "No. You will rock it whatever way you want to do it." I have no doubt.

After a moment, she says, "Hmmm, this is nice. I actually do not feel sick. It's nice just taking a moment for whatever this is with the baby." It comes out gentle.

My arms tighten more around her. "I think so too."

"Boy or girl?"

"No clue. Do you have a feeling?" I ask because the app told me that the women tend to have a better feeling.

"Hmm, I have some theories. But I don't think I want to find out, do you?"

"I guess this was a surprise already, so what's one more?" I mull it over.

"Hopefully, he or she has your nose," she comments gently as she becomes dead weight in my arms as she has completely relaxed.

I smile at her comment.

We enjoy being in the moment for another minute or two. Finally, guru lady hits a gong and we hit the end of that class.

Walking out of the class we find ourselves on the street corner with the sounds of cars whizzing by.

"Not sure that was for us?" She tries not to laugh.

"You mean guru lady and energy? Yeah, she was a little eccentric," I admit and give her a knowing look.

We begin to walk.

Layla gives me the side-eye. "Thank you, it means a lot that you came."

"Of course, anything. We will try anything you want."

It is in that moment that I realize I really do mean anything. I am drawn to her. More than just physically. Anything is everything. That includes us and any possibility we may have.

I give her a side glare but realize she did not pick up my subtlety.

"I am happy I did. Not only for the entertainment, but it is good to do these things together...for the baby." My hands find my pockets, but our arms slightly graze the other.

Her lips part and the corners of her mouth twitch to almost form a smile. We look at each other for a moment.

"It's time, Josh," Layla states and I know what she means.

I stop walking and grab her arms to ensure we are looking at each other. "To tell Noah?"

She nods yes. "I can't keep it from him. He is my brother. A big part of my life. Your life too."

My lips curve in, but I nod. She is right.

"Okay. We tell him when he is back from his business trip next week. Maybe take him to lunch?" I suggest.

She smiles. "Yes, a very public place is a good idea. I am not sure what is going to rattle him more. The fact I am unexpectedly pregnant or the fact it's with you."

We continue to walk, and our arms graze one another.

"Definitely it's me," I state, and my mind is going to the many scenarios of how I will need to play this.

———

THE NEXT DAY, I am sitting in my office, clicking away on my laptop, and Layla knocks on my door.

"Hey baby daddy," Layla whispers loudly.

I smile to myself before looking up from my laptop at her. "Yes, baby momma," I respond with the same tone.

Fuck, she is wearing an olive green sweater dress thing. Would match perfectly with that bra and panties with the same color that I have seen her in. Those ankle boots with little heels are asking for a trip around my neck too.

But we are trying not to complicate things and we are doing a damn good job of floating into something positive.

Layla stays leaning against the door and looks at me with a coy look. I get up out of my chair and walk to the front of my desk for my usual spot to sit and watch.

"Hey, why are you here? I thought you were only going to come to my office once a week to do Mindy's work."

Layla takes a few steps forward. "I didn't come to work. I thought I would stop by... to see if you want to go out to lunch?"

My face is a mix of surprised and impressed.

Wow. She is taking initiative and it seems like those

prenatal vitamins are giving her that extra dose of vitamin D to put her in a good mood.

"Yeah. That sounds good." *Really good.*

Layla steps closer and there is only a step or two between us. Her eyes sparkling as they look up to me. There is a pause, but a breezy pause. The air filled with a light and playful mood.

"To strategize telling my brother, *of course*." She struggles to keep a straight face. Because admitting what she wants and enjoys is far too difficult for Layla Wells.

Our eyes hold.

"*Of course*," I confirm.

I want to take her lips to mine right now. It could be a quick one that nobody would see. Enough to knock her brain into a frenzy.

But my attention turns to Karen, my assistant, who comes running to my door with a look that I have only seen on her twice. Both times were for the same reason and both times did not bode well for me.

A breathless and panicked looking Karen starts to speak, but I already know what is coming. "S.O.S. Josh, your sister has been trying to reach you and—"

My hand goes up to stop her, I do not need her to finish that sentence. My hand then travels to my forehead for a rub of fuck-me-I-am-in-trouble frustration. Layla looks at me, perplexed.

Karen shrugs her shoulders. "Sorry," she offers her sympathies and walks away.

I motion my finger to Layla to give me a second, as I grab my phone that was laying on my desk. There are nine missed calls from Harper and one from my mother.

Damn you, silent mode.

Quickly, I touch my phone screen and Harper picks up after one ring.

"I am so sorry. Mom and Dad like to surprise you, you know that," she begins.

Yeah, because my family likes to surprise me for a visit. Has happened twice now, hence why I know Karen's look of terror when she came to my door. She does not like to deliver that news. My family is great, but timing is not their forte.

For example, now when I have a woman in my office who I want to desperately fuck and who is carrying my child, their grandchild. Yet we still have not figured out how we are going to do this going forward nor have we told her brother slash my business partner. My parents decide now is good timing. In fact, great timing for a freaking family visit.

Shaking my head. "When do they get here?"

"This afternoon. They have a layover in Chicago on their way back from Mexico before returning to Connecticut," Harper explains.

I look at Layla who is trying to figure out what is happening.

"Pretty confident they could have gotten a direct flight back to Connecticut. Tell me you didn't tell them?" I plead to my sister on the other end.

"No way! I only said you had a lot of changes coming your way... that could be anything!" Harper tells me innocently. My head sinks to my hand again.

"Talk later, Harper. Thanks for this one. I will be sure to repay you around your wedding date." Before she can respond, I hang up annoyed and agitated.

Layla looks at me with lines on her face and hands on her hips. My mouth quirks quickly before returning to my frown and sitting on the edge of my desk.

"Uhm... everything okay?" she reluctantly asks.

My jaw moves side to side. "So, my parents are making an unplanned surprise visit."

"Okay? When?"

"Today." My voice hitches and Layla's face goes blank as she swallows.

"I will just skip this visit? I stay? I hide? What do you want me to do?"

Quickly, I grab her hands in mine. Not caring if anyone can see.

"I know we haven't told Noah yet—he is back next week. Maybe we just introduce you on this visit then share the baby news later?" I suggest as my eyes try to read her face.

"That's a good plan." She tries to offer me a faint smile. Then her head bounces softly side to side. "But who am I to you?"

She may kill me in a second. Any bridges we were building may burn. But there is only one way we may survive Geraldine and Henry Ives.

"Uhm Layla, did I mention my parents are quite conservative?"

Her finger comes up to indicate she needs a second. Her face turning a shade of white.

"Sorry. I think our baby is making me really dizzy," Layla tells me as she falls forward and my hands grab her arms to catch her in my arms.

As she falls forward, I see that we have an audience at the door to my office.

"You're going to be a father?" my mother's voice exclaims in shock with my father standing next to her giving me the stern eye.

Timing. They really have impeccable fucking timing. Their forte.

24

LAYLA

S itting in the back of the taxi with Josh, we are on our way to meet his parents for late lunch. I experienced a slight victory by managing to escape his office to be sick in the bathroom and fix my face to appear somewhat respectable. Meanwhile, Josh managed to get his parents to leave. After finding me, he let me know that his parents would meet us at the restaurant. While he did offer me an out, one look at his face told me that even I cannot leave him alone in the trenches.

Plus, they will be part of this baby's life. Just like Josh will be there when I tell Noah. I should be there for him in return. Also, I am completely intrigued by his family. He mentioned they are conservative people. Conservative people raised Josh and his sister? I struggle with that as Josh seems like someone who did not follow rules and broke many hearts in the process. He is not the kind of guy waiting for marriage to screw someone into space.

"Really, I am so sorry for this. It didn't even register that they would pop up unannounced," Josh apologizes profusely as I throw a mint in my mouth.

"It's... okay. But why do you care so much what they think? Where is your my way or the highway personality today?"

"Says the one who is afraid to tell her brother."

I hold my hand up "Okay. Fair point. So how do I play this?" I look at him curiously.

His look tells me that I should prepare myself. "Right... so can we just for the sanity of us all in this moment pretend that we are together... together. We can explain it better in a few months after they adjust to the idea of a baby out of wedlock is on the horizon." Josh scratches the back of his neck.

I continue to freshen up my face with a fresh coat of lip gloss. A laugh escapes me.

"Fine," I tell him, not entirely thrilled. But no point making this situation worse. "Josh, I don't do half-ass performances. So, if I have to do this, then I am going all in," I warn him.

He rolls his eyes and I am not sure if he is worried, scared, or excited about that prospect. He should be all three.

"What's our backstory? Give me something to work with. What am I channeling for my performance?" I snap my fingers.

He leans his head against the window already exhausted from today and puts his hand to his forehead with a sigh. "Layla, they are not idiots. They know we obviously had sex to create a baby."

"Okay, so your son had his way with me many ways for four days straight is the story I run with," I tell him seriously. But when he looks at me and shakes his head slightly, I cannot help but let my eyes give him a funny look and his mouth curves up. The humor he finds in me in this moment makes it well worth it. Maybe a little relief overcomes him too.

The taxi is a little rough on the turn and I slide down the leather seat into Josh's warm body. He leans forward to get the driver's attention.

"Hey man, a little easy, please. We have delicate goods back here." Josh slightly shakes his head to himself as the driver holds a few fingers up to show he heard.

I can't help but let my lips tug into a small smile. The way he indirectly keeps on taking care of me is sweet. I'm not sure he noticed my face soften.

I touch his thigh. "You're going to be okay?"

"Yeah. This just wasn't part of the agenda for the day, but it will be fine and if it's not, then I still don't care."

My head rolls against the headrest to look at him. "Ah, so you are relaxed. Because I was going to offer you a blowjob to calm you down."

His head rolls against the headrest to look at me with a neutral look. "Great. Now I have to arrive to lunch with that thought in my head. You may be trying to kill me. Thanks."

Arriving at Two Tomatoes, a favorite spot amongst our circle. We are ushered to a booth in the middle of the restaurant. Geraldine and Henry Ives are sitting on one side with iced teas, and Josh and I slide in on the other side.

Mrs. Ives has perfectly dyed brown hair that she must get permed to match her perfect makeup. Accompanied by gold earrings and chain necklace to match her turquoise pant and blouse outfit. It is when I look at Mr. Ives that I see a resemblance to Josh. Maybe not physically, but in behavior. Even the retired version of Josh wears a light-blue button-down shirt with suit coat and has foxy gray hair. My guess is he still charms the ladies at their country club, which Josh explained quickly in the car about conservative he meant appearances not religious.

I throw on a smile. "It is so lovely to meet you both, apologies for earlier. It's been a little shaky with the pregnancy."

"Don't need to apologize, dear, perfectly understandable." Mrs. Ives attempts a smile as she looks at me as if I dropped from the sky.

Mr. Ives clears his throat. "This is, uh, a surprise."

Josh straightens his posture. "We were going to wait to tell you both, but yes, Layla and I are having a baby."

"I thought for sure Harper would give us our first. This is a shocker, but we are going to be grandparents Henry." Mrs. Ives beams and touches her husband's shoulder and seems to be getting emotional.

"I just didn't know you were in a serious relationship. You did not mention anything during your last visit. You two must have been together quite a long time for this to happen. How long have you been with Layla?" Mr. Ives tries to put the pieces of the puzzle together.

I struggle to not let myself laugh. "Do tell them, Josh. How long have we been together?" I loop my arm with his arm and he gives me the death glare.

"We have been together for a while. Layla and I have known each other a few years as Noah is my business partner, as you know. It was a slow burn then finally Layla succumbed to my charm and the rest is history," Josh explains rather calmly.

"Yes. A romantic trip to New Orleans and his appeal was just overbearing. Magic just exploded between us. You really trained this one well on the charming front, Mr. Ives." I give Mr. Ives my flirty smile and my hand finds Josh's thigh under the table to sink my nails into his flesh as he clears his throat.

"I did teach the boy well." Mr. Ives has a suave, proud look on his face. "Don't get me wrong, Layla. We are happy to see a beautiful and successful woman on Josh's arm. The fact you are Noah's sister is also perfect. Just—we are a little lost about what this all means."

"You will be on his arm then at his sister's wedding in a few months, right?" Mrs. Ives gives me a hopeful look.

"I will…" I draw it out as I look to Josh for a clue who gives me a gentle nod. "Most definitely will be on his arm at his sister's wedding. Fat as a whale." *Will I be on his arm?*

"She will be the most beautiful whale there is." Josh kisses my cheek and I flutter my eyelashes at him.

"I mean, you both will be married before Harper, I assume. Something low key and soon?" Mr. Ives suggests more than he asks. All the while, indicating to the waiter passing by for a scotch, which Josh adds on another one to the order.

"No, actually. Layla deserves a beautiful non-rushed wedding; we will wait until we can have the wedding of her dreams, even if it means after the baby comes." Josh gives his parents a tough look.

"But you are engaged? I mean, we can tell our friends and the guests at Harper's wedding that you will be married soon, right?" Mrs. Ives questions, but she does not seem like she actually is that bothered by that fact.

I step up to the plate for my big monologue. "We are engaged and let me tell you—your son did a real number on me with that proposal. Wow. Hotel, dinner, he is such a great dancer too and even breakfast was a treat with my favorite foods."

Josh cuts in, "She loves southern biscuits for breakfast."

Mr. Ives is lapping this up and I almost feel bad we are so convincing. "How did my son ask?"

I nudge Josh's arm, then take his hand in mine. "Well, where we were and when, I think we will leave that out of the story. I mean, the grandkids will have to hear this one day, right? Let's just say we had a lovely room." I wink to his parents as my fingers slide along Josh's arm, and then I look to Josh to give him a playful nod.

His look is priceless and if he is annoyed with my antics, that grimace is telling me otherwise. He is having fun.

I continue. "The rest of the story, you tell them sweet pea. It was your voodoo magic that got me to say yes." My eyes give Josh a daring look.

Josh looks at me to let me know he has accepted the challenge then back at his mother. "I held her and said Layla, 'you were a headache to me all these years. Every conversation with you is a witty and playful challenge, and I love challenges—especially when I get to look at your beautiful face. When you let me defuse our issue that one time then I knew, I knew that you had to be my wife. So, Layla Wells, will you marry me?'" Josh drinks from his iced tea like it was a piece of cake that just came out of his mouth.

Me? I am falling. To where? I do not know. But the destination is looking promising.

My body melts a little and my heartbeat picks up. There is a strange scrape in the back of my throat, because in my mind I am impatiently waiting to hear how our dream proposal ends—because it sounds lovely.

Then I am snapped back into the reality that we are putting on a show.

"Of course, she said yes. I mean, it is me. My good looks and charm does it every time for her." That cocky look spreads across his face as he points to himself.

Mrs. Ives wipes a tear away. "Just so happy, my baby boy

finally has a great love and you're both going to have a baby."

Perfect time to direct us to baby talk. I need to move us away from the dream scenario of Josh and me. The growing human in my body is making me think and feel that the dream scenario could be quite marvelous.

Grabbing my phone, I pull up the app with the ultrasound photos and video.

"Here. Here is the little one." I show the future grandparents my phone and Mrs. Ives asks if I can send her the photos, which I answer of course.

"We don't want to find out until the end what we are having, but we know that he or she is probably going to be strong-willed." Josh beams and gives me a nod.

Both grandparents seem to be a little emotional and genuinely happy. Even Mr. Ives, that old fox, is letting his eyes swell.

"You will have to let Harper and me arrange a baby shower for you, my dear. You should already start a register somewhere. Helen from the club just became a grandmother and the stroller her daughter wanted took twelve weeks for delivery. Twelve weeks!" Mrs. Ives is now in excitement mode.

The waiter finally comes to take our order, because we shooed him away about three times already. Even the college-age kid could pick up on the deep conversation vibes happening at our table. Owe him an extra tip for his patience.

BLT for Josh's father, Oriental salad for Josh's mother, club sandwich for Josh, and chicken wrap for me. Mr. Ives asks for a bottle of champagne to celebrate the next generation in my belly. As the waiter leaves, Josh stops him.

"Can you make sure in the wrap there is no blue cheese

and the chicken needs to be cooked really well. Thanks," he says it so casually as if it is nothing.

But it is something, and it makes me warm inside. He remembers all these little pregnancy facts that even I forget, and he follows through like he cares. No, he does care because the man only knows genuine. If he is a big jerk, it is probably because he genuinely is in that moment. If he does something to show he cares, it is because he does.

It's not pretend when I bring his hand that is interlaced with mine to my mouth for a gentle kiss.

As the meal continues and I play with my wrap—because nausea again—I listen to Josh with his parents. He may be annoyed by them and they may seem a little stuffy to some, but they are good people. A solid family. His dad asks him about work and seems to be truly proud of Josh and his career.

Since they know Noah already so well, they know about my parents. They make a point to let me know when the baby comes that they will be glad to help care for the little boy or girl when I recover and if there is anything else to just say. Mrs. Ives—Geraldine—since I am now on a first name basis shows me photos of Harper's wedding preparations and tells me how excited she is. They both seem like they hit the jackpot as in the same year a wedding for one child, a baby for the other with a wedding in the cards.

It gives me a sour feeling in my stomach that we are deceiving them about Josh and me—our relationship. And I cannot figure out what bothers me the most. The fact we are lying to them or the idea that our somewhat fake relationship is something that I think I may want to try.

25

LAYLA

Walking along the sidewalk after saying goodbye to Josh's parents, I squeeze Josh's interlaced arm with mine.

"Not so bad, was it?"

Josh sighs. "I guess not. Almost entertaining, but I would not expect anything less from you. Thanks. You were a star in there. Totally believable," he compliments me, but in truth, I am not sure I was pretending the whole time.

We stop walking and we look at each other.

"No problem. They are really lovely people, Josh. You are lucky to have them. This kid will have grandparents that seem very excited for him or her," I tell him whole-heartedly in a soft voice.

He looks at me with parted lips. "They are. Just they see things a little to the right and I didn't want to have a blowout quite yet about you and me—"

"I get it. I do. But I feel a little bad. We painted them a lovely pretend love story that one day they will realize isn't true. Guilt here," I admit and raise a hand.

He nods slowly. "Right, all pretend." It comes out so

gentle that almost I sense there is a thought or feeling behind the tone.

We begin to walk again, and we pass a baby store. Both of us look at each other and an agreeing look is shared. Stopping, we both look at the window display.

"I already see a discussion point." Josh indicates with his finger to the two onesies hanging on little hangers against the white backdrop. One is a blue Chicago Cubs onesie and the other is a black and white Chicago White Sox onesie.

A scoff escapes me. "A no-brainer. Cubs all the way." I grin.

His hand finds his forehead and pretends to wipe his head. "Phew. That is a relief."

I laugh and we continue to walk.

"By the way, Harper really wants you to come to her wedding. Even if it only as my plus one, fake future marriage aside. But I understand if you say no. No pressure." His look is endearing, and I should be more anxious, but I am calm.

"If you want me there then sure. I mean she is this kid's aunt and judging by what she sends you via text then something tells me her wedding will be a little crazy," I accept his offer.

He holds a laugh in, and I look at him. "In the last four hours alone—you agreed to lie to my parents and come to my sister's wedding. We even agreed on the best baseball team in the world."

Holding a finger out to him. "Hey, I didn't say they were the best baseball team in the world only in the city. And yeah we are more bearable around the other, borderline pleasant, maybe even enjoyable on a good day. Having a baby maybe does that to you." I smile.

"Is it just the baby?"

It's not. Really is not. It's been this way for weeks.

I am done playing games today.

"I-I don't think so." I'm truthful and his lips twitch.

He interlaces our fingers and electricity goes through my body as I smile to myself. We walk a little more in silence. A calming silence where the air dances around us and we take in the sounds of the city and the evening lights. Our hands connected to confirm the other is still near.

A yawn escapes me as I'm so relaxed around him.

"We should get you home, you need sleep." Josh takes out his phone and requests a cab via the app.

While we wait, we stand there looking at each other. A bit lost in a relaxing silence.

When the cab arrives, we slide into the back seat.

"I set it in the app that we drop you off first then I go to mine," he mentions.

"Yours. I want to go to yours." I grab his hand and he looks down at my hand then back to me with a smile forming.

"You're trying to ruin my app rating." He pretends to be annoyed.

A sly smile forms on my face as I undress him with my eyes. "Something tells me you won't be caring about that in twenty minutes."

He quickly leans to the front seat to tell the driver the change of plans. I pull Josh back to the seat. Pulling his hand closer to my body and resting it on my lap.

Our eyes meet and it is different.

We both move toward the other with looks of lust and a need to pounce on each other. His hand finds my thigh and he must feel my radiating heat, my hands touch his arms as he angles his body to me, and we lean in.

This kiss is going to be impressive, hot, and we will not stop until we reach his place when we actually will need to part to get out. The taxi guy even has some Motown on the radio. This night was meant to be.

Josh kisses my forehead and whispers against my skin, "Not here, let's wait until we are alone."

I like the sound of that.

It is too early to sleep, and we agreed we would only have sex after we figure out what we are doing with us, the baby, and how we will arrange that situation.

But I feel like I am starting to figure out things. I am certain there are possibilities worth exploring.

————

WE ARE quiet on the short ride back and in the elevator too. When Josh closes the front door behind him and we take off our jackets, I turn to him. My fingers slowly touch and run up his shirt then rest at the top where the top two buttons are unbuttoned. My eyes peer up into his and our eyes lock with one another.

"Layla, we said we wouldn't make this complicated and we agreed we would only do this again if..." he informs me, dead serious, yet his hands find my cheeks as he looks down to me.

This time has to be different is what he is reminding me of, and he is right.

"I know," I confirm and then let my face lighten as I grip his shirt tighter. "I know." My smile should tell him that I understand.

He *is* a smart man and his mouth slants into a grin as he moves in.

His mouth comes down to capture my bottom lip and our lips meet for a slow, soft kiss. My arms circling his neck as we deepen our kiss.

We have had sex together a few times now, we are having a baby together—but we have never kissed like this. As if it is our first kiss as two people who care and see a chance.

Our tongues meet in a slow tango, our lips gently brush and press the other's. Mouths angle to get more, more of the other. Remembering each other's taste and taking in the warm, firm softness of our lips. His hands move to my hair, because intensity takes over and we soar into a new unknown direction.

Josh lifts me, and my legs wrap around his waist as he walks us to his room and I feel his hard cock pressing against me which only sets me on fire more. When he lays me on the bed, I know this will be different.

We quickly take our clothes off and get under the covers.

He leans on his side and his hand comes to my stomach that is ever so slightly changing where he immediately begins to let his fingers dance on my skin, and it feels as if feathers are brushing me.

I quickly move to straddle him, completely aware that his twitching cock is wanting me as my arousal teases his length. "Please tell me you are not one of those guys who are petrified to screw someone with a baby inside them." My mouth slants to the side.

He gently laughs at my humor. "No way. But you will be my first someone I am screwing with a baby inside them."

"Oh good, we are confirming that's what we are going to do," I say seriously.

He grips my hips and flips me to my back, because he likes to take charge in the bedroom. His eyes roam me up and down as his hand rests on my hip. He seems hungry for me and I am thirsty for his mouth on me again.

"Yes?" I wonder.

He smiles. "Trying to figure out what position to take you in."

"Any. I am not that big yet. But can we just get this started, please?" I try to rile him, but really *please*.

My legs spread open to welcome him and he comes between my legs with his hands supporting his weight on each side of my body. Placing a kiss on the flesh of my breast and the pulsating between my folds intensifies. He reaches for his nightstand, but I stop him.

"Uhm Sherlock, unless there is something I don't know. You can't get me more pregnant, so we don't need a condom," I remind him with an elated smile.

"True. Great fact. Phenomenal news and I am safe." He gives up on the condom and I nod.

His lips find mine for a controlling yet decadently soft kiss with my hands finding his face as our kiss deepens and my legs wrap around his waist. His hands find my arms and he pins them against the mattress softly as his mouth drags down to my very sensitive and firm breasts. My hum filling the room.

"I think I'm going to really like how these change," he teases as his teeth catches a straining nipple before his tongue swirls and it sends a thousand little shocks to my inner walls that release silk.

"Me too," I moan, because I could come just from his mouth sucking on my nipples.

He treats each nipple as equally satisfying treats. Before letting his cock slide along my slit and rub against my clit making me ache for him. My hips roll to try and gain friction from his long shaft and he grins at me as he brings a hand to my cheek.

"Please take me now. I just want you inside me tonight," I whisper and he nods. We do not need foreplay now; we need to feel as close as possible and joined together.

The moment I feel him enter and move deeper, my mouth gapes open, but no sound comes out as my body may be in shock from such a magnificent feeling. My flesh wrapping around him as he moves inside me. His teeth gently tease my bottom lip to check I am still in this moment.

He slides into me so naturally and I close my eyes to enjoy the full feeling of him inside me and bare. Something I never do. My inner walls clutch around him from that realization that he is my first.

"You have no idea how much I've always wanted to feel you this way, I want to fill you up, Layla," he whispers into my ear sending a wave of tingles down to my nipples and clit.

"Mmm, that sounds *really* excellent."

"This is the way it should have always been between us," he adds with warm breath hitting my skin.

My hands come up to cup his face and to look into his eyes. I gently nod in agreement before leaning up to steal a quick kiss. He grabs my hand, kisses my inner palm in an almost sweet manner then lays our interlinked hands on the pillow. My head turns to see our hands together. The image intensifying a feeling in my chest. But I don't think, because the feeling of him sliding in and out of me as he grunts brings me back to the moment.

He starts slowly before finding a pace that has us both taking in every thrust that touches every nerve-ending.

"Is now the time to confess that I was thinking about you all the time when you were away and every time that we don't share a bed to sleep?" I whisper with a grin.

He beams as he moves in and out of me. "A great time to tell me. I should confess that you didn't leave my mind. You never leave my mind."

I lick my lips as I sink into our rhythm, my breath growing ragged. "Still a good time to confess? You are actually really likable, and I like you a lot. Like *really* a lot."

It makes him grin, but he does not lose focus on the task at hand. "I confess I think you are enjoyable too." He hits a deep spot in me.

"This is so... oh-oh." I am struggling to speak as my eyes roll to the back of my head. "You feel so good."

He moves in and out of me with my nails gripping into his back. When he hits that special spot that makes me yelp in pleasure, I let my thoughts float away. Instead I float into the feeling of his body as he has a way of taking control of my body that feels spectacular.

He does not go too fast or too slow, he knows how to find right.

"Come with me," he urges as he picks up the pace. The feeling of his pelvis rubbing against my clit as he is deep inside me helps me ride the wave with him.

Our mouths find each other again and our hands clasp firmer together. I am not sure how we got there, but when he let's go inside me. I already know I am quenched.

Completely satisfied.

We lay there like two lifeless limbs holding each other as he stays inside me. I feel his release leaking out of me, but I don't even care.

"Hey there," Josh whispers softly as his lips graze my cheek.

"Hey." It comes out drowsy before I nip his shoulder with my mouth.

"You okay?"

"Completely." My breathing shallows.

Our eyes meet and we can't help smiling at each other in bliss from this new tide that moves between us.

He kisses my cheek quickly before telling me he will be right back. He quickly returns with a wet towel for me. After a few moments of cleaning and readjusting, I lean on a propped elbow to look at him.

"Is it different?" he asks, giving me a sheepish look.

I have to laugh. "You mean because I am pregnant? Or the fact I am doing it with my baby daddy? Because both throw a spanner in the works."

He adjusts so he is laying on his side looking at me.

"Ah so that is where your mind went." His finger traces the outline of my hip.

I nod. "Is that bad?"

He shakes his head no. "But I guess this wasn't our first time having sex with you pregnant," he recalls.

I laugh. "You are never going to let it go that you tied me up pregnant, are you?"

He laughs with me. "No. It is too good of a story actually."

Josh goes to lie on his back with an arm coming out to motion to me to join him—I do. I lean against his chest and an arm comes around me as the faint beating from his heart is near my ear.

For a few minutes, we lay like this. His lips occasionally kissing my hair and his fingers brushing along my arms. I pepper kisses across his chest.

Josh lets out a sound under his breath. I peer up to him to study his face and he notices. "You know my father isn't my biological father?"

Immediately, I lean up on my arm to look at him. "No. No idea." This news almost astonishes me.

"My biological father was never in the picture. Didn't want to be a father, I guess. My parents were never together. My mother married Henry when I was a year old. He raised me, even adopted me. I only know him as my father." Josh doesn't look at me and I get the feeling he doesn't share this often; I don't think Noah would even know.

"Wow. I would never have guessed. It is so clear he loves you as his own. Is that why you are a go-getter in business, to make him proud? It's what he does in his own work, right?" I try to put the pieces together.

Josh slightly laughs. "Do you mean if it's the reason I am an ass to some? To impress my father? —I don't know. Maybe. He owns an IT company and does well. Finally, about to retire. Maybe I do want him to see that I learned from him. Never thought about it in that way."

"Is it also why you jumped right into the pregnancy? No doubts. You don't want to be like…" I do not dare say it as I do not want to remind Josh.

"No. No I don't want to be like my biological father—who I have never had contact with. And I also do not want to be like my dad. He is great, but he was not always around due to work. That's not what this child is going to get from me."

I give him a reassuring smile. "I know. I can see it already. I have no doubts."

I admire that he is so confident with his train of thought. At peace with the past. It makes me want to be open with him too. I lean against his chest again.

"When I discovered I was pregnant, I thought that I would finally get to rebuild the family that I was missing. It is hard some days knowing my parents will miss this, the pregnancy, a grandchild. Everything."

"Is that why you had no doubts too?" he asks, bringing his arm around me.

"Yeah, and the fact it was you. I know you," I admit. "Actually, it's more." I almost blush and try to not look at him. "I think one reason why sex is so good with you is because I feel safe with you. Even the first time. That does not happen a lot with me. I can let go with you."

"You can."

His eyes have an almost glint and it seems like he is really taking in my words. Almost as if he wants to speak, but he doesn't. Instead, Josh moves me so I am on my back and he brings himself over me to cage me in underneath him. Our lips meet for a brief and tender kiss.

"Look at us having a deep and meaningful conversation," he teases and my fingertips cradle his face.

"True. But I think we have talked enough for tonight. Can we just keep having sex tonight and worry about everything else later?" I state and realize it is the only answer I have that does not involve a decision or label of where we are heading.

"At your service," he confirms.

26

LAYLA

S topping in front of the upscale baby store, Josh grins at me and drags me with him as we head inside. After sleeping in from our night last night, we decided to go for a walk and ended up at the baby store.

"Are we sure it isn't too early?"

"We will just look. You're almost in the second trimester, the train is a rollin', Layla," he assures me as he does not let go of my hand and drags me inside.

The store is… overwhelming.

Everything beautifully displayed along white tables and flooring. Besides the usual clothes, toys, and bed linens that I am used to browsing through when friends have baby showers—I seem to notice the little things. Things I would never have thought of. Ten different types of cream you may need, items for the baby sleeping at home, items for the baby sleeping on the go, items for the baby sleeping in the summer, bottles, lots of accessories for bottles…

Babies need a lot.

But when a little elephant stuffed animal catches my eye,

I turn all googly-eyed and an audible 'aw' escapes me. I head straight to the elephant sitting on a perfectly displayed table with other toys and books. Josh following in tow. I pick up the soft elephant. The size of a teddy bear, but an elephant. Perfect shade of gray-blue fit for a surprise baby that we do not know if it is a prince or princess.

"He is cute, no?" I ask, waving the elephant at Josh. He smiles, licks his lips then takes the elephant from me.

"Yeah he is. Shall we get him for the baby?"

I look away, but cannot help my smile form as I look back at Josh. "I mean, it is only one thing, right?"

He nods and smiles as we go farther into the store. Commenting on items and Googling what half the stuff is. When we reach the strollers, Josh's eyes light up.

The smiling assistant comes to us. "Looking for a stroller?"

Josh looks at me and shrugs a shoulder. "We are *maybe* browsing. Figuring out what we want."

"Wonderful. There are many options. Do you want an all-around, city driver, one that's good for running, one that can accommodate more kids? Collapses on the plane? Do you need one to accommodate sand if you are at the beach?" The assistant lists and puts her hands together.

My face and stomach turn to panic. I'm overcome with a thousand questions running in my head. I can't even sugar-coat this. I'm freaked out.

My arm waves at my side. "Josh, I'm out. I cannot even. The stroller? No way. I leave that all to you," I tell him and indicate that I am going to look in the corner at cribs.

As I walk away, I hear Josh mention that he is looking for the Tesla of strollers. *Yeah, he's got this.*

After a few minutes, I calm down and look at cribs,

admiring the different options. Different designs, the color of the wood, the sets of neutral-colored linens. Taking into account the size and where it will go. My thoughts drift to what the baby room will look like.

The tags on the cribs send me into a flurry when it mentions delivery times depending on address. My head goes into a reality check of the thought that has once or twice popped into my head.

The where do we live when the baby comes thought. Do we try to live together? Surely, that is better for the baby. But are we living together as two parents or more?

I am snapped back to present when an arm snakes around my waist. Looking at Josh, he hands me a perfectly wrapped bag with tissue paper and a yellow bow. Glancing at the contents, I smile at the elephant and it seems Josh added a Cubs onesie too.

"Ready to go?"

I nod and we start to walk. "Did you give up on the stroller?" I ask, amused.

"No way. I already knew which model we are going for before we stepped in here," he confesses and wraps his arm around my shoulders.

We step back out into the weekend afternoon sun and a yawn escapes me.

"How about you go back home, and I will meet you there in a little while?" Josh suggests as he studies me.

Putting a hand on my hip, I look at him, curious. "Trying to get rid of me already?"

He shakes his head no as he smiles. "Not at all. But I need to do a few things for tonight and you could use a nap. You may also need a nap for what we will do later." Josh wiggles his eyes as a warning, which makes me crack out a laugh.

"Sounds like a plan."

AWAKING in my bed from an afternoon nap, I am quickly overwhelmed by something smelling quite edible from my kitchen. Rubbing my eyes and stretching out on top of my bed, I look at the clock. I got a solid two-hour nap in. Dragging myself out of bed, I look in the mirror and decide I should probably freshen up a bit. Looking in my wardrobe, I quickly decide that I should take things up a notch and I smile to myself.

Five minutes later, I walk into my kitchen and I stop in my tracks.

"This isn't my apartment," I state amazed as I take in the view around me. Josh cooking in my kitchen, candles on the table and a solid playlist playing.

Flowers. There are fresh flowers in a vase and red rose petals on the dining table with lit candles.

Josh looks up to me as he just pulled something out of the oven. "Your oven looks like it hasn't been used in years," he comments.

Walking into the kitchen to get a better view of what he is doing, I admit. "My bad. I used the oven once maybe six months ago to bake a frozen pizza. Didn't end well."

He chuckles as he continues working on the food in front of him.

As I investigate what is in front of me, I squint an eye. "This is…"

He looks at me to check if I am going to smile. "My attempt to cook."

I laugh. "Oh yeah, you mentioned something about that once. A hidden skill for when you want to get laid," I taunt him as I hug his arm and kiss his cheek.

"Go sit and I will bring you some moussaka."

Walking to the table, I grab a bottle of water on my way. "This looks impressive. Please take no offense if our kid doesn't agree." I slide into a chair and admire the perfectly set table.

"None taken," Josh confirms as he brings the food to the table.

Soon we have very edible food on our plates, and it tastes scrumptious.

"You are glowing today, by the way. Extra beautiful," he tells me.

I slam my fork onto the plate and let out a deep laugh. My hands go out in protest. "Okay. What the hell is this? Have you always been a romantic or are you laying it on extra thick to get laid?" I tease.

He laughs as he takes his beer bottle in his hand and leans back in the chair. "Getting laid is easy. All I have to do is piss you off and then I know I am getting some action." That cocky swagger is in his tone. "So, guess I am a romantic, impressed?"

Playing with my water bottle and letting my eyes search him as my cheeks tighten. "Maybe."

"Just maybe? I guess I need to up my ante."

"Okay. I am impressed. But really, have you always been a romantic?"

He takes a swig of beer and debates what to say. "I don't know. It has been a while since I was in a relationship. Admittedly, it wasn't my priority for a while."

"I figured. I hear the rumors next to the coffee machine at Ives & Wells and it doesn't paint you well."

This seems to make him proud. "Oh yeah? Nice. Anything good?"

My tongue circles my mouth as I pull my knees to my chest on the chair. "Nah. Only that you date a lot and I think half of project management thinks you're easy on the eyes. There is a debate on the size of your dick, but nobody has been able to prove it, so the bet is still ongoing."

He bursts out laughing. "I hope you're making this up."

I shake my head no.

After a moment, he shifts the conversation. "I had a look at your sketches on your desk. Are they for the baby?"

"Yeah. Thinking of maybe drawing something on the wall near the crib." That I have yet to figure out where it will go.

"Already nesting?"

I look away to laugh. "I don't know. I am a lot of emotions lately."

He puts his beer bottle down and grabs my hand on the table. "Happy? Is that an emotion you are lately?"

"Yeah—I think I am." I come off my chair and slide onto his lap, looping my arms around his neck, nuzzling my nose to his cheek.

"Good. You need to be relaxed and happy."

We take a moment to look at each other and we get lost in the moment. I kiss his cheek and then his forehead.

"Were you always attracted to me?" I wonder aloud.

He looks at me. "Yes." He is direct, I will give him that.

"Why didn't you make a move? I am not sure it really bothers you what Noah thinks."

His fingers run through my hair. "Layla. I was always cautious, but if I had any indication from you that I had a green light then I would have done something earlier. But the idea of you and me seemed to be a big deal to you because of Noah, so I respected that."

Logical, endearing, respectable, and this guy is pulling me in.

"I can't change the clock. But I can give you the green light now to do deliciously dirty things to me," I offer as I stand up. Pulling my long sweater dress up and off my body. I am left in the olive green lingerie set from New Orleans. Returning to his lap, I sit on top of him and encircle my arms around his neck. Already, I feel a strain in his jeans rubbing against my thin laced panties.

He draws in an audible breath. "This is… a very promising green light." He nearly purrs as his mouth finds my neck.

As he slides his mouth up my neck, I inform him, "this is the last time you will see me in this for a while. My breasts are getting too big. Better make it count."

With that, his lips land on mine. Things quickly escalate and he lifts me up and lays me on the table. There is a feeling of rose petals against my skin and the uncontrollable urge to raise my hips to him as he kisses my little round bump on my belly that popped out in the last week and his mouth drags lower.

"I love this. Soon everyone will see what I did to you," he admits in a firm, low voice as his fingers caress the edges of lace.

I laugh. "It turns you on that you marked me. Why am I not surprised?" The thought that he is claiming me brings a throbbing feeling between my legs.

Suddenly, the smell of smoke overpowers my nose. My eyes catch a glimpse of the candles next to me.

"Whoa there, Casanova," I warn him and place my hands on his shoulder to guide his head back to mine. "Your flowers and candles are about to set the fire alarm off."

Josh draws his eyes to my view and we both realize that our desire for the other overtook the basics of fire safety. We both start laughing hysterically as we quickly try to stop the candles burning the flowers by swatting with a kitchen towel and pouring water from a water bottle. Luckily, we manage to stop it from setting the alarm off.

His hands cup my face. "Never a dull moment with you, Layla. Never." We meet for an affectionate kiss that is as good as any dessert he has stored in the fridge. I'm happy and hopefully my brother senses that when I tell him.

27

JOSH

Sitting at Cups and Jars, the popular hotspot for Sunday brunch. Layla and I sit at a cozy table for two. The place is packed. Waiters walk by with plates of pancakes and eggs to tables filled with tired parents and screaming toddlers. Plates of avocado toasts arrive at young couples who are childless and probably planning which weekend market to check out. But none of it matters as I am focusing on Layla in front of me who is glowing as she looks at a menu.

"Know what you want?" she asks.

"Yeah, I do." It comes out subtle because I don't mean my brunch option. Already for weeks it's been on my mind, but the last forty-eight hours just knocked some sense into me, it confirms I have a chance.

The middle-aged waitress arrives to take our orders.

"Good morning, what can I get you two on this fine sunny Sunday?" The waitress with a nametag Katie smiles.

Layla smiles at her. "Good morning. I will have the momccino and the hangover supreme."

Katie lets a laugh escape. "That's quite a combo. Sounds like you are having a party."

I must admire the scene in front of me because there is never a boring moment with Layla.

"Oh, we did. Hence why the momccino is needed and the hangover special is because the idea of ice cream, bacon, and waffles sound pretty good right now. Can you just make sure the bacon is extra cooked and also the eggs too please?" Layla beams as she hands the menu to our waitress.

"And for you, young man?" Katie asks me.

"I am drinking for this one," I say, indicating my head to Layla. "So, let's do a Bloody Mary and since I am drinking for this one—" I indicate with my thumb to Layla. "Then it most definitely is not a virgin Mary and I will do the eggs benedict." I hand Katie my menu as she writes on her paper.

"You two seem fun." She smiles and walks away.

"You're really into these momccinos, huh?"

She puts her hands together in excitement. "It's the highlight of my pregnancy."

My hands go out to my sides. "Here I thought sex with me was the highlight of your pregnancy." I give her a fake frown.

She smiles at me. "Can't complain."

There is a pause and here is my chance to knock that momccino off the podium.

"Layla, we need to talk." I take her hand on the table. Her eyes shoot up to mine. "Where are we going?"

She bites her bottom lip and looks away then back at me. "Ah. *This* talk is upon us."

"Yeah, hence for my Bloody Mary order. The last two nights have been great but we need to think about what happens in the long run and when the baby arrives." I look at her intensely to study her and she looks at our hands.

"Right, the long run." It comes out slowly from her mouth.

"Tell me, I'm not still the guy who annoys you, but you love to fuck?" I ask, slightly amused and equally scared of her answer.

"You don't annoy me. Well, you do, a little. Just less. Sometimes only a tiny bit, like not even enough for a microscope to pick up. But since I give you a run for your money on the irritation front. I don't think that's the issue." She is being honest and a look that I can only describe of vulnerable spreads across her face.

Katie returns with our drinks. Layla swirls a spoon in her cup and I dip the celery in my Bloody Mary.

Taking a sip of my drink. "Yes! This is strong." I enjoy my drink; I need that extra kick now. "I think we should try."

"As in you and me?" It comes out gently from her parted lips.

My eyes lock with hers. "Yeah. As in not just sex."

Almost a glimmer of a smile forming graces her lips, but she seems a little taken aback from my boldness.

"I just don't know how to do this." She is almost radiant.

My tongue circles my mouth and my fingers go to circle the back of her hand on the table. "Leave it to me?"

She gives me a puzzled look.

Giving her a look that has secured me many digits from ladies across the city, I do my best to charm her. "I'm the boss, remember. Just listen and I will make sure we close the deal."

Layla looks away as a smile forms almost ear to ear.

"Careful there, boss, you may be marketing yourself as a romantic. I would hate to be disappointed." Still, she tries to rile me up.

I lick my lips; she is not going to give me an easy answer.

"I work in marketing; pretty positive I can persuade you."

She looks at me and with a smile that has her biting her inner cheek.

"Can I quickly run a market research survey by you?" Layla asks as she leans back into her chair and plays with the spoon in her momccino.

"Of course."

"Where is this coming from? It isn't just because of the baby, right? I mean that evolving feeling of two parents making it work for the child is a strong feeling."

"Oh so you listened to that podcast too?" I quip and she is amused.

Taking a sip of my Bloody Mary, I speak. "It's not because of the baby. I already told you last night that I've always been attracted to you. I think it was always on my mind the moment we kissed in New Orleans—you and me, but someone at this table was insistent we would only have a few days of sex only."

She rolls her head and looks at me as if she is debating what to say.

It was sex, but the way I enjoyed being around her already in New Orleans had been growing on me. I did not just want to see her to go at it hard and good. I wanted to see her smile and listen to her constant retorts that made me laugh. Watch her as she fell asleep.

Grabbing something from my pocket. "Plus, I think if it was just sex then I wouldn't have been holding on to this all this time." I hand her the napkin with her drawing and lipstick stain from that first night in New Orleans. Something in me already urged me to take it with me when I left the table. Completely unexplainable.

It catches her by surprise as she looks at what I just pulled out of my pocket.

Nice play Josh. Nice play.

Her eyes slowly slide up to meet mine with a smile forming as she realizes that I am telling her the truth.

"You kept it?"

I nod yes and her face lights up

"Okay." Her voice is feathery.

"Okay?" I double-check.

Nodding her head up and down. "Okay. My green light from yesterday is a green light for everything. Let us date, romance, upgrade our fling, whatever the hashtag is for it these days."

My face that managed to stay confident and strong collapses into the face of the guy who is falling for the woman in front of him.

Taking her hand, I bring it up to my lips for a kiss. "Well then, let's get started."

————

WAKING up to Layla in my arms is different this morning.

We've crossed the point of no return.

Even though—it's Monday morning—I decide to pull in my ownership card and play hooky. I mean, I will check my emails, I'm not that reckless, but I am not leaving my place this morning.

The sheets begin to rustle from the movement of a naked Layla waking up. A mumble escaping her mouth as I pull her tighter to me and my hand resting on her belly.

"Mmm… maybe we stay in bed all day," she murmurs.

"Would love to and we can, but we are meeting your brother later for dinner to tell him the news." If that does not feel like ice waking you up then I don't know what will.

She wide eyes as she looks to me. "I think we got this. We are professionals after dealing with your parents."

I have to chuckle slightly. "Different species, Layla. Anyhow, how are you feeling this morning? You've been better the past few nights."

Her eyes peer up to me and she grins. "It's sex. It must be the cure."

"It isn't just sex. It is sex with me and that is on another level," I tease her and she pinches my stomach.

"Your arrogance woke up strong today. But anyhow, I am starving."

"Really? That is great. Shall I order breakfast in? Croissants, beignets, egg sandwiches…"

"Burger. I want a burger for breakfast."

Kissing her forehead, I gently lay her back and roll out of bed. "Let me see what I can do. Stay in bed, rest. I will let you know when food is here."

I do what any sane guy who has a feisty Layla Wells knocked up would do. I order burgers for breakfast accompanied by momccinos.

I got this.

Twenty minutes later, I am leaning over the kitchen island with only sweatpants on, I check my phone for my latest emails and the Cubs score from last night. The doorbell should ring any second with our breakfast order. Then later today, we will meet Noah and break the news to him. Crossing that off the list.

When the front desk phones to tell me our delivery is here, I tell them to send it up. Heading to the front door, I don't bother throwing on a shirt as I know the doorman and since he sees Mr. Smyth on the sixth floor walking his dog in boxers, then my guess is my well-trained physique is a welcome change. Opening the door, I can already smell the burgers and special coffee. An unusual breakfast combo, but what Layla wants, she gets because her pregnant and moody is not a walk in the park.

"Hey Clive, thanks," I already say as I open the door, then stop in my tracks. "Hey Noah." That one comes out awkward. Maybe because Noah is unexpectedly here, and his sister is naked in my bedroom.

"Mr. Wells arrived as your breakfast arrived," Clive mentions and while I should question why my ridiculous monthly resident fees should guarantee no surprise visitors, Noah is on the approved anytime list.

That move came back to bite me.

"Thanks," is all I manage to utter, and Clive heads off after he hands me the bag of food and tray of drinks. Noah looks a little rough and I cannot think of why he is here at this time of day, but I can't shoo him away.

Noah follows me in. "Sorry man, it was a long night, and had no idea what to do, and Karen said you were working from home." He sounds somber.

"Are you okay? Thought you were flying back in this morning and we would meet for dinner."

Noah slumps onto a stool at the kitchen island as I begin to unpack the food at the counter. It looks like I got enough food for a family of ten. But figured Layla would need options.

"Rachel and I broke up." It comes out blankly and already I know that the guy needs an ear. But damn, this is actually good news. We were not Rachel fans. Still, I need to play the role of supportive friend.

I look hesitantly toward the hall to my bedroom, hoping Layla figures out we have a guest and stays put. Noah must pick up on my glance.

"Oh man, I'm sorry. You have someone over," Noah apologizes.

I interrupt him before he tries to leave. "Uhm yeah I do, but this is big news, Noah."

"Yeah, I mean, maybe I saw it coming. Wait—I didn't know you were seeing someone. Is it the woman from your phone?" Noah's face almost turns excited.

"It's, uh, well it's—"

Before I can finish my sentence, an oblivious Layla comes prancing down the hall in my shirt.

"Yay. Food at last," she sings. Then her face immediately drops when she sees our guest. In fact, all of us freeze in what would be considered a stand-off fit for a Western movie.

"Noah," she gulps out.

Noah looks between Layla and me.

"What are you doing here?" Noah asks with a hardened look. "And why are you in Josh's shirt?"

Match lit.

28

JOSH

L ayla holds her hands up, but I decide to intervene.

"This isn't how we wanted you to find out," I admit with my hands sliding through my hair.

Noah hops up from sitting. "Find out what?" He shoots me a murderous stare as his hands stay firm on the countertop.

Layla puts a hand over her mouth, and I see a familiar look. Her face turning pale and in thirty seconds she may just vomit. She quickly runs off and it leaves Noah's gaze to focus on me.

"It just happened," I begin. Deciding to play this cool because you know what? She and I are happening no matter Noah's opinions. I finish unpacking the takeaway box. "Want something to eat?"

"Are you kidding me right now? You want me to easily move on from the fact you are sleeping with my sister?" He raises his voice.

"Yeah."

Play this cool and casual.

And then without thinking. "You can have whatever you

want, but the burger is Layla's as it has extra pickles." I turn to look at Noah who looks at me confused.

As he should be because I literally walked us into a landmine there without thought.

"Extra pickles? Sounds like she is pregnant or something," Noah jokes bitterly and then his head snaps up.

Unable to think of a response as Noah stares at me.

Noah's face changes.

It drops.

Eyes glare.

This situation is a pin dropping and the city of two point five million turning silent.

This is bad.

"Tell me she isn't pregnant?" Noah demands as he slowly begins to walk toward me. I stand taller and square my shoulders. His eyes blaze and my eyes stay firm.

"She is—uhm—she is not *not* pregnant?" I crack out and my face must be looking quite cartoonish.

Real cool man, real cool.

Noah's face turns red. "And how would you know this?"

The man is fuming, boiling, and ready to explode. I should probably clear anything that resembles glass or utensils to the side now.

Oh man Josh, just suck it up and face the man.

"Because… it's my baby. We are having a baby." My eyes gently close then open, before I can register the face waiting for me. Layla returns.

"False alarm. What did I miss?" She looks between us and then her face sinks as she slumps against the counter and realizes the gravity of the situation.

Noah's brutal look doesn't leave my pathway until it does and his eyes glue to Layla's stomach that he gapes at before looking to Layla's face. "I don't know. Maybe the news you are pregnant as confirmed by your unusual burger request for breakfast or the news that my business partner and you have been together for how long it is?"

Layla sighs. "This isn't how we wanted to tell you."

Noah quickly looks at Layla. "How far along are you?" His gaze returns to me.

"It happened in New Orleans." Layla looks to the floor, not that she is ashamed, more that she is waiting for her brother to let it sink in.

Noah drops his face to his hands and grumbles. "This is fucking unbelievable. I don't even know where to begin. On a business trip, you two got together. And you have been together since and hiding it from me?"

"Well," Layla drags out. "Together since is stretching it a bit, we were trying to figure out some things."

Noah's nostrils flare and his eyes fume with a new dose of anger. Raising his voice again. "Fuck you, man. You use my sister for sex, have unprotected sex and knock her up—"

"We used protection!" Layla and I say in unison.

"He didn't use me for sex. I do also make decisions on my own, you know," Layla defends.

But it's my turn to speak. "It isn't like that and before you go all macho on me. I will support Layla in every way possible. We should have told you sooner, but we knew you would act crazy. *Point proven.* Maybe you need to cool off. Celebrate the fact that you're going to be an uncle." I'm equal parts cocky and relaxed. Confident with my words.

Layla grabs her burger and offers one to Noah.

"Lost my appetite," Noah snickers.

Layla quickly begins to attack her burger while standing by the counter. "Well, I didn't. I'm starving and haven't eaten normal in weeks."

"How can you eat during this conversation?" Noah ponders.

Layla is busy pouring ketchup on her plate. "Because in all honesty, my mind has narrowed in on one thing only the last two hours. A burger. If I have to choose between you two cooling off right now or eating my burger. The burger wins hands down." Her seriousness in that declaration makes me chuckle and even Noah lets a glimmer of a smile form.

"You haven't been feeling well?" Noah sounds concerned.

Layla is busy eating her burger and cannot talk.

"No, she has really bad morning sickness, which is not only in the morning by the way. No clue why they call it that," I explain softly as I lean against the sink with ankles crossed.

"But everything is okay?" Noah asks.

I nod yes.

"Please, can you two hash out your differences later? Now, I really want to enjoy my burger in peace, and I think I will even manage a second burger," Layla begs. I cannot help but smile to myself. "Why are you even here now?"

"Oh yeah, I even forgot. Probably because this bombshell tops my own," Noah admits as he rubs his forehead. "Rachel and I broke up."

Layla looks at Noah with bulging eyes. "And? You should be celebrating." She speaks with a full mouth and I admire her candid answer.

Noah looks to me and I shrug a shoulder. "I mean yeah, she wasn't the one, was she?" I ask with doubt.

"You both didn't like her?"

Layla and I look at each other then back to Noah to shake our heads no. "It's honestly Monday, so I am not going to lie," Layla tells him as she grabs a fry.

"Why didn't you tell me before?" Noah asks, confused.

"Because I thought she made you happy," Layla answers.

"And I thought you two hated each other, but now you are making me an uncle." Noah seems to be lightening up.

"Oh no." A hand finds her mouth and I know where this is going. "What have you done to me?" She looks at me before running away. Seems the burger was a bad idea.

Noah and I watch her disappear down the hall. Leaving us alone and we look at each other. An eerie silence filling the kitchen.

"Want a coffee? Or a normal non-pregnancy inspired breakfast?" I ask as I head to the coffee machine. I do not wait for an answer, I make two cups.

Noah lets out an exhale as he leans against the counter. "Okay man, Layla is away. This is where brother bear comes out like the bear from *The Revenant*."

Turning to him, I am ready for this stand-off. "Let's hear it."

He points a finger to me. "Never mind the fact that you and I are business partners. But you both work together in some way. What would you say if I slept with my direct report on a business trip?"

"I would say good for you, you deserve a good night of action." I am a little arrogant there and that was a shitty line to say given the facts of the reason we are having this conversation.

Noah charges at me. "Is that all she is to you? I swear to God if you did this because it seemed like a great thrill then there is no point even continuing this conversation."

My hands come between his arms to push his arms away. "It isn't. Layla and I are happening. So, either get on that bandwagon or stay away."

Again, not doing great on the word front today.

I should not be telling the guy to stay away from his sister.

"No way am I staying away," Noah confirms as he shakes his shoulders and begins to pace the room.

Adjusting my shoulders, I continue. "Good. Because I am going to try with Layla, really try. So would appreciate your support as your sister is not exactly a piece of cake when it comes to me. Crap, that was the wrong phrase to use." Because she is like a piece of cake that my mouth would devour every last crumb of, which her brother most definitely doesn't want to hear.

"What I mean is, she is going to make me work for it. She is moody, hormone-crazed, and our child is having a party inside her. Not easy terrain for me to drive."

"Now you have the audacity to ask for my help?"

This can go many ways; I cannot read him right now.

It's a solid minute before the guy gives me a clue. "Fine," he answers, but it's short.

"Good. Settled. Anything else?"

"Yeah, asshole. We are in a pickle. The fact she is my sister—fine, we settle that in private. But the fact she and you... well... while she works here. Yeah, this is tricky," Noah explains.

"Is it? Many couples work together. I think it is more you and your stupid employee handbook that has a problem with it. You do realize that in our office of forty people under the age of forty that nobody cares. I'm confident Jared from IT is boning Bonnie from projects which is even more scandalous than your sister and me," I try to justify, because I am positive if he ditched the handbook then none of this matters and he would make a play for Lauren.

He continues on. "What is the game plan for the office?

Are you two out in the open or what? I don't want staff uncomfortable."

"You mean are we screwing on my desk or—?" I have to ask to rile him, which this isn't the right time, but was too tempting.

Noah brings his hands to his forehead. "Oh my god this is my future life. You both messing with me at every chance."

"No, we aren't in the open other than Lauren nobody knows and my parents by chance. It doesn't need to be a secret. Besides, she is starting to show in case you didn't notice just now."

"Yeah, I noticed."

"*I definitely* noticed," I admit, and it comes out dirtier than it should. Probably because I told her in the shower yesterday morning how her stomach and breasts are growing, which is not a deterrent to my hands or mouth.

"Dude, I think I liked it better when you both despised the other. Now I feel like you both will always mess with me."

"Nah, I'll behave."

"What about Radnor? Shouldn't he know the two main people working on his big account are together?"

Shrugging a shoulder and scratching my chin, I answer. "Don't see why we need to disclose that, but Layla isn't going to travel much anyway in the coming months."

"You decided that or she did?" Noah gives me an arched eyebrow.

"Not her. So yeah, she went ballistic. But even you must see my logic." I smile to myself, remembering how annoyed Layla was.

Noah holds a hand up. "Got your back there."

Finally, a small win.

There is a pause as his steely eyes stare at me.

"I swear Josh, if you so much as don't support her in any way then our relationship as business partners is done."

Raising my voice slightly. "Noah, do you really think that is even a question? Do you really think I wouldn't support her?"

Noah looks away and then back to me. "She doesn't deserve anything less than A-game effort for romance and a long future with someone. If that's not what you can offer her, then I'd rather you both focused on co-parenting or some situation like that."

"You're right and A-game effort it is," I promise with a scout hand in the air.

Noah adjusts his shoulders as he takes his coffee cup. "I'd love to say do the honorable thing and marry her, but she would freaking hang me out on a BBQ. Just please don't break her heart," he pleads.

How can I break her heart? She has not even given it to me, has she?

Nonetheless, I say, "I won't." And somewhere inside me, something warms in a place I never felt before. Maybe it's the gravity of the situation pulling a string in me. It's the idea of her giving her heart to me, it swirls around my own.

"Nothing should change between me and you," I mention to him.

He looks at me and thinks for a moment. "Don't hurt my sister and it won't." Noah is firm and I understand. "Give me some time to cool off, we have a lot to talk about and you better believe I will be watching you like a hawk."

A half-smile forms on my face. "I wouldn't have it any other way."

Just then Layla returns and this time in jeans and a T-shirt.

"No fists thrown? No throw-down out in the back alley?

I'm disappointed," she jokes as she comes to lean next to her brother at the counter.

My eyes looking between them both.

"How are you feeling now?" I ask with a worried look.

Her shoulders sink. "Biscuits, I really only can tolerate southern buttermilk biscuits. Lesson learned." She pouts.

"Geez, what creature have you two created?" Noah jokes at last with a lightened look.

Layla goes to give him a hug and I can tell they need a moment. So, I head to my bedroom to finally throw on a shirt. Stopping in the hall when I hear them speak.

"It's okay. I am fine. Especially now that you know," she assures him.

"I know you will be. But you're my responsibility—" Noah begins, but Layla interrupts, "I'm an adult now. You did an amazing job taking care of me when I still needed some-one, but now it's my job to take care of someone else. He or she is currently residing in my belly, but I need the next months to mentally prepare for this."

"You will rock it, Layla. And as much as I want to murder Josh right now, he will be a good dad too."

"I know he will," Layla says with a soft voice and although I cannot see her, I imagine a warm smile on her face. It makes me feel soft inside.

"I'm going to be an uncle, I guess?"

"You mean my free babysitter? Absolutely," she challenges.

I go grab a shirt quickly and walk back to the kitchen picking up on the conversation again.

"I feel like I need to create a handover for Josh if he has to put up with you for the rest of his life," Noah jokes, but in my head, I am thinking how I'd gladly take that handover.

"Just promise me, you will go easy on him. I know you. I

know you will have a big brother speech to give him. But for weeks I've been scared to tell you, because I don't want to come between you two. So please promise me that it will be okay."

I arrive in the kitchen to Layla smiling at Noah.

Noah holds his hands up and he looks at me. "I'll try. I will be tough, but not as tough as the Tom Kane argument."

In that moment, my heart sinks. My eyes move to Layla, whose face has turned pale and her bottom jaw drops.

"What did you say?"

An oblivious Noah answers, "Tom Kane, the client that Josh turned away."

Layla's eyes immediately move to me, and her face is unreadable. Already I know that something has changed between us. Until ten seconds ago, Layla knew I turned away a client, but she didn't know that the client I turned away was her ex that she hadn't seen in years.

29

JOSH

Barging into Noah's office first thing the next morning, the guy looks at me as his feet rest on the desk. He has been waiting for me.

"Tell me she is okay?" I head to his floor-to-ceiling window to look out.

Noah swivels in his chair to look at me and our eyes meet in understanding.

"She's okay. Just needs some space," he confirms, and relief fills me.

I haven't heard from her since she left my place after yesterday's bombshell.

"You know she finally told me about what her ex did, but I am wondering why you didn't tell me first?" Noah asks.

"She told you?" I am skeptical.

Noah nods. "Yeah. She wanted me to understand why I shouldn't be mad at you about letting Tom Kane go, but I told her it is already water under the bridge. I can't figure out why as someone who has a sister that you didn't tell me to begin with and we wouldn't have had the argument."

I sigh. "I debated, but Layla told me once that she never told you and I felt I had to respect that."

"Why didn't you tell her?"

"Why make her have a bad day?" My shoulders sink.

"Explain to me what happened," he requests.

"I was prepping for my meeting with Tom Kane and Lauren came into my office and noticed my screen. She mentioned that he and Layla used to date. Obviously, my body went into jealousy mode even though I had no claim to Layla and I tried to remain professional. But when Lauren commented that I should watch my drink then I knew it was him. The asshole who drugged your sister's drink once."

"You still put Layla in front of me. You didn't tell me."

"I wasn't going to break her trust," I admit.

Noah leans back in his chair and crosses his arms to listen. I walk around his desk and grab his hacky sack from the desk to toss between my hands and begin to pace.

"I knew what I had to do when I went into that meeting,"

Sitting across from the asshole Tom Kane is not the highlight of my day, week, and probably year.

"We are not going to represent you," I say firmly as I lean back in my chair at the conference table. Remaining poised and confident considering I'm internally telling my fist to stay down.

Tom laughs with his hands in his pockets as he looks out the floor-to-ceiling window of the view of Lake Michigan. "Why is that?" He turns his head to me with arched brows.

"I think you know why." My face remains neutral.

"No, I don't. Other than you are asking for business suicide when word gets out, you turned me away." This asshole is arrogant and we are still only on the surface.

I propel myself out of my chair and walk toward him with strong strides.

"You could go around saying that, but let's cut the bull-shit. You only wanted to work with us for one reason and Noah may not realize it but I sure as hell figured it out."

"He has no remorse, Noah. He really thinks he did her a favor."

Noah's hand goes into a fist. "I will kill him."

"Maybe that is why I didn't tell you." I give him an understanding glare. "Anyway, I took care of it."

My fist clenches at my sides and suddenly I feel satisfied with my boxing sessions in my twenties.

"Whatever you think you know you have it wrong, I am sure. Layla too."

"Are you kidding me right now? Positive she didn't get her drink getting drugged as wrong." I step closer to the douchebag with my muscles flexing underneath my shirt.

Tom holds his hands up. "Whoa. Relax. It was a long time ago, I am sure we can all look back on it and realize it wasn't a big deal. She and I were dating for a few weeks and she was a little uptight, needed to relax, I wasn't going to do anything to her. Was just helping her—"

I raise my voice. "Uptight? Her parents just passed away, you bastard. You drugged her unknowingly. She had no fucking clue." I shove him in the chest.

He looks down where I just pushed him and that disgusting smile returns to his face.

"Ah, I get it now." He looks at me and seems to be studying me. "You're screwing Layla... guess she finally relaxed." He begins to walk away, but not before I step in the way and grab his arm with force.

"Stay away from Layla," I snarl. "Find whoever the hell you want to represent you, but it's not us."

He jerks his arm away from me and licks the corner of his mouth before he walks away.

"He won't speak negatively about us, otherwise he knows we have a story to counter that isn't good for him. I already asked the police if they could do something since I have his confession, but too much time has passed."

Noah stands up and comes around his desk to perch on the front of his desk next to me and nudges my arm.

"I had no clue they ever dated. And I am thankful you did what you did. You put my sister in front of the business and that's a big thing. Especially as if the timeline serves me correctly then I don't think you even knew she was pregnant then, which means you really feel something for her even if there was no baby."

I take a moment to take in that thought. But there was no question in my mind, I hadn't seen Layla for a few weeks then but I felt the need to turn into Hercules to protect her.

"I do. She's been an unexpected surprise. And maybe I should fully disclose that I kissed her a while back and never told you," I admit.

Noah laughs and bites his inner mouth that makes his dimples show. "Wow, you really are going full transparency in this conversation. But maybe it's good you never told me, otherwise I would have never let you and her go to New Orleans together." His hand slaps my back.

"True. Then there would be no baby maybe," I reflect.

We take a moment to enjoy the silence. But I am still at a loss.

"She isn't answering my calls and I don't want to show up at her place if she doesn't want to see me. We were heading somewhere good, and I hope this didn't knock us back two steps."

"Really, just give her some space. I think you two will work out. I may even be joining team Josh, so I am rooting for you," Noah admits, and the corners of his mouth curve.

"I'll be waiting right here for when she is ready. Speaking of which, I want to cut down my travel. I do not want to be away from Layla, especially as she gets further along," I add to this already surreal conversation.

"Absolutely."

There is a pause and we look at each other.

"Are we good now?"

Noah lets out a sigh as he hops off his desk. "Yeah. But Josh, if you ever well—you know, put a ring on it. Then you better plan a full spread breakfast meeting to discuss it with me first." Noah is serious, but soon a smile forms on his face.

"No other way," I confirm with my face relaxing and lips tugging.

I shake his hand and we head in for a manly side hug.

"Now get the hell out of here and go distract yourself—it will be okay."

As much as he is offering sage advice, it doesn't help.

———

TALKING to Harper via video call, I have a glass of whiskey filled to the rim in my hand as I lay on my sofa. Harper seems to be cooking in her kitchen, and I hope for her other half that it isn't rabbit food.

"This is a mess," I confess.

"She is probably overwhelmed. Needs space. She must be getting kind of big now, right? I mean, I hear that is when women kind of lose the plot when it all becomes real, their minds can't think clearly," Harper offers her knowledge.

"Harper, she isn't that big yet. And it's a bit more complex. Finding out your current boyfriend had words with your ex who is an asshole can be complicated and I don't want to get into it with you to respect Layla, but geez, there are horrible men in this world."

Harper gives me a sympathetic look.

I continue, "but wish she would talk to me. Even if it is to tell me that we are going nowhere, or she is scared the baby may have my scowl. Anything."

"Sounds like you were watching out for her. Are you more upset about not hearing from her right now or the thought that you and her, well maybe it's only a parenting future?" Harper points her carrot at the screen.

"I guess the future part." I shrug before taking a generous sip of whiskey.

Harper jumps up and down. "This is great. You love her. You want it all with her, don't you?"

Thinking about it for a moment or two, I let a sound escape from the back of my throat. I do not think I have ever felt this. This uncontrollable want to have someone around me who I want so desperately to make happy as if it is the only way I can be happy. In the future, there is no one else I would rather wake up with. I cannot imagine someone who makes me laugh the way Layla does. How much fun we have. Sure, doing the whole family thing with her is a thought. But everything else consumes me almost more. Because before we knew we were going to be parents, something in my heart jumped when I thought of her.

I always wanted her and always put it down to want. But I think somewhere that want turned to love.

Hell, I really fell in love with her.

No point denying it. Holding my hands up. "Yeah, I do. I want all the bells and whistles. I love her."

Harper turns matter of fact as she aggressively cuts into the carrot with a sharp sound from the knife. "Okay. Give her a day to chill out and then if she doesn't come running to you then you do one grand final romantic gesture to let her know you love her."

I click my tongue gently. "Seems like solid advice. I may just follow it."

JOSH

I sit at my kitchen counter and look at the documents, brochures, and paint samples spread out. Trying to distract myself, I decided to dive into the world of pregnancy and baby preparation. Bad move on my part, as it is a headache. The half glass of scotch in my hand is making me question my day drinking habits as it's only four p.m.

My head freezes when I hear the soft click of my front door and the light pitter-patter of feet walking in, making me look up. The blood rushing in me is heading in only one direction—my heart.

"Hi," Layla says softly as she stops in the middle of the kitchen. She looks like she hasn't slept.

"You're here." She must hear the relief in my voice.

Immediately, I get up and walk to her. My hands finding her arms to soothe her and I pull her into a tight hug as I kiss her head. Although she lets me hug her, she isn't very receptive. She steps back, but my hands don't leave her arms.

"Do you want something to eat or drink?" I offer as I need to know she is staying healthy. I try to read her face and my own face is moving in all directions to study her.

"Maybe some water."

I go to grab her a glass of water as she sits on a stool at the counter. I know we need to talk. I come to sit next to her at the counter.

"Layla, I need to know where your head is at," I plead as she focuses on her glass of water.

"I'm horrible with feelings." She states rather bluntly.

I can only nod slowly.

"It takes me a while to wrap my head around things." She bites her bottom lip. "Why didn't you just tell me?"

"What was I supposed to tell you?"

There is a long silence as we look at each other.

"I don't know, but it's the reason you and Noah had an argument. You could have told him to avoid it."

I touch the top of her hand. "Wasn't my place to say."

She looks up at me with watery eyes. "You could have told him, and he wouldn't have argued with you. You could have told me so I wouldn't freak out so much about coming between you and Noah plus I would have…"

"You would have what?"

"I-I wouldn't have told you that you and I… you and I."

"We would have what? Tell me," I demand gently.

"I wouldn't have said we should cool off," she admits, and it takes a moment for my eyes to blink at her realization.

My upper lip twitches up. "But you did. I didn't want you with me because I was the hero. I wanted you with me because you wanted to be."

"You should have told me," she whispers.

My hands move to cup her face. "I was protecting you."

"I wasn't yours to protect," she barely speaks.

My mouth drags along her temple. "You're mine to protect. Both of you."

I can hear her hiccup a cry and I move my head back to look at her. My thumb catching a tear.

"It's okay," I assure her as I pull her close again.

"It's just I didn't think I would have to think about it again and then it kind of hit me yesterday. I guess it affected me more than I thought. You know that whole time in my life."

I kiss her forehead. "Layla, I think because I knew it affected you more than you thought was the reason I did what I did."

She nods.

"There is a lot happening right now. This, Noah finding out, the baby. I'm overwhelmed."

"It's okay. That's reasonable."

She lets me hug her and we stay in a long embrace. Finally pulling away and her mouth corners hitch up as she looks at the contents on the counter.

"Is this what you have been reading?" She sounds hopeful.

I nod and she smiles slightly. Her hands begin to shuffle the papers around and she picks up a brochure.

"We should probably plan some of this stuff, right? Maybe a good distraction right now."

I shake my head side to side and decide to roll with it. "If that is what you want."

Thirty minutes later, we are in a peaceful conversation over planning. It does the charm of distraction.

"Okay, so what do we still need to do?" I ask and realize I just accidentally pulled the trigger.

Her face flares and she looks like she may go back to putting me on the jerk pedestal that she had me on a few months ago.

"What don't we have to do? Open a baby register for the

shower your mother is adamant we are having, find childcare, decide on a birth plan, order the crib, think of names. What about baby stuff? Do we order two of everything? Where do we ship it to? Where does the baby live? Does the baby have your last name or mine? What is the theme of the nursery? Where is the nursery? What are we doing?" Whoa, she lists and rambles there, her hand running through her hair and letting her hair fall in layers around her face.

I grab her hands. "Are you okay? It's all going to be fine."

She looks like she may break, and I am not sure what is happening.

"What are we doing Josh?" Her eyes look at me glazed.

Oh shit, *this* conversation is upon us. Because when it rains, it pours.

The how are we together once the baby arrives conversation, living situation and all. But I am ready for this like white on rice.

Pulling her to my chest, I wrap my arms around her and hug her tightly.

"Hey, it's okay. Let's talk about this," I suggest, and she gently pulls away to look at me.

"When the baby comes, what are we…"

I look at her with soft eyes and a gentle smile. "I'm not messing around, Layla. You and me."

My hands find her face so we can look directly at each other.

"For the long run," I add with a soft smile. Then I frame her face with my hands. "I love you, Layla. I'm absolutely in love with you."

She looks like she wants to speak, but words are stuck in her throat. Instead her hands shove my hands away. "Maybe I should go."

What? Didn't see that coming. Thought for sure that this

would be when we profess our deep feelings for the other and then are incredibly deliriously happy that we don't make it out of the kitchen because we can't contain what our bodies want to do to each other.

"Don't go. We need to talk."

She pulls away and hops off the chair at the counter. "Just-just give me some more space," she pleads, and then she leaves me there clueless.

I am lost again.

31

LAYLA

"I just got so overwhelmed and a flood of emotions came over me. It is all happening, it's really happening. I felt I had to get out of there. To make sure that I am thinking clearly, you know," I sob as Lauren passes me another tissue.

We are sitting on my sofa where the past ten minutes, I have gone through a box of tissues that now lay scattered around my body clothed in pink sweatpants and a black tank top. Last night, I laid awake almost all night thinking about everything. Today, I tried to go for a walk to clear my head, but thoughts of Josh kept overpowering my ability to find any shred of Zen.

Lauren arrived and my floodgates opened like Niagara Falls. A mixture of hormones and good old-fashioned lessons from the school of life.

"It's a lot. Finding out about Tom, an unexpected baby and a guy all at once. You must be feeling that you now need to make decisions?" Lauren prompts me as she touches my arm.

"Exactly. Living together. Being together. Not for fun, if we do this then it needs to be for the long run. It's a jump."

Lauren offers me her warm smile as she pulls her hair into a bun. "Ah. So, it's the jump that is scaring you. If it's right or not?"

I sniffle and nod.

"Do you think he is the one?" she dares to ask, but hard love is what I need today.

My lips part and I think about it. In the last months, I have laughed more than the last five years combined. I go to sleep feeling so safe and adored, waking feeling excited to roll over to find Josh lying next to me. When he talks to his sister and parents on the phone, I want to listen to hear if he talks about the future with the three of us and he does. It sends a tingle of pure joy through my body. The way he cares for me, it feels as though I am soaking in the warm sun. I do not want this to be temporary. Every time the door closes when he leaves, I am counting seconds until I see him again. I want more of him. I want everything with him.

"We will always be connected. We are having a baby."

Lauren shakes her head. "Not my question."

After a moment, I nod softly. "Yes."

Lauren forms a half-smile. "So, Mr. Jerk is the one—"

I interrupt. "He is not a jerk. Far from it, actually. He put me in front of Noah even before we were anything. He is so kind, caring, sweet. He makes me happy. His protective streak also does a number on me. Oh, and his body, well yeah, bonus points."

Lauren and I are startled by the knock on my door. I look at her with a confused look. She hops off the sofa and heads to the door. Returning, my brother is following her.

"Alright, what is going on? I received an S.O.S. message from both you and my business partner. I am praying we haven't hit a freaking iceberg and shit just got complicated again," Noah grumbles as he throws a box of cookies and cupcakes on my coffee table. He throws his jacket to the side and comes to the sofa next to me. Lauren goes to sit in the cushioned chair on the opposite side.

"She was just telling me about Josh's body, I am sure you would like her to continue." Lauren gives Noah a mischievous grin.

Noah rolls his eyes and angles his body to me by leaning against a propped arm against the back of the sofa. "Let's leave body parts out of the discussion, please. Why do you look like my box of cookies from Beans isn't going to save the day?"

I sob loudly and snicker. "I am a human, not a pregnant pet that responds to baked treats."

Lauren and Noah look at each other and shake their heads.

"Layla, I thought things were going really well before this weekend? I have never seen you so happy even when I had no clue the reason why. Hell, I have never seen Josh so happy. And I know finding out what he did was a shocker, but when you and I talked about it, it seemed like it wasn't a big issue what he did," Noah begins.

"I am happy and I don't blame Josh, although I wish he'd told me—I get it. I-I just now the baby and decisions and living and love and names…"

Noah brings his hands out. "I don't understand? Can't you speak normally?" He gives me a hopeless and humorous look.

Lauren grabs a sprinkled white cupcake and flops back into the chair. "She ran away from the inevitable where do they live when baby comes conversation, which opened a can of worms of topics. Now she realizes she is in love with the guy. You're caught up and you're welcome." Lauren bites into her cupcake.

"Ah, so my sister is in love and freaking out. Don't think I have witnessed this yet." Noah smiles, entertained.

I blow into a fresh tissue. "I am a horrible person, Noah. I called him a jerk for months and he is the best thing to happen to me." Words start to flow out of my mouth.

"But you used to think he was," Lauren chimes in.

Goading the other was our game. Our way to deal with attraction. For a while, I made myself believe he was bad news. It made it easier. Because Josh Ives always sent electric shocks through me. Under the surface there were two people desperately wanting the other. Even when we found ourselves going at each other like two wolves in mating season, we were fusing together as two people crossing the lines to more.

Our lines shifted from the moment our lips met. He was more than a thrill, no matter how much I tried to put on a front that it's all it was. Every kiss, I wanted more. Not because the guy has some magical talents. No, it was because I knew the way he makes me enjoy every conversation with him and makes me laugh that he had the ability to make me deliriously happy.

"It was all a charade. I didn't want to get in the way of Noah and Josh. I did not want to admit what I felt. It was easier to make him an incredibly sexy jackass who had the ability to turn me on—"

An undistinguished sound escapes my brother's mouth. "Geez, I am sitting right here still. G-rated please." He rubs his face in aggravation. "Sure, if I had known before my business partner and you decided to roll around in the hay, then I probably would have protested. But since you both went with your own tune then I am too late to the game on that. And what Josh did, he handled it the way I would have and can't fault him. He put you first in front of his own business partner. He chose you. Now you are having a baby and I want nothing more than for you to have a happy family. More importantly, I want you to be happy. I'm not a roadblock, so I give you my blessing."

My lips try to slant up, but they are still exhausted from my crying.

I give Noah a hug. "You're the best brother, Noah. I am lucky to have you, and it means everything that you say that. You're part of Josh's life too and soon this baby's life. Both of you," I tell Noah and Lauren as I pull away from the hug.

"I think I was scared that I would fall in love with him all along. Hence my craziness on the jerk factor and the reasoning that Noah would go apeshit. But none of it matters, I've been falling in love this whole time," I admit aloud and relief floods me.

"Finally, you admit it. Because I have been watching your sappy face for weeks now and the way you talk about the guy —it's been obvious." Lauren smiles.

"What happens now?" Noah asks as he puts his feet on the coffee table and hands behind his head as he leans back.

"I guess two people in love and having a baby together maybe should try living together. I guess that's his place since we will need more space," I reflect and for once do not feel panicked.

"Shouldn't you first tell him before you move in," Noah jokes.

I stand up and a burst of energy comes through me. "Yes. You are right."

Quickly, I run to my room to throw on a dress and leggings. Grabbing my phone and bag, I run back into my living room. I am a crazed woman now.

"What's happening?" Noah is confused.

"I am going to Josh's to…" I debate how honest to be.

Lauren interrupts. "She is going to Josh's to talk and to

probably do all the things you don't want in your head, Noah." Lauren is now teasing Noah.

"Yeah. That." I point my finger, then zoom to my front door, then quickly turn around and run back to the coffee table.

I grab a chocolate cupcake and a cookie. Looking at the two guests in my living room. "I'm just going to take this for the road. Probably need it for energy and all." I smile before running back to the front door and heading out to find my future.

32

LAYLA

It's almost eight by the time I reach Josh's place. I decide to just show up and use my key. Element of surprise seems to work for us. Slowly opening his front door, I see that the lights are off except for a line of light coming from his bedroom door along with the sound of indistinguishable words.

Knowing he is in his bedroom makes this easier. I am quiet as a mouse and tiptoe down the hall to his bedroom where the door is slightly ajar. I can hear that he is on his phone talking to someone, it sounds business-related. Taking a deep breath, I decide to still go with my original plan.

Pushing his bedroom door open, I appear in his doorway. He immediately looks at me as he is sitting up in bed—shirtless—on the phone with the duvet at his waist. His face tells me he is curious and relieved I am here.

"Listen, I will call you back in the morning. Something important has come up." His thumb touches the screen of his phone then he throws his phone to the side, his eyes never leaving me. I hold a hand up when he moves to get out of bed.

"Stay," I politely demand as I stand in the doorway.

Looking to the side of the room and letting an audible exhale escape. "Make space for me in bed?"

"Only if you tell me if this ends well even when we wake up." He doesn't blink and doesn't seem like he will throw me a bone for ease. *Understandable*.

Stepping into his room, I take a few steps until I am in between the door and his bed. "How does, I think we should move in together and I have fallen in love with you too sound as ending well when we wake up?" I tell him as I begin to strip in front of him by taking off my leggings.

"I would say that you need to be quicker to getting undressed otherwise I will rip it all off you in record time." His face remains unchanged, but his eyes give me a sparkle.

Pulling my blue tunic dress up and off. I stand there in my black bra and panties. Our eyes meeting. I love that he is still sitting in bed watching me. I unclasp my black bra and let it fall to the floor as he watches with an approving look. Finally pulling down my matching black panties and kicking them off. Standing there naked as he looks at me with eyes full of lust and want.

After a moment of him eyeing me up and down, he lifts the duvet on the bed to welcome me in.

Sliding into bed, he lowers the blanket when I am lying next to him. The soft bed sheets already warm from his body that gives off a layer of heat. His eyes never leaving me as he re-positions, so he is laying on his side toward me.

"Why did you leave?"

"I had a realization, and I needed space to think. Okay, I completely freaked out. It's scary. I've never felt this way. For years, I've avoided emotions like the plague. You've managed to make me cross boundaries. I was always skeptical of love. But I am completely in love with you. I think the obstacle this whole time was that I was more scared that I would fall in love with you because it was happening the whole time," I confess as my hands stroke his cheek.

He gently closes his eyes then opens them again as if he needs to take in what I am saying. His hand then finds the nape of my neck as his thumb rests on my cheek.

"Layla, I am serious I am not messing around. I want it all with you. No games. No circles. No running away when you need space. You run to me. I've been falling for you for a long time now too. Even when you annoy me, you have me. When you're angry, I'm there. If you need a challenge then you know I can deliver. I want to be everything to you. We can go slow if that's what you really need, but I don't think I can contain myself with how much I want it all with you."

I give him a reassuring look. "Did you miss the memo when I said I want to move in with you and that I've fallen in love with you?"

He kisses my forehead with a grin.

"And you are not an evil prince, I don't think you ever were. You are anything but. Gosh, you have been so patient with my craziness. Yes, we can challenge each other. And we make every day interesting. This baby and I are so lucky to have you. We are a little family, and I am so happy it's with you," I tell him in between peppering kisses on his face.

"And I also realize that I am so at ease because of you. You destressed me even when you annoyed me. But it is also not even the sex. It's you, Josh. When I found out I was unexpectedly pregnant instead of having a major freak-out, I only had a semi-freak-out because the idea that it was with you was calming, comforting… exciting."

His finger touches the tip of my nose then grazes my lips. "Every sentence with you is exciting, Layla. While I always thought you aggravated me; it was the total opposite. You entice me and captivate me."

There is a moment as we look into each other's eyes and acknowledge our commitment and declarations.

"I love you," I whisper as I stroke his cheek with my thumb. My eyes must be glimmering, and my face elated.

"I love you, Layla, so much." He barely finishes the sentence as his mouth collides with mine. A deep and longing kiss full of love.

We pull away gently to look into each other's eyes before kissing again.

His lips drag down my neck to my breast before finding my emerging belly where he places a kiss before coming up to kiss me again.

My thighs open wide and he comes to settle between my legs. Already I can feel he is ready.

"Make love to me," I request softly with a gentle smile.

He moves and comes to lie behind me. His front pressing into my back. Kissing my shoulder ever so gently. His finger hooks under my chin to tilt my face up to look behind me so our eyes can meet.

"It's the only plan I have for you tonight, but you are carrying something pretty special. So, I am going to take you this way from behind and hold you tightly as our mouths don't part and my hands move between your beautiful breasts and belly," he informs me softly, sensually, and loving.

My leg props up over his thigh as my hand reaches behind me to grab his hard shaft that has already found a path and my hand guides his tip to my entrance.

"I think I would like that a lot," I confess with a raspy voice before letting out a moan as he enters me slowly. Pressing in, pulling out, then diving in deeper. Doing it several times as our mouths meet and our hands clasp together to move between my breasts and my evolving belly. We get completely lost in each other again and again until we fall asleep still connected in our embrace.

JOSH

The last few months have been running smoothly. My girlfriend has a growing belly that sends my cock into a tailspin. My mother and sister now text Layla, which feels like I have a team of women conspiring against me. Work is one win after another. Even people around the office have noticed my new mood.

Arriving in our conference room, Trey Radnor is waiting at the end of the long table. Admiring the view out the window as he sips coffee. He stands when he sees me enter.

"Hey Trey, good to see you." I offer my hand, which he gladly accepts.

"Yeah. We saw each other last in New Orleans, right? But I am loving the work, really happy. Can't wait to start on the next hotel. Layla will join us?" he asks.

I scratch my upper lip and smile to myself. "Layla is here, yeah. But she won't be working on the next hotel rollout," I begin.

"What? No? I really love her work," he starts.

Holding a hand up, I stop him from going further. "I know, but there is a good reason. Trust me."

Right on cue, the most beautiful radiant pregnant temptress there is walks through the door. The woman who charmed us both a few months back.

"Hi Trey, so good to see you again, thought I would stop by." She smiles and walks to shake his hand. Of course, he pulls her in for a kiss on the cheek. I can't help noticing his brief glance at her belly, but like any sane man—he says nothing.

"No, I didn't eat a big lunch. I am pregnant," she clarifies as she pats her bump.

"That's some news." Trey grins, then offers her a seat.

Layla looks at her stomach. "Yeah, it is. Don't know if Josh mentioned it, but I am cutting down on my work before maternity leave. I won't be able to focus on your project from start to finish, but Josh will still make sure you are taken care of." She looks at me with a warm smile and I come to sit next to her.

"A full team is waiting for you," I tell Trey as he still looks at Layla.

"Okay, sounds good. If I had known in New Orleans, then I would have ensured you had the whole pregnancy package available to you."

Layla takes a drink of her water and smiles to herself. "Oh, but I wasn't pregnant then, but thanks to your hotel, I came back with a keepsake." She shrugs a shoulder and smiles as she looks at me, and I reach over to touch her shoulder.

Trey looks taken aback but an entertained smile forms as he looks between Layla and me. "What? You mean you two are having a baby together?"

"We are indeed," I confirm.

Trey begins to laugh, which makes Layla and I look at each other.

"You two really took your market research seriously. This is pure marketing genius. The full romance package at the Sweet Dove. Where romance happens, I am sure you both found a way to spin it. Definitely find a way to throw this into the marketing material. You have to come back for a baby-moon and honeymoon." Trey seems ecstatic.

I look at Layla who looks slightly taken aback and I scratch the back of my neck. "Maybe." I try to move us on, because the guy just threw the marriage talk into our hemisphere and we have been flying past that with ease so far.

We follow up on a few matters, all the while, I cannot help noticing that Layla is quieter than normal. By far way more reserved than she normally is, and I think I know why. But we will save that topic for another day.

————

A FEW WEEKS LATER, Layla smiles as she knocks on my office door. "Hey baby daddy."

Getting up from my chair, I immediately walk to meet her in the middle of my office and my hands clasp the sides of her head to pull her into a kiss.

"Mmm, you taste good. Chocolate craving today?" I ask, not letting my hands leave the sides of her head.

"Maybe," she replies sheepishly. Then takes my hands and guides me to the sofa where we sit, and she places my hand on her belly as she has done many times in recent weeks. "Feel it?" She beams.

Feeling a flutter under my hand, I nearly jump. "Strong today."

She nods. "Yeah, this bambino responds to chocolate."

I must be glowing as I feel the little jabs against my hand. "It doesn't hurt?"

"No. They say it hurts more later when they hit your ribs. Gosh, we are already more than halfway there," Layla reflects and looks down at her belly.

"Yeah. Yeah, we are." It comes out soft and gentle.

A warm silence fills the room as we look at each other.

"A good time for a babymoon, no?" I ask.

Her head pulls back and she looks at me confused. "Since when did you get on the babymoon train?"

Holding a hand up. "Now, I must admit that I have a meeting down in New Orleans and thought you could come with, as you are at a good time in the pregnancy."

"You mean not throwing up and not quite the size of a whale? Yeah, it is a good time. But you know last time I went to New Orleans; I fucked my boss *a lot* and came back with a memento." She gives me a knowing look.

"Sounds like a scenario to replay," I suggest, throwing on the charm.

"Sign me up." She grins before kissing me quickly and leaving as she is having lunch with Lauren.

A few minutes later, I am walking down the hall satisfied and confident. Knocking on Noah's door, I lean against the doorway.

"You look elated," Noah comments, looking up from his laptop.

"Breakfast meeting tomorrow? The full works, me and you?" I give him a knowing grin and he understands. His cheeks raise and he tries to not let his grin show, because I know the man secretly wants me permanently in the family. Who wouldn't with my good looks and charm?

"Expensive champagne, Josh, only the best," he reminds me as he continues to click away on his laptop.

I chuckle to myself and walk away.

———

ARRIVING at the Sweet Dove Hotel, Layla has not stopped smiling since our plane landed. We head straight to the room where we slept together for the first time where a bottle of non-alcoholic babymoon champagne was waiting for us next to a plate of buttermilk biscuits and beignets—because this place has every scenario figured out.

After freshening up, we head out for a walk and when we come across Luna Ray's tarot cards, I mischievously smile at Layla and pull her hand with me as we walk toward the shop.

"We completely underestimated her last time, so let's see what's in store for us this time." I smile.

Layla laughs. "Well, she was kind of right last time, so why not."

We head into Luna Ray's where the parrot and the bell greet us before a colorful Luna Ray emerges from behind the door of beads.

"Welcome back, my children, shall we begin?"

A skeptical Layla asks, "Really? You remember us?"

Luna Ray gives us a knowing grin. "Of course."

We head to the back room and sit around the table.

"I sense a change between you two. Did something unexpected happen?" Luna asks with a knowing look on her face as she shuffles her cards.

Layla and I look at each other. "Definitely," I confirm.

The first card appears on the table. "Ah the card everyone wants. Lovers. Need I say more?"

We all softly laugh.

Luna pulls a card to the table. "Two of cups visits you both again. Sign of commitment and love. The two of you will cater to each other's needs and have a lasting union."

"Hmm, sounds like a lot of people get this card. So frequent at your table," I comment in fake doubt.

Another card appears on the table. "Ah this one is new for you both. Ten of cups. The card of family and it seems very fitting. It also can mean you are in the presence of your soulmate and your future is very fulfilling," Luna explains, focusing on Layla.

"I guess that isn't too crazy, the card of family," Layla comments as she pats her belly and looks at me convinced.

The next card. "Ace of cups. Romantic gestures are on your horizon." Luna gives me a knowing look because I've got only romance A-game planned for this evening.

"Well, sounds like my future is sunshine and unicorns," Layla sarcastically says.

After saying thanks, we head out to the street and laugh for a solid two minutes. I ask if she wants to go for dinner somewhere or the hotel and she quickly confirms room service is what she wants. A great answer.

And just like that night all those months back, we go back to the room and get passionately lost in the other. We enjoy lying in bed as the fan twirls on the ceiling and the French balcony doors are open to allow the night heat and sound of locusts come through.

This time instead of having space between us as we lay, she is tightly in my arms with a warm hard bump between us and a sheet twisted around our waists.

"What is next on the agenda for the babymoon?" she innocently asks and leans toward her nightstand for the literature left by the hotel on pregnancy massages. The literature we helped design.

In the meantime, I quickly grab the little black box that I hid under the pillow and still very surprised she didn't come across it yet when she clawed the pillow earlier as my mouth ravished her—but I guess she was preoccupied.

When Layla lies back down and turns to me, her jaw drops.

"What about those cards, huh?" I grin as I hold the box open with a damn fine ring inside of it. Her eyes that were glued on the ring shoot up to meet mine and a smile tugs on her mouth.

"Seems like Luna Ray gave us another accurate reading again," she remarks, almost breathless.

Maybe Luna Ray is gifted or *maybe* I paid her an extra fifty… because you know I needed this to go down smooth.

"Does that mean you will agree? Because I was not lying that one day when I said you were a headache to me all these years. Every conversation with you is a witty and playful challenge and I love challenges—especially when I get to look at your beautiful face. When you let me defuse our issue that one time then I knew—I knew that you had to be my wife. Layla Wells, will you marry me?" I ask her and her face glows.

It beams.

"I believe that story ended with me saying yes, and I really liked that ending. So yes, Joshua Ives, I can't imagine a life without you being the thorn in my side and making me feel unbelievably happy. Yes."

Her lips crash onto mine for a luscious kiss and when she pulls away, I slide the ring onto her finger.

"Phew. I can make you an honorable woman," I joke.

She looks at me slightly concerned. "You're not asking because you knocked me up, right?"

I laugh. "Whoa, the look on your face. No. No, I am not. You had me falling for you before you even knew you were pregnant. In fact, I kind of forgot that there is a baby hearing this whole evening until you just mentioned."

Her look turns to relief. "Do you think we scarred the kid by what he or she may have heard transpired ten minutes ago?" Layla pretends to be concerned but struggles to contain her smile.

Putting my hand on her belly. "Nah. Remember guru lady said the baby should feel our connection as parents." I smirk.

Layla's laugh fills the room as we adjust our position to look at each other and her leg props over my hip.

"I know I knocked it out of the park that day we told my parents our romantic proposal. But we never got to hear what kind of wedding you want."

Layla's lips quirk out as she considers. "True. Instead you told them that we would wait so I have the wedding of my dreams." She remembers and then her fingers come to draw lines on my arms. "But, I don't want to wait, and I don't want a big wedding." There is that malice on her face that I was waiting for.

Those momccinos are no longer going to be the highlight of this pregnancy.

"You mean like a wedding with only your brother, Lauren, my parents, sister and her husband in attendance?" I offer with a fake questioning look.

She looks at me impressed "Yeah, how did you kn—" She stops mid-sentence and then her face catches on and she clicks her inner cheek with her tongue.

"The thing is, Layla. You and I, we like tit for tat. When I asked your brother for your hand in marriage—because that was the protocol to follow. I knew, *I knew* you had your own scheme planned."

She looks away, entertained, then pushes me to my back and comes to sit on top of me with her hands resting on my chest to look at me knowingly. "And you figured out that I would surprise you with those people coming to New Orleans for an impromptu wedding."

"I figured if you are going to arrange the wedding then I should arrange a damn good proposal." I grin.

Her smile spreads before she comes down to kiss my lips.

"So, this time tomorrow we update the babymoon package to the honeymoon package?" she asks with a look of happiness never fading.

Gently—because baby on board—pulling her tightly down to me and rolling her to her side, my fingers cup her cheek.

"Damn straight," I confirm.

EPILOGUE

Josh

I t was a small intimate wedding at the Sweet Dove Hotel. Complete with all the ladies crying, Sazerac for the guys and a dinner complete with southern biscuits. Trey Radnor ensured we had the best champagne and cigars to accompany the cake of beignets that Layla wanted. Who was making me want to send everyone away because she looked amazing in a white dress that fit snuggly over her skin and showcasing her curves. The lace barely covering her shoulders teasing me during the quick ten-minute ceremony.

As her pregnancy progressed, she got a little moodier as her belly grew. She also was more insatiable in bed, and I was not complaining at all. We got the baby room ready at my place and the Tesla of strollers was delivered on time. The instructions to put it together took a rocket scientist and a solid one week to figure out, during which Layla watched me and Noah in entertainment.

I remember it clear as day our *dressgate* number two. This time knowing I wouldn't be the moron I was during *dressgate* number one.

Heading out of my meeting, I text Layla.

Me: How was handover?

She was going to stop by the office today to hand back work to Mindy who returned from her leave.

The Mrs: Fine. But why don't you ask in person?

Ah, right, because she is hopefully waiting in my office for me with a little attitude and the look that melts my heart every time.

Turning the corner of the hall, I see the best view in the city waiting in my office. My beautiful wife looking out the window, her hand with a shiny diamond ring on her left ring finger resting on her belly. Slaying it today in a blue skintight dress that is snug in all the right places and emphasizing the bump that highlights to everyone how much of a good time we had on that one business trip. She turns to me when she hears me come into the office.

Layla holds a hand up. "Don't you dare ask. Just don't." She was nearly barking.

I hold my hands up in surrender. "Okay. I will not be asking how you are feeling, how was handover, or how is the baby doing today. Shall we skip to what can I do to annoy you, so I screw you like crazy in hopes of getting this kid out?" I mention casually as I place my phone on the desk.

The glare on her is strong today as she rests her hands on her hips. She *may* be a little cranky too.

We look at each other and say nothing for a few moments. Sitting on the edge of my desk, I drink up the view and she is absolutely beautiful. A smile tugs on my lips as I admire the image of her in a dress.

She gives me a questioning look and I slowly approach her. Testing the waters if she is about to erupt. But she sinks. Sinks into my eyes, drowning her in admiration. I step to her and my hand glides along the nape of her neck and hair.

"You look absolutely radiant today. Just like every other time I have seen you in a dress."

Layla nibbles on her bottom lip. "Like when?" she asks innocently.

"The time I was a moron and said nothing. The time in New Orleans—all those nights when I most certainly made up for the fact I was once a moron. When you became my wife. Every time I see you in a dress and wonder if you will give me attitude or kiss me senseless, but I like both. Today when you look beautiful with our baby in your belly."

Her smile spreads as she leans up on her toes to kiss me with her arms looping around my neck. Our lips brushing before settling in the perfect rhythm of tongues and mouths tangling together.

"You really know how to make a girl love you, huh?" Layla whispers.

"Nah. I didn't have to do a thing; you were always going to love me," I tease her and it earns me a pinch on the arm to which I let a rumble of a laugh bounce in the back of my throat.

"Hey. I love you," I whisper.

"I love you."

We look at each other and move in to kiss again. Admittedly, we spice it up with a powerful kiss that my business partner most definitely would not approve of. My hands begin to wander through her hair and down her body as her hands follow suit. We are on fire and I am thinking about the fastest way to get us out of here.

But we won't be heading home today…

I reluctantly pull away from her mouth when she puts her palms to my chest. "Uh, Josh."

"Yes?" I continue to kiss her neck.

"I'm wet."

"Yeah, that happens a lot when you are around me." I grin against her skin as I move to kiss near that spot next to her ear she loves.

She pushes me back again, and she cups my face with both hands to get me to focus.

"Josh. I think it is time." She smiles at me and her head slowly looks down.

I follow her line of sight and then back up with my eyes wide. I nod slowly and grin. "Always knew my kisses would do the trick."

Stepping back, she looks down at her soaked blue dress.

Me? I turn on Superman mode. I grab my phone and jacket, all the while yelling for Noah to hightail it in here.

"What the hell, what is—" Noah is speaking as he comes running in, adjusting his shirt, which tells me he finally grew a pair and is hooking up on his lunch breaks with Lauren from accounting.

"It's game time," I declare.

"Is that like from… her?" Noah's still in a daze and points to Layla's dress.

Layla looks at both of us with her face flaring in annoyance. "Both of you—I am not a museum exhibit. Let's get rolling. This baby is coming." She is far too relaxed and already ordering us around.

Ten hours later, a beautiful Layla is lying in bed—a tad on the tired side—waiting for me. The rumors that pregasauruses are real have been witnessed. My wife turned into a spitfire that screamed, bossed, and pushed out the best souvenir ever.

Coming to sit next to her in bed, I slowly bring the mint green blanket-wrapped baby to her and place the sweetest little bundle in her arms. Layla's face glows into a smile I have never witnessed on her.

I kiss her forehead tenderly and whisper, "You did it. Our

little girl is here." I stare at my wife then baby Luna who we unexpectedly created.

"You're in trouble," she tells me weakly before tears fall from her eyes.

I am absolutely in trouble. They both already have me wrapped around their little fingers for the rest of my life.

THANKS

A big thank you to you the reader. I hope you enjoyed Josh and Layla's story. Their story honestly wasn't planned. It came to me one day and three weeks later their story was complete. They are truly one of my favorite couples and stories of all time.

Anyone who shares this story on their social media or tells a friend. You rock!

It was a long — well worth it — journey for these two. It started with Kimberly from Revision Division for beta reading. Thank you for helping me decide to publish this one.

Things got fun when I looked for a photo for the cover. Thank you Lindee Robinson for the photography and the models that are the perfect image for this story. To Tash for creating the concept, and Kate for following through when we lost Tash too soon.

My Brother's Editor, thanks for taking me on and it was worth the wait. The icing on the cake. Magical sorcery really.

My other half and our little offspring, thanks for letting me really take writing during a pandemic to a whole new level of crazy! Who would have thought I would knock out a lot of words? I know I avoided folding a lot of laundry so I could write, and I promise it's worth it ... I'll fold the laundry eventually.